RACHEL

HER STAGE LIFE AND HER REAL LIFE

Rachel
From a portrait by Müller.

RACHEL

HER STAGE LIFE AND HER REAL LIFE

BY

FRANCIS GRIBBLE

AUTHOR OF

"THE PASSIONS OF THE FRENCH ROMANTICS," ETC.

WITH SIX PHOTOGRAVURE PORTRAITS

WILDSIDE PRESS

RICHARD CLAY & SONS, LIMITED,
BREAD STREET HILL, E.C., AND
BUNGAY SUFFOLK.

PREFACE

THEATRICAL biographies, in England at all events, are usually written either by actors and actresses or by their stage-struck admirers. The impression which they convey (whether accidentally or by design) is not so much that all the world is a stage as that the stage is the only part of the world which is of much importance. The picture drawn is apt to lack proportion, and to be a picture, as it were, of the theatre surrounded by other things, and of actors and actresses surrounded by other people. In the case of the majority of actors and actresses it is, perhaps, necessary to stand at the point of view from which the picture assumes that shape in order to persuade oneself that it is worth while to write their lives. Examples illustrative of the truth of the remark will occur to every one.

There have been a few actors and actresses, however—actresses more particularly—to whose case the remark does not apply. They have been great enough to be classed, not with public entertainers, but with public institutions; their personalities as well as their performances having counted in the social life of their times. Rachel's personality counted, beyond question, in that way. If she had not the whole world for her stage, she had the greater portion of the civilized world for her audience; and she held her audience, not merely as an artist, but

Preface

as an individual. Her contemporaries discussed her
caprices and her character no less eagerly than her im-
personations; their descendants have not yet desisted
from the discussion. Her biographer, therefore, has
no right to flatter himself that he has finished his task
when he has compiled a list of her professional
engagements and buried her beneath a tumulus of
adulatory press notices. The case is one of the few
in which it is worth while to try to go further,
drawing the portrait of an actress, and composing
a picture of the social medium in which she moved.

To do so, indeed, is not only worth while, but may
even be edifying—a word which an author has as
good a right to use as a reviewer, seeing that he, at
least, knows not only what he has put in his book, but
also why he has put it there. It is a word, at any
rate, which is used here for a definite reason, and
with a full sense of responsibility. Edification is a goal
which may be reached by many roads, but the road
of hypocrisy is not one of them; and though there
may be occasions on which hypocrisy should be
classed with the venial sins, it would be difficult to
prove that there is anything to be gained by adopt-
ing a hypocritical tone when writing about the
theatre. On the contrary, the advantage in that
case is all on the side of candour.

Let us consider. We live in an age in which the
theatre tends, more and more, to be regarded as
affording an appropriate career for the daughters
of professional men. Young women come to the
career, in increasing numbers, even from the Manse
and from the Rectory. Neither they nor their
parents know, as a rule, anything whatever about

Preface

the conditions of the calling. Their chief, if not their only, expectation is that they will be beautifully dressed, much admired, frequently photographed, and encouraged to regard themselves as artists. Their picture of the life on which they are about to enter is derived from theatrical novels, in which the heroines are invariably as virtuous as they are gifted, and from theatrical biographies in which the actual facts of the case are concealed by the thick smoke of ascending incense. There is no edification there. Not "edifying" but "misleading" is the really applicable epithet for the works which complacently favour such agreeable conventions; and the matter is one on which it is exceedingly undesirable that the Manse and the Rectory should be misled.

As long as the Manse and the Rectory ignored the theatre there was, perhaps, no useful purpose to be served by directing their attention to its particularities; but the case is different now that the theatrical impresario includes them in his recruiting grounds. It is not to their interest to be deceived—the price ultimately to be paid for the pleasure of the deception may be too high. It is no kindness to them (though it may soothe them) to write of the life of an actress as if there were nothing in it but the acting and the applause. They want (or at all events they ought to want) the complete picture. The details in the picture of which they disapprove are precisely the details of which it is most important to them to inform themselves. They want to know something about the theatrical atmosphere, the theatrical point of view—and the point of view of the admirers

Preface

of the actresses; something too of the effect of the theatrical life in titillating vanity, subduing sentiment, and hardening the character. A theatrical biography, faithfully written, may supply materials for the drawing of conclusions on all these matters; and the conclusions may be the more convincing if the writer leaves the actual drawing of them to the reader.

Three new books about Rachel have recently been published in France : *La Vie Sentimentale de Rachel*, by Mlle. Valentine Thomson; *Rachel et son Temps*, by Mme. A. de Faucigny-Lucinge, and *Rachel Intime*, by M. Hector Fleischmann. Each one of them contains documents of interest previously unpublished; and the author has to acknowledge obligations to all of them, and also to a biographical study by M. Henry Lecomte, entitled *Un Amour de Déjazet*.

FRANCIS GRIBBLE.

CONTENTS

CHAPTER I

Contents

Contents

LIST OF ILLUSTRATIONS

RACHEL

CHAPTER I

The Leit-motif.

A WORD may seem to be due, at the outset, to any irresolute readers who stand, as it were, titubating on the threshold, reluctant to pursue Rachel's acquaintance until informed what sort of a person she was.

To such readers it must be freely admitted that Rachel did not, in conduct and deportment, conform to the ideals of certain admirable English actresses—admirable one means, of course, in the matter of their domestic relations. The facts forbid us to picture her grouping a fortunate husband's children about her knees when she hears the footfall of the photographer on the staircase. She never married, and the art of the photographer was in its infancy in her time. Nor was there anything in her way of life suggestive of the Rectory, the Church and Stage Guild, or even the Bedford College for Women. In view of the circumstances of her up-bringing there hardly could be. She came, as has been said, to the stars from the gutter; and she was not very careful to brush the mud of the gutter from her skirts on her arrival.

B   I

Rachel

All that has to be granted, and will have to be illustrated as we proceed, but without emphasis, and in no censorious spirit. A Life of Rachel, truthfully undertaken, is bound to be, in the main, a book neither of blame nor of approbation, but of pity. She seems to have pitied herself. "La pauvre Rachel!" is a refrain which runs through her letters, now playfully and now pathetically uttered; and the reasons for her melancholy are tolerably clear.

It was something more than the melancholy of the race which wandered so long in the wilderness and afterwards was carried into captivity and scattered over the face of the earth. It was also the melancholy of the weak and weary, who feel that their strength is inferior to their genius and fear that it will prove unequal to their task. She had hardly begun to taste the intoxicating joy of her artistic triumph when she received her first warning that her course from the dark to the dark would be brief; and her life, thenceforward, was a race against time: a race in which there was to be little leisure for repose or contemplation.

That fact is the clue to a great deal in Rachel's career and character. She was famous when she was young, and was exalted to a very delirium of delight; but the clouds were already stealing up, foreshadowing the night when no man can work and no woman can be admired. Her chilling instinct of their advent grew gradually to a certain knowledge, and there were times when she spoke of her terror. Once, at a rehearsal of *Adrienne Lecouvreur*, she burst, without apparent reason, into a flood of tears. Asked why she wept, she replied that it was because of her premonition that she, too, like the actress whom she was impersonating, was destined to die young and see the cup of rapture snatched from her lips almost before she had tasted it.

And therefore she made haste, racing against time, declining rest even when she was longing for it. The day came when she saw her error and admitted it.

She had been born in a position in which life is an ignoble struggle for the means of living. She had risen, almost without effort, as one who runs lightly up a ladder, to a position in which every morning and every evening of life might bring fresh pleasures. Having achieved that position, she wanted all that it could yield : glory, the homage of princes, wealth, and, if not love, at least that passionate make-believe which goes by the name of love. So she pursued glory from Paris to St. Petersburg, and from St. Petersburg to New York, and took lovers and bore children to them, and having earned one fortune by her talents, acquired a second by spoiling the Egyptians.

Not, it may be objected, a very sympathetic person. Probably, and indeed almost certainly, Rachel was not sympathetic. That epithet " sweet " which is deservedly applied to so many of our English actresses would not have been very applicable to her. For she had genius; and the temperament of genius is rarely sympathetic. The essence of genius is to be egoistic, if not hard,—avid of experiences rather than passionate,—ready to drop an experience when it has yielded all that can be got from it, and pass

on complacently to the next. That was the way,
for example, of Napoleon, of Chateaubriand, and
of George Sand. But genius, in the very eagerness
of its pursuit of experiences, may sometimes over-
shoot the mark, and miss the best experience of
all; and that seems to have been Rachel's case.

It is related that Rachel, in the days of her
glory, when she queened it at supper-parties,
trailing rich lace sleeves in richer sauces, once
confided to the company that she could not remember a time when she had been what the world
calls "innocent." That, one may justly say, supposing it to be true (which is uncertain), was rather
her misfortune than her fault; for respect for the
innocence of young women is not numbered among
the traditions of that gutter in which she passed
her early years. The trouble was that, whether
in consequence of the premature soiling of her
innocence or for other reasons, no one of her love
affairs ever seemed to her of supreme and exclusive
importance.

There was a *bourgeoise* in her who had died young,
as there always is in even the most Bohemian women :
we shall come upon clear traces of that *bourgeoise*
when we come to examine some of her letters. But
there was no romance in her life, only restless
avidity of sensation. "I have never belonged to
any man," she exclaimed, in the heat of self-defence,
when certain revelations (of which more hereafter)
decided the Faubourg Saint Germain, after taking
her to its bosom, to drop her like a hot potato; and
the true inwardness of the boast seems to have been
that, though she had given herself to many men,

Rachel

in the pursuit of pleasure or of presents, she had given her heart to none.

That, truly, was not a very sympathetic way of asserting the self-dependence of genius; and it is by no means for the sake of such stories (though it would be idle to try to avoid them altogether) that one attempts a fresh book about Rachel. Equally little does one assume the task on account of the strength of her family affections, though it can justly be said that she looked after the interests of the Tribe of Félix as devotedly as Napoleon looked after those of the House of Bonaparte. Her claim on our attention is simply and solely her genius.

On the whole one hears rather more of the genius of actresses than is warranted by the circumstances of their case. They like the use of the word, and they lay themselves out to make things pleasant for those who please them; so that critics are apt to sacrifice truth to them, as courtiers sacrifice it to kings and queens. In the case of Rachel, however, one can employ the word without any sacrifice, and even without any economy, of truth. Her power overwhelmed Charlotte Brontë at Brussels; poor, prim little Charlotte's only doubt being whether she merited moral approval. Fanny Kemble, who saw her in London, declared that neither Ristori nor Madame Bernhardt was worthy of being mentioned in the same sentence with her. Yet she needed praise from neither of them, for her achievements were definite and tangible.

Just as Napoleon, when quite a young officer, restored order to a troubled France—just as Chateaubriand, almost with his first book, made religion

Rachel

fashionable in a community of atheists—so Rachel, as a mere slip of a girl, came to the rescue of the National Theatre at the darkest hour of its fortunes, and restored the classical drama to favour at a time when the revolt of the Romantics had almost expelled it from the stage. Like Napoleon, too, she triumphed early, without the help of any of that mysterious " influence " which, alike on the stage and in the army, is so often requisite to give the young their chance. The parallel, in short, between her career and Napoleon's may be made to seem very close; and one is the more interested in drawing it because it is through her, as will appear, that the blood, if not the genius, of Napoleon has been transmitted to an esteemed contemporary manufacturer.

Her figure, therefore, is, for these reasons, well worth recalling and reviving; and it will be proper to write of her real life as well as her stage life because she herself drew a sharp distinction between the two. She burst into tears, one day, on withdrawing from the boards to the wings; and when asked the cause of her trouble, she replied : " It is because I have to live the life of others and not my own."

Exactly what dreams of a life of her own she cherished it might be difficult to say. Occasionally, it would seem, they were the dreams of a *bourgeoise*— dreams of marrying and settling down, nursing babies, darning stockings, and feeding poultry, in some quiet country place. Such dreams appear to have visited her more particularly in the later years of her brief life, when she was ill and tired, and the pursuit of wealth and glory had become an effort. But she never realized them; and she never

Rachel

tried to realize them, although a simple man, who was also a devout lover, offered her the opportunity. She dallied with the idea, but always put it off until the morrow which never came.

It was borne in upon her at last, indeed, that she was a shadow pursuing shadows, but the habit of the chase had hold of her, and she could not desist. Always, it seems, there was to be one chase more, " the best and the last "; and so she went on, with the melancholy which they said was the melancholy of the race upon her brow, " faint but pursuing," till she fainted by the way. *La pauvre Rachel!* That is the *Leit-motif.*

CHAPTER II

Rachel's birth and childhood.

QUESTIONS having been raised as to the accuracy of the register, it is uncertain whether Rachel was born in 1820 or in 1821. The place of her birth, however, is known to have been the village inn at Munf, in the Canton of Aargau, in Switzerland; and her father, Jacques (or more properly Jacob) Félix was a Wandering Jew—a pedlar—" un homme qui colportait," as the aforesaid register describes him.

It is said that he was rather a superior person for a pedlar, and that, in his promising youth, he had been intended for the honourable calling of a rabbi. If so, that was Rachel's nearest approach to the Rectory—that source from which a perennial stream of highly regarded English actresses flows now-a-days as from a fountain. And Jacob Félix did certainly show himself a man of acute intelligence in his more prosperous later life—albeit mainly in connection with the amassing of pieces of silver. In 1820, however, he had very few pieces of silver in his possession, and peddled for a precarious livelihood.

His papers, including his marriage certificate, were in order; and he carried his wife, Esther Haya Félix, in the same cart in which he stored his soap, scent, ribbons, laces, popular illustrated almanacs, and other wares. Madame Félix, it appears, attended

Rachel

to the branch of the business which concerned ladies' wardrobes, laying up at an inn, from time to time, to bear a child. Thus babies—a perpetually increasing company of babies—were added to the contents of the cart. When Rachel arrived, Sarah was already there; and afterwards there came Rebecca, and Dinah, and Leah, and Raphael—a considerable quiverful, and rather more than a reasonable cartful.

On one occasion Rachel, happily well padded with blankets, fell backwards out of the cart, and lay, for some time, in the middle of the road, without being missed by either her father or her mother; but a passing peasant picked her up, ran after the cart, and restored her to her family. But for that peasant's thoughtfulness, it has sometimes been said, Rachel would probably have been brought up in a Swiss charitable institution and begun life as a general servant; but that is as it may be, for it seems a more reasonable hypothesis that her father would ultimately have remarked her disappearance, and returned to look for her. He was an intelligent man, as has been said, and not like the birds that cannot count their eggs.

That is the only story of Rachel's infancy which has been preserved. Getting a little older, she is said to have helped to peddle, and there are stories to the effect that she and Sarah sang and danced, and played the guitar, and collected coppers in the country cafés to which the peddling pilgrimage brought them; also stories to the effect that she was soundly slapped for begging, and that, once, having lost her way in the streets of Rheims, she was brought

9

home to her parents in the basket of a tradesman's errand-boy. Rachel herself used to tell such stories at the supper-parties of the glorious days when, as has been said, money being no object, she trailed her sleeves in the sauces, regardless of expense; but it would be hard to say how much of the stories was remembered and how much invented or imagined. Everything, in short, is vague and legendary until we find the family settling at Lyon.

Jacob Félix, one may suppose, felt the need of settling somewhere because his family was outgrowing his cart; for his wife bore him ten children who died young as well as the six who grew up. For what reason he chose Lyon in preference to any other town one does not know; but he soon displayed there all the ingenuity of his race in devising means by which every member of the family, from its head to the latest baby, might do something to earn a little money. He himself turned from peddling to tuition, and gave German lessons to such pupils as were satisfied to have an ex-pedlar for their tutor, though he occasionally reverted to his old calling, and hawked opera-glasses outside the cafés. His wife called on the ladies of Lyon with a view to purchasing, altering, and reselling their cast-off clothes, offering, at the same time, to tell their fortunes with a pack of cards which she carried in her corsage. The elder children were sent out to sing and dance for coppers at the street corners. The baby—there always was a baby in that prolific family—was exhibited on a costermonger's barrow to excite the commiseration of the charitable.

One feels the influence of a master mind in this

Rachel

elaborate co-ordination of remunerative activities; and one also feels that it would have been strange if pieces of silver had not been accumulated when so many tentacles were stretched out to gather them in. They were accumulated, if not to any great extent, at least sufficiently to pay for the removal of the family to Paris, where they took a poor lodging, behind the Hôtel de Ville, and opposite the house of the popular novelist Paul de Kock, a few days after the outbreak of the Revolution of July 1830.

At first, however, the life at Paris was only the life at Lyon over again : tuition and the hawking of opera-glasses for the father; old-clothes dealing, diversified by fortune-telling, for the mother; street singing and entertaining for the children; poverty, though not actual destitution, for all. It was in those days, no doubt, that Rachel, hungry but beginning to be conscious of the fire within her, acquired some of her cynical disdain for the manners and moral and social standards of a world which, as she said, when explaining how she felt herself in the very skin of one of Victor Hugo's heroines, "would let a woman starve to death while she was pure and innocent, but would overwhelm her with flattering attentions after she had lost her honour." She acquired it unconsciously, however, and, in the meantime, she twanged her guitar and sang :—

J'ai deux femmes dans mes maisons
Pour m'habituer aux poisons,
    C'est ce qui me désole !
Mais pour dissiper mes ennuis
Je bois beaucoup de vin de nuits,
    C'est ce qui me console !

Rachel

Arsène Houssaye,[1] afterwards the manager of the theatre at which Rachel was the leading actress, quotes that as a part of her lost repertory. Probably it is a favourable specimen of it, for the street songs of Paris are apt to plumb much lower depths. The child who sang them was a pale and scraggy mite, plain almost to ugliness, with thin dark hair and a disproportionately large forehead, though also with "certain fires of sunrise in her eyes." She had a deep voice, too, which sounded absurd, coming from so small a body; but, somehow or other, she held her audience. There was an unusual intelligence in her *gaminerie*. She acted while she sang; so that her humble admirers offered her, not only copper coins, but also sweets, oranges and fried potatoes.

One day, however, there was added to the audience a radiant, clean-shaven man, of quite a different class from the others. He stopped to listen for a moment on his quick, firm walk towards success in life, and he remarked the intelligence of the child's performance. He lifted her up, and kissed her on the forehead. "Little one," he said, "I love children, and I love artists. Here is a piece of silver for you. But you should not sing those very shocking songs. Here is something better, a little piece of my own. Take it and sing it to any tune you like. Good-bye, my little one!"

Having said that, the radiant, clean-shaven man

---

[1] *La Comédienne*, by Arsène Houssaye, is a fanciful biography of Rachel under the name of Esther. It is not a trustworthy work. The volume of reminiscences entitled *Les Confessions* may, however, be followed with more confidence.

passed on, resuming his march towards success in life; and the child, hugging her piece of silver, inquired whether any one knew who the kind stranger was. The question was passed round the ring until some one was found to answer it : " His name is Hugo—Monsieur Victor Hugo. He is a very clever gentleman who writes books."

Such is the anecdote as Arsène Houssaye relates it. We may believe it if we like; or we may believe, if we prefer, that Rachel and Victor Hugo imagined it in collaboration, as a happy piece of symbolism, in the later years when they met as equal potentates, claiming respectively to be the greatest poetical creator and the greatest poetical interpreter of their generation. Another street encounter of the period, however, is historical, and also important, since it put an end to the street singing and placed Rachel on the path which was to conduct her to glory. Choron, the great music teacher, and head of the Conservatoire of Sacred Music, happened to pass, and was so pleased with her voice that he offered to take her into his school and train her.

Would she still be allowed to sing ? she asked, not knowing what kind of a school he kept. Yes, he replied, but she would be taught to sing psalms and hymns instead of comic songs. Would there be opportunities of taking up a collection ? was the next question. There would be no need for that, was the answer. Not only would her parents have nothing to pay for her at his school, but he himself would give her a piece of silver every week as pocket-money. The one condition which he made was that she must drop the Israelitish name of Rachel, which

Rachel

did not become a singer of Christian music, and content herself with her other name, Elisa. The condition was accepted, and Rachel made her first start in life.

It was a false start, though not an unhappy one —much better than the false start which she might easily have made, under her mother's guidance, as an old-clothes woman or a fortune-teller. Rachel's voice, as it turned out, was only moderately good, and she had no disposition to diligence. "They have nicknamed me Pierrot," she wrote home to her mother, "and I deserve the name, for I am up to all sorts of nonsense like a true Pierrot"; and the stories preserved of her stay at Choron's school are chiefly to the effect that she played truant. She wrote to Choron—he kept the letter on account of its quaint mistakes in spelling—begging him to excuse her absence from his class on the ground that her mother wished to take her to have a bath; and it transpired that there had never been any question of a bath, but that the promising pupil had spent the time in the Bois de Boulogne, where she had gathered a group of strange children about her, and entertained them by mimicking the methods of her teacher with the conductor's bâton.

Some teachers would have been angry, but Choron was good-natured—" has a thousand kindnesses for me," she wrote in one of her letters home. His most useful act of kindness was his recognition of the true direction in which her talents lay, and the trouble which she took to put her in the right path. He met, one day, his friend Saint-Aulaire, an actor at the Comédie Française and a professor at the

Rachel

Conservatoire, who also kept a private school of elocution.

"Saint-Aulaire," he said, " I want you to take over one of my pupils."

" My dear fellow, I have quite enough unsatisfactory pupils already," the comedian objected.

" I dare say. But this is a great actress, and I am going to pay her fees for her."

Perhaps he told him at the same time how Rachel had sold her umbrella (informing her mother when questioned on the subject that she had lost it) in order to be able to purchase a copy of the works of Racine—a story which could not fail to melt the heart of a French actor. Whether he did so or not, at all events he persuaded him. Saint-Aulaire heard his friend's pupil recite, thought her promising, and admitted her to his class. But he made one stipulation. The child must drop the name of Elisa and call herself Rachel—for that was the name for the theatre.

The stipulation was agreed to, and Rachel, at the age of fourteen, was thus started on the road to glory.

CHAPTER III

SOME of the girls at Saint-Aulaire's Dramatic Academy left their teacher from time to time in order to flit, gaily and gracefully, down the flowery track. So Arsène Houssaye tells us, hastening to add, however, that against that danger Rachel was immune.

Not, indeed, that she had the temperament of a nun—a great actress never has. But she was ugly, and she was proud; and she had the instinctive perception belonging to genius of the goal for which she was bound, and of the fact that certain roads did not lead to it. The flowery track, she divined, was for the *théâtreuse*, not for the actress. The path of pleasure was not the way to glory, though the path of glory might be the way to pleasure. Moreover, as she was a plain child, the temptations were probably inconsiderable.

She wore a calico frock—it was the only frock she possessed—of a red ground with white spots. Her boots were abominably coarse and clumsy. Her black hair was drawn tight, so that her huge forehead bulged, and hung, twisted into meagre pigtails, down her back. She hoped, with a longing like despair, that she would grow up to be beautiful; and she wondered what she could do to make her-

Rachel

self look like one of the Greek statues in the Louvre galleries. In the meantime, however, she did not look in the least like any of them, but was a puny freak with a voice like a big bassoon.

She was intelligent, however, and she could act; and Saint-Aulaire was a teacher who found his pupils opportunities of showing what they could do. They gave public performances under his direction in the Salle Molière, paying him fees for the privilege of appearing—from one to ten francs according to the importance of the part—and recouping themselves by selling tickets for the entertainment to their fathers and mothers and uncles and aunts, and, no doubt, their admirers if they had any. A list has been compiled from the register of the school of thirty-four rôles from Molière, Corneille, Racine, Shakespeare and other dramatists of the repertory which Rachel sustained between the ages of fourteen and sixteen.

The bulk of the audience was doubtless ignorant, if not uncritical; but not the whole of it. It sometimes included the friends of the professor as well as the friends of the pupils—actors, theatrical managers, and amateurs of the arts. All of these were eager to "discover" a new actress—some of them for purely professional reasons, others for the satisfaction of their vanity, or in the hope that the gratitude of the actress discovered might manifest itself agreeably. So intense is the French interest in matters of art, especially when there is a reasonable chance that there will be a pretty woman in the case! Rachel, as we know, was not yet a pretty woman; but she nevertheless began to attract

c   17

attention. The list of those who remembered in later days that they had conversed with her in Saint-Aulaire's little theatre is rather long; and she became, of course, so celebrated that the most trivial incidents of the days of her apprenticeship seemed worth recalling. Even the gentleman in the French consular service who recollected that he had once said to her : " My dear, here is a penny for you. Go and buy yourself some fried potatoes ! " came to regard himself as the possessor of a valuable piece of exclusive information.

One of the amateurs who remarked her was Berryer, the famous orator of the French bar—the Sir Rufus Isaacs or Sir Edward Carson of his time and country. He is said to have gone home with her more than once to the fifth-floor garret in which Madame Félix refurbished ladies' cast-off wardrobes, in order to give her hints in elocution. Dr. Véron, equally famous as a newspaper editor and a man-about-town, was another who observed her. He was to know her more intimately before long, but, at the moment, he only noticed the profundity of the voice in which, in reply to some one who asked her what she was doing, she replied : " Monsieur, je poursuis mes études." Samson, the actor, who was presently to be her tutor at the Conservatoire, also saw and spoke to her; but her talents seem to have impressed him less than the fact that her presentation to him interrupted her in a game of hopscotch. Spectators with more insight were Monval the actor, who noted her as a possible recruit for the Gymnase, and Jouslin de Lassalle, director of the Théâtre

Rachel

Français, who ran up to Saint-Aulaire in the green-
room and remonstrated with him—

"What on earth do you mean," he asked him,
"by letting that girl play soubrettes? Can't you
see that the child has all the makings of a great
tragédienne?" and he proposed that Rachel should
be transferred to the Conservatoire.

She went there, and he forgot all about her. She
came under the tuition, not of Samson, but of
Provost; and Provost was a terror to all his pupils
and to Rachel more than to most of them. He
mocked her; he bullied her; he shouted at her, as
some of our own stage-managers are said (no doubt
unjustly) to shout at awkward extra ladies at
pantomime rehearsals. He told her that she had a
voice like a costermonger, and he concluded in his
most magisterial manner—

"Child, what were you doing before it occurred to
you to study for the stage?"

"I was selling flowers, sir," Rachel answered
humbly.

"Then you had better go back and sell more
flowers. You are far more likely to excel as a
flower-girl than as an actress."

The time was soon to come when he would have
to eat those words, pretending that he liked the
taste of them with profuse apologies; but, in
the mean time, his rasping tongue drove Rachel from
the Conservatoire, though it did not drive her back
to the street industry which he specified. Poirson
of the Gymnase, who had heard of her from Monval
of that theatre, offered her a three-years' engagement
at £132 a year. Her father, who was in a hurry to

see his talented daughter contributing to the support of her family, insisted upon her accepting it. *La Vendéenne*—a drama based on the plot of *The Heart of Midlothian* — was written for her début. She made her first appearance on July 24, 1837.

All the Children of Israel in Paris—all those of humble station at all events—rallied to the support of the Tribe of Félix on that occasion. If *haute finance* was not in evidence in the stalls, the pit and gallery, at any rate, were packed with the loyal hawkers of opera-glasses and the vociferous dealers in old clothes. Among them, if in no other circles, the intimation had been passed round that this particular daughter of Israel was destined to be one of the glories of her race. They shouted themselves hoarse in their enthusiasm; and the critics also spoke kindly, especially Jules Janin.

He was the dramatic Aristarchus of his time. He wrote for the *Débats*, a journal which, in those days, was quite as important as the *Times*; and his good word carried at least as much weight as the good words of Mr. William Archer and Mr. A. B. Walkley combined. Moreover he cultivated a genial, friendly style, aimed at the hearts rather than the heads of his readers—a style akin, in some respects, to that of the late Clement Scott, and in others to that of the friendly contributors to the dramatic columns of the *Referee;* and he was also a critic who liked, sometimes, to encourage an actress by putting his arm round her waist.

His desire to encourage Rachel in that way was presently to get him into trouble with a rival patron

Rachel

of the arts; but that story belongs to a somewhat later date. Rachel, as yet, was too immature to attract a man of Jules Janin's extensive opportunities, and he took a purely professional view of her. Poirson, he wrote, had introduced " a new-born babe " to the public; but this new-born babe was no " infant phenomenon," and there was no need to " write her up as a prodigy." She had " soul and heart and intelligence," but " very little skill." Her voice was " harsh; " her hands were "red." She was not "pretty" but she "pleased." There were "tears, interest and emotion" in her acting. It seemed reasonable to predict a future of some distinction for her.

And so forth with the interminable verbosity of the man whose life's work is to make much ado about nothing. It was a satisfactory, if not a gushing, notice; and the critic remembered afterwards, though he seems not to have noticed the matter at the time, that the actress achieved one moment of supreme triumph when she chanted, or intoned, instead of singing, a lyric included in the piece—

> *Je croyais encor l'invoquer :*
> *Vers moi soudain elle s'avance,*
> *Et du doigt semble m'indiquer*
> *Une ville inconnue immense . . .*
> *Un seul mot rompit le silence :*
> *"Paris !" et puis elle ajouta,*
> *Comme en réponse à ma prière :*
> *"Vas-y seule, à pied . . . car c'est là*
> *Que tu pourras sauver ton père."*

" The *Marseillaise* of my days of misery," Rachel called that song in after years—we shall see why as

Rachel

we proceed. They tell how she recalled and recited
it, on a bed of sickness, in a dimly lighted room, and
burst into tears when she had finished, because she
knew that her triumphs were over, and she had
only to wait for death.   But that is to anticipate.
The actual triumph of the first appearance was of
very brief duration.   *La Vendéenne* failed, and had
to be withdrawn.   *Le Mariage de Raison*, which
succeeded it, was equally a failure, and afforded no
scope for the display of Rachel's special gifts.

It became clear that the Gymnase was not the
theatre for her.   She was as little in her element
in the light pieces of its repertory as would be,
say, Mrs. Patrick Campbell in *Pink Dominoes*, or
Miss Lena Ashwell in *Charlie's Aunt.*   Poirson
recognized this, and offered to release her from her
engagement, while, at the same time, using his
influence to facilitate her admission to the Comédie
Française.   Before she could enter there, however,
she had to go back to her lessons; and this time she
asked Samson to take her as his pupil, and Samson
agreed to do so.

Samson was an admirable man, a good actor, a
true gentleman, and the greatest dramatic teacher
that the world has ever seen : a man of whom it
may justly be said that he dignified his profession
in the confidence that, if he did so, his profession
would dignify him.   He had known Talma; he was
to be the link between Talma and Rachel—the two
greatest tragedians of his country.   He had
thought highly of Rachel even when Provost
had hustled her out of the Conservatoire with his

injunction to go back to her flower-selling; and he had protested against her removal to the Gymnase as the probable ruin of her career. When she returned to him, brought back by her father, he realized at once that, in training her, he would have the chance of a lifetime. But he also realized that he had to do with a very ignorant little girl whose training must begin with the elements.

Rachel in those days could hardly read. Whatever she had to read, whether it was a letter, or a newspaper, or a book, she read aloud. It had not even occurred to her that it was worth while to read anything more of a piece than her own part in it; and her parents complained that she neglected her studies in order to play with a skipping-rope. All these faults Samson, treating her more as a daughter than as a pupil, set himself to eradicate with the patient care which his widow describes in her interesting volume of theatrical recollections entitled *Rachel et Samson*.

First he insisted that the skipping-rope should be destroyed. Then he showed his pupil how impossible it was for her to understand a part unless she studied the play as a whole. Finally he required that she should take lessons in the French language, and arranged that the governess of his own children, a Madame Bronzet, should instruct her at the cheap charge of twenty francs a month. And all this, be it observed, solely in the interest of art, and without any of those "ulterior motives" by which the men, whether actors or patrons of the drama, who hold out helping hands to actresses are sometimes influenced.

Rachel

One feels assured of that by the absence of even the faintest gleam of jealousy from Madame Samson's narrative. Both she and her husband often quarrelled with Rachel in later years, but they always quarrelled with her simultaneously. In the meantime she was their prodigy, of whom they were jointly proud. They invited her to their suburban villa as well as their Paris flat; they admired her efforts, already beginning to be successful, to make herself beautiful by " living up to " the statuary in the Louvre; and they were very sorry for her because she was so poor. Two glimpses at her poverty may be taken from Madame Samson's book :—

" Her French governess," we read, " used to tell us that she often found her sitting before a small fire watching a saucepan. She sat on a small three-legged stool, studying a Racine which she held on her knees, while her hands were full of carrots which she was scraping to put in the *pot-au-feu*."

And then, on another page—

" It was when she was coming to our country place. One day she arrived later than usual. I began to reproach her, but she said naively—

" ' It is not my fault, madame. This is the only dress I have,' and she pointed to a little gingham frock, flowered with lilac. ' I had to wash it this morning, and then I had to dry it and iron it, and that is why I am late.' "

But she was getting on; and presently Samson

made her recite to Vedel,[1] who was now the director
of the national theatre.

" After she had finished "—we are still quoting
Madame Samson,—" Samson turned to him and
asked him what he thought of her.
" ' She is very small,' he said. ' Her physique is
rather fragile.'
" ' Never mind about her physique,' replied
Samson. ' What do you think of her reciting ? '
" ' Very intelligent, but hardly rich and full
enough as yet.'
" ' Quite so,' rejoined Samson. ' You can't expect
a full-blown talent at her age. But do you think
her good enough to be introduced at the Comédie
Française, or, at all events to be engaged by the
theatre with a view to her appearance a little
later ? ' "
" Vedel agreed that she was good enough, and
a few days later offered her an engagement at
£160 a year."

Then followed a further period of probation during
which Rachel enjoyed the privilege of free admission
to the theatre. She was still so poorly dressed that
she sometimes had trouble at the box-office; and she
complained to Samson that the clerk there tried
to relegate her to the pit or gallery on the ground
that she was not sufficiently ornamental for the
dress circle or the stalls. " A little girl like that ! "
the clerk objected when Samson spoke to him; but

[1] Promoted from the post of treasurer to succeed Jouslin
Lassalle.

Rachel

Samson warned him that that little girl would soon be in a position to bring about his eviction from his box-office merely by remarking that she did not like the colour of his hair.

She was, too, an impatient little girl. She had not associated with the Samsons without getting to know how grand was the status of a leading actress at the Théâtre Français; what praise awaited her, and what presents, and what opportunities of diverting herself in the society of the nobly born, and at their charges. It seemed to her that that good time could not begin too soon. Vedel, in his article on Rachel in the *Revue des Races Latines*, tells us how she tried to hasten it :—

" On the 10th of June," he writes, " Mlle. Rachel, who often used to come to see me, said to me—

" ' I am tired of this sort of thing. I want to make my début. I wish you would let me appear.'

" ' When you like,' I said. ' Will the day after to-morrow suit you ? '

" A sudden blush came over her face, and, with a look of pleasure which I shall never forget, she answered, in eager tones—

" ' Yes, I shall be delighted.'

" ' In which of your parts would you like to appear ? '

" ' In whichever you prefer.'

" ' Camille in *Horace*, for instance ? '

" ' That will suit me very well.'

" ' All right, my dear. Tell M. Samson, and your début shall be advertised to-morrow for the day after.'

Rachel

" ' But I haven't the dresses ready.'

" ' Never mind.   I will attend to that for you.'

" And, on the following morning, I supplied her with what she needed."

The début duly took place on June 13, 1838, with exactly £30 2s. 6d. in the house.

CHAPTER IV

Début at the Comédie Française—State of the French stage at the
time—Effects of the Romantic Movement.

IF Rachel had failed, or even if she had been
only moderately successful, the matter would have
concerned no one but herself. As things turned out,
her appearance and signal success marked an epoch
in the history of the French stage; so that it will be
proper to interpose here some remarks on that branch
of the subject—remarks, of course, to be passed over
by any reader who is only interested in the personal
aspects of this work.

The point to be made is that Rachel, without
meaning to do anything of the kind, and without
even knowing what she did, suddenly stemmed the
rising tide of the Romantic Movement in the theatre.
So we must go back once more to the Romantic
Movement.

The Romantic Movement began in prose with
Rousseau, and was continued by Bernardin de
Sainte-Pierre, Chateaubriand, Madame de Staël, and
George Sand. These writers evolved fresh harmonies
out of the French language, and gave a new emotional
turn to French literature. In the matter of romance
they substituted first sentiment and then passion
for gallantry. It was their boast that they wrote,
not with ink, but with tears and their hearts' blood.

Rachel

They put themselves into their books, and sounded
the personal note on the house-tops. The departure
was one from which no return was possible. The
ball, once set rolling, had to roll on until the
Romantic Movement became the Realistic Movement; for Realism was only a new kind of
Romanticism—the result, not of a counter-revo-
lution, but of a supplementary revolution — the
further overthrow of certain literary conventions
which the Romantics had left standing and certain
others which they had set up. The writers of
the eighteenth century conventional and classical
schools can hardly be said even to have shown fight
against them.

Where the prose writers had led the way the poets
followed; first Lamartine, then Alfred de Vigny,
Alfred de Musset, Sainte-Beuve, before the poet in
him died young and left him a critic, and finally
Victor Hugo. They not only devised new metres
and made new music; they also introduced new ideas,
new emotions, and new points of view, bidding the
world wake up and find itself modern, calling upon
it to feel instead of thinking. Their lives were, as
one may say, successions of nervous crises, and their
verses were the reflection of their lives. Between
them and the intellectual literature of the eighteenth
century the French Revolution lay like a great gulf.
The classical and conventional subjects of poetry
did not appeal to them. Such subjects, they felt,
were only fit for school-boys' themes—the real
purpose of literature was self-expression.

They expressed themselves, at first in tears, and
afterwards in frenzy. The history of their Movement

can almost be summed up as the transition from the
tears of Lamartine to the frenzy of Victor Hugo.
The sobs of Alfred de Musset, the sighs of Sainte-
Beuve, and the spleen of Alfred de Vigny are land-
marks on the journey.   Only, of course, neither the
frenzy nor the tears are of the essence of the matter.
The essence of it is the resolve, or the instinct, of
each writer to be, and to express, himself : to see life
with his own eyes, and feel it with his own heart, and
render it accordingly, without regard to the rules and
traditions of the men of old.

Acting by instinct at first, by degrees they became
self-conscious.   When they became self-conscious
they became militant; and when they became
militant the theatre was the principal object of
their attack—just as it is the principal object of the
attack of certain fiery young English " intellectuals "
at the present time.   And this for obvious reasons.

For the theatre in France occupies, or at all events
occupied at that date, a very different position from
the theatre in England.   An English intellectual of
this age might reasonably say, if he chose to, that
the contemporary drama concerns him no more than
does contemporary ballet-dancing, or conjuring,
or plate-spinning.   A French intellectual of the
Romantic School could not possibly take that line.
The theatre was not to be poohpoohed by him as a
mere place of popular entertainment.   It had to
entertain, of course, under penalty of losing money
and being compelled to close its doors; but its appeal
was to persons of taste, and not to the vulgar herd.
It was, in short, a Temple of Art.   The national
theatre was an endowed and established Temple of

Rachel

Art—the repository of artistic traditions, officially stamped as the best. The Romantics were bound, therefore, to feel that, so long as the national theatre upheld the classical traditions, it stood in their way, and in the way of progress. They could also depend upon it, as an old conservative institution, to resist their attempt to overthrow it.

The fact of the matter was that French dramatic literature had hardly progressed at all since 1789. Stage plays like *Le Mariage de Figaro* had helped to prepare the way for the Revolution; but no new dramatist of mark had come to light since Beaumarchais. The best literature of the intervening period had been what Professor Brandes has called " the literature of the *émigrés*"—the work of the men and women who fled before the revolutionary storm and the subsequent despotism—Chateaubriand, and Madame de Staël, and Benjamin Constant, and Sénancour. Some of them amused themselves with amateur theatricals in their exile —notably and chiefly at Coppet; but their real interests were far removed from the theatre; and the few writers who remained in Paris and wrote for the stage found themselves engaged upon a thankless task.

There were too many competing excitements— life itself competed. In the days when the guillotine was " going always," and in the days when every morning brought the bulletin of a fresh victory, people did not need to exercise their emotions at the play. The theatre retained, indeed, a certain ceremonial importance because Napoleon was a playgoer and was believed to have commanded Talma to coach him in imperial deportment. But dramatic art made no advance. The old plays were good enough for the Emperor—he had not an idea beyond Racine, if indeed he had an idea beyond Corneille; so that tragedy, in his reign, did not progress beyond the point at which Voltaire had left it. The revolution was not attempted until after he had been sent to Saint Helena and the Bourbons had come again into what they regarded as their own.

Then Stendhal began. He is not properly to be classed with the Romantics; but he did some of their work for them when he wrote his pamphlet, *Racine et Shakespeare*. His thesis was, roughly, that Shakespeare, being exempt from the limitations which had hampered Racine—freer in his choice of subjects and unfettered by any notion of dramatic " unities "— should be regarded as a greater man. This in the city in which a play of Shakespeare's had just been hooted off the stage on the ground that the author was " Wellington's aide-de-camp."

Next Victor Hugo followed where Stendhal had shown the way, producing, in the famous preface to *Cromwell*, what may fairly be styled the romantic dramatists' Petition of Right. There was no need, he urged, for the tragedian to confine himself to " noble " subjects. No subject was common or unclean, and any subject could be made noble if the artist knew how to treat it. And the so-called " unities " were ridiculous. To confine a writer within their four walls was like compelling a workman to work in chains. Et cetera, et cetera, in a long and furious manifesto.

Rachel

So the new school was founded. Adherents were recruited as fast as special constables are sworn in on a day of riot; the militant company sallied forth to war. Enthusiastic young poets began by translating Shakespeare, and then proceeded to imitate him. Alfred de Vigny's translation of *Othello* marks a date in the movement; but the most important date of all is that of the production of Victor Hugo's *Hernani*.

Other theatres—the Porte Saint-Martin and the Odéon, for instance—had already yielded to the assault. *Hernani* was designed to conquer the national theatre itself; and it achieved the victory in the face of opposition alike from the old-fashioned players and from old-fashioned playgoers. Mlle. Mars, who had ruled over the theatre for so long, showed, at rehearsals, a disposition to " guy " her part, and was amazed to find that the author had the courage to ask her to resign it if she were not prepared to play it as he wished.[1] The Old Brigade rallied at the *première* to boo and hiss, and there ensued a battle royal between the rival claques.

All the world knows the story of that battle : how Gérard de Nerval and Théophile Gautier raised an army of Romantics in the studios; how Théo. the long-haired ordered a new red waistcoat [2] for the occasion; how that red waistcoat served as the Oriflamme of the Hugolaters, who streamed into the house with complimentary tickets; how the Hugolaters and the Old Brigade shouted against each

---

[1] The final quarrel occurred because she presumed to amend the author's text, resenting a portion of his vocabulary as unclassical.

[2] According to some accounts he also wore green trousers.

Rachel

other and almost came to blows; how the Hugolaters triumphed and remained in possession of the
field, declaring that the classical drama was "played
out" and that Victor Hugo was the greatest dramatic
author that the world had ever seen.

All the world knows, too, how the triumph of
Hernani was followed by the triumph of Alfred
de Vigny's *Chatterton*.

In that case also there was an Opposition to be
subdued—an Opposition which included both Louis-
Philippe and his Minister of Fine Arts. These
objected that the national theatre was no place for
the emotional methods of Marie Dorval. They
insisted that the part of Kitty Bell ought to be played
in the cold-blooded classical style by the venerable
Mlle. Mars. Their arguments were repeated, with
sarcastic predictions of failure, in the *coulisses*; and
the author had to threaten that, unless he got his
way, he and his piece and his leading lady would be
transferred to the Porte Saint-Martin.

He got his way; and *Chatterton* was an even
greater success than *Hernani;* the upshot of the
matter being that the classical drama did really
seem to be on its last legs in France. The public
was not merely impatient of inferior writers of
the classical school—such writers as Marie-Joseph
Chénier and Néopomucène Lemercier. It was tired,
or supposed itself to be tired, of Corneille and Racine
themselves. Tradition kept their works in the
repertory, but they ceased to draw. It looked as if
their removal from the repertory could only be a
question of time.

*   *   *   *   *   *

Rachel

That was the state of things when Rachel made her first appearance as Camille in *Horace*, with £30 2s. 6d. in the house; and even with that figure the nadir was not reached. On her second appearance in the same part the receipts amounted only to £14 18s. 10d.; and on her third appearance she played to a house holding no more than £12 2s. 6d. Her triumph was near at hand, but it was still to be delayed a little longer.

So little importance had been attached to her début that the Press had not been invited to witness it. It had taken place at the beginning of the dull season, when the men who made public opinion in Paris were all at the seaside. Or, at any rate, only one of them had remained in town; and he could not make public opinion by himself.

The one was Dr. Véron—the inevitable man with a *flair* for important artistic events which would give him something to talk about in after-life, as keen as that of the penny-a-liner for a street accident or a fire. He turned into the theatre casually, he says, searching for a cool and quiet place in which to spend a sultry evening, and he found only four persons besides himself in the stalls. His attention was drawn to the stage by " a strange and exceedingly expressive countenance, a prominent brow, a dark eye, deep-set and full of fire." He remembered that he had seen that face before either at Saint-Aulaire's Academy or at the Gymnase. He remembered a certain deep voice answering the question what the owner of it was doing in the words : " Je poursuis mes études."

And now the studies had been pursued with so

Rachel

much success that Dr. Véron perceived the student
to be a prodigy of genius.   If the prodigy whom he
had discovered had been merely a poet or a painter,
he might have kept his discovery to himself until he
had forgotten all about it.   As she was an actress,
and of a certain haunting beauty, he felt the need of
telling all his friends.   " When," he assured one
of them—and probably, indeed, assured several of
them—" the twelve or fifteen hundred men of
taste who make public opinion in Paris have seen
her and taken the measure of her talents, that
child will be the glory and fortune of the Comédie
Française."

A true prophecy, corroborated by an interesting
entry in the diary of a colleague, the actor Joanny :
" I played very well to-night, and that little girl,
Mademoiselle Rachel, seems to have the right stuff
in her."   But not a prophecy which could be fulfilled
immediately.   Dr. Véron, as has been said, could
not make public opinion by himself, though he tried
hard to do so.   Jules Janin, who could, was taking
a holiday in Italy; so that Rachel went on playing
to empty houses.   The best house which she played
to on the first eighteen occasions on which she
appeared was only £52 4s.; and the average receipt
was a few pence under £29.

Moreover the actress who had had to stand aside
in order that Rachel might appear in leading parts
was becoming impatient.   She wished to resume
those parts, saying that Rachel had been favoured
sufficiently; Vedel had his work cut out to appease
her.   He did appease her, however—unless it was
that he intimidated her—for he had confidence in

Rachel

his new star, and was resolved to keep her in the foreground until Jules Janin had seen her.

And now it was the middle of August; and Jules Janin was on his way home; and there were people waiting to tell him—a few men of taste amid the multitude who waited for a lead—that there was a little débutante at the Théâtre Français, making a curious impression there, though not yet causing a furore, and that he had better make haste and inspect her, and tell Paris what to think.

CHAPTER V

Rachel's reception by the public and by the critics—Jules Janin and
Alfred de Musset quarrel about her.

RACHEL, it is to be observed, though seen in leading
parts, was not yet definitely fixed in the position of a
leading lady. She was entitled, as were all débutantes,
to appear in such parts a certain number of times, to
show what she could do in them. What happened
afterwards would depend upon how her playing
affected the fortunes of the box-office; and, for three
months, in spite of the plaudits of the pit and the
enthusiasm of two or three men of taste, the box-
office derived no perceptible benefit from her performances. She was still a struggling neophyte,
relegated to the worst dressing-room in the theatre,
and so poor, Madame Samson tells us, that she had
to dispense with the services of a dresser or a maid,
carry her own chair up to it, arrange her own dressing-
table, and fix her own mirror in its place.

The prejudice against the classical drama was
strong. The Romantics were in possession, and
were not to be dislodged in a day. A clarion blast
would have to be blown on some newspaper man's
trumpet before the walls of Jericho would fall down
flat. Frédéric Soulié, best known as a writer of
sensational stories of mystery and crime, who was
doing Jules Janin's work for him during his absence,
was committed to the Romantics, and could not be

Rachel

expected to blow it. But Jules Janin was coming, and he could do so, being committed to no party, but always anxious to find something which he could gush over with the fiery fluency of the late Clement Scott.

He came; he heard of Rachel; he went to see her; and, for a moment, he hesitated to trust his judgment. Was it possible, he asked himself, to praise Rachel without affronting the great Victor Hugo? And, if not, was it right and proper that the great Victor Hugo should be affronted? He took a day or two to think these questions over carefully; but then, at last, he grasped his courage in his two hands and plunged.

" Take notice " (he wrote in his weekly feuilleton) " that, at the very moment of writing, at the Théâtre Français itself—the *Théâtre Français*, mark you—an unexpected victory is being won : one of those happy triumphs of which a nation like ours is rightly proud, at the hour when, brought back to honourable sentiments, noble language, chaste and self-contained love, it makes its escape from nameless violences and barbarisms which never end.

" What a joy it is, indeed, for an intelligent people suddenly to find itself once more in possession of its masterpieces, so long and so undeservedly misunderstood! O gods, and goddesses, be praised, you who have made the masterpiece at once immortal and indulgent. It is indulgent precisely because it lives for ever. In vain is it overwhelmed with insults and outrages. In vain is it subjected to humiliating comparisons. In vain do men cease to remember

Rachel

and admire it. It disdains insults, and despises oblivion. It replies to affronts with a smile. It is calm, it is patient, it is solemn; and when at last we call upon it, there it is extending its royal and paternal hand to the ungrateful who cried aloud in their boredom : *Lord, save us ; we perish !* "

So much as a prelude and a declaration of policy, an intimation that the critic proposed to back the dead against the living : the old Classics against the new Romantics. And then :—

" This time we find ourselves in possession of the most astounding and amazing little girl which the present generation has ever seen on the boards of a theatre. This child—take note of her name—is Mademoiselle Rachel."

And then, after reminding himself and his readers that he had already discovered the child once, at the Gymnase, and suggesting that he was probably the only playgoer who remembered her appearance there :—

" And now this child is listened to, encouraged, applauded, and admired. She is appearing at last in the only kind of drama worthy of her precocious genius. Picture it, and think of it ! A slip of a girl, quite ignorant, without art, without training, drops into the world of our old tragedies, blows on their august ashes and makes them burn up, and compels flames and life to burst from them. Oh, it is marvellous. . . .

Rachel

" Ask her no questions about Tancred, and Horace, and Hermione, and the Trojan war, and Pyrrhus, and Helen. She knows nothing about these things; she knows nothing about anything. But she has something better than knowledge—she has rays of light emanating from her person. When she steps on to the stage, inches seem to be added to her stature. She is tall enough for a Homeric heroine. Her head is uplifted and her bosom expands; her eye is brightened, and her walk is like that of a queen; she gesticulates, and it is as if her soul spoke. Her voice vibrates, swayed by the passions of her heart. . . .

" Wait till she grows up, this little girl who is accomplishing a revolution without knowing what she does. Wait till she finds a young man as inspired as herself to play with her; and then the gods of poetry will come back to us, and we shall see the extinguished torch of Corneille and Racine rekindled. . . ."

And so on and so forth, and so forth and so on, in the best Clement Scott style, with many vain repetitions and mixed metaphors, as if the writer's pen had been wound up to go, and could not stop going till it ran down.

But the notice " did the trick," and the walls of Jericho were levelled. Parisians returning from their country houses, and from the spas and watering-places, tumbled over each other in their hurry to see and admire the new star signalled on the horizon during their absence. One has to listen very intently indeed to catch a jarring note in the sudden chorus of delight; but the one jarring utterance which is audible may as well be preserved :—

" October 20, 1838 : Yesterday I went with Pauline to the Comédie Française to hear Mlle. Rachel, who is now causing so great a sensation. I was not at all pleased. They all acted very badly, though Mlle. Rachel is not so bad as the rest. They played *Andromaque*, in which she took the part of Hermione, the part of irony, scorn and disdain. She went through it accurately and intelligently, but there is no sympathy or attraction in her acting. She has a thin voice, is neither pretty nor beautiful, but very young, and might become an excellent actress if she had good training. I was very bored, and returned home benumbed."

So the Duchesse de Dino noted in her recently published Diary. But the queue at the pit door was of inordinate length, and began to form hours before the door was opened; and the records of the box-office are eloquent. For Rachel's first eighteen appearances, as we have seen, the receipts averaged no more than £29—the most profitable night producing £52 4s., and the least profitable only £12 2s. 6d. ; but the next eighteen performances showed very different results. The highest receipt was then £256 8s. 4d., the lowest £85 3s. 4d., and the average £197 11s. 5d.

It was immense for the house and the period : a veritable hail-storm of pieces of silver. The Head of the Tribe of Félix heard the grateful sound and hurried to the spot. "Was für Plunder !" he reflected

Rachel

in the words of Blucher taking stock of London from the dome of Saint Paul's. His daughter being a minor, he was entitled to draw her salary for her, and he was resolved that it should be a salary worth drawing.

In vain did Vedel spontaneously raise her stipend from £160 to £320 a year; in vain did he add perquisites bringing her total earnings to about £800 a year. That was not good enough for Jacob Félix. He suggested a salary of £1600 a year, and he brought his demands to Samson. Samson pointed out that Rachel had a contract with the Comédie Française; but Jacob Félix laughed in his face. A contract, indeed! What was the use of a contract with a minor? Such a contract was not worth the paper it was written on. He would repudiate it; he would tear it up; he would go to law about it. He really appeared to think that he had right and reason on his side.

" For you see, Monsieur Samson, since my daughter has talent, it is only just that I should make something out of her," was his way of putting it.

Whereupon Samson struck attitudes of noble indignation. First he took a statuette which Rachel had given him, as a thank-offering for his teaching, from the mantelpiece, and smashed it to fragments in the fire-place; and then he turned to Jacob Félix, saying, as only an actor of the old school could say it—

" That is the way out, sir. Let your shadow never darken that door again."

So the Head of the Tribe of Félix withdrew. But he nevertheless went to law, as he had threatened to do, on his daughter's behalf, and retained Crémieux, afterwards Governor of Algeria, and won his suit— got Rachel's contract declared to be void, and imposed his own terms on the theatre.

That was one of the proofs which Rachel enjoyed of the importance of the position to which she had sprung almost in a night.   Another was vouchsafed when the critic who claimed to have made her, seeing her again as Roxane in *Bazajet*, printed some unkind remarks in striking contrast with his previous eulogies.

" Affaire de lit et d'argent," was Sainte-Beuve's brutal summary of the incident.[1] He intended, apparently, to imply that it had been intimated to Jules Janin that it was unnecessary for him to try to encourage Rachel by putting his arm round her waist—that this privilege was reserved for admirers who brought presents in their hands—and that Jules Janin had made his feuilleton the weapon of vengeance for the *spretæ injuria formæ*. The insinuation cannot be verified, though one suspects that there sometimes are such wheels within wheels in the relations between dramatic artists and dramatic critics.   What we do know is that Rachel, being put on her mettle, played Roxane a second time and triumphed; and that she found a formidable champion in an unexpected quarter.

Jules Janin was not the only critic who had praised her performances.   Alfred de Musset had also done so in the *Revue des deux Mondes ;* and he now took up his pen once more in a combatant and aggressive mood.   He said that Roxane was Rachel's best

_____
[1] In a letter to the Oliviers of Lausanne.

part. His heart had told him so, and the judgment of his heart was not to be influenced by cabals. It was her destiny, he felt certain, to be as great as Malibran. He had observed with pain that she had been attacked. He felt it his duty to defend her to the best of his ability; and he was very indignant against those who had " tried to destroy in the heart of a child the divine seed which cannot fail to bring forth good fruit."

It seemed to Jules Janin that this was meant for him, and that it was incumbent on him to reply; so he, too, took up his pen, and took it up in an even more angry and aggressive temper than his supposed assailant.

Beginning with general principles, he soon got to personalities. First he repeated his censures, and said that he adhered to them—" C'est mon opinion et je la partage." Then he proceeded to ridicule those whom he styled " the newborn babes of criticism." He pictured them " spreading out their tails like peacocks before a reputation which they cannot even understand." He protested that such persons compromised the noble art of dramatic criticism by their extravagant exaggerations; and having thus worked himself up into a white heat of passion, he concluded—

" When I see these retired novelists and these third-rate poets picking up the critic's pen with a smile, I am reminded of the worthy ancient who picked up a violin. ' Can you play the fiddle?' some one asked him. ' I don't know,' he answered, ' for I have never tried.' "

Rachel

Then it was Musset's turn. He rejoined, not in print, but in a private communication, which ran thus :—

"Saturday, Dec. 8, 1838.

" SIR,

"In the *Revue des deux Mondes* I expressed my opinion of Mlle. Rachel with politeness and sincerity. There was no reference in my article to you. You have replied to it with unbecoming violence. Your article is coarse and unmannerly. In your capacity of man of letters you are a child who ought to be muzzled. In your personal capacity you are a buffoon who ought to be forbidden to enter the Théâtre Français. Avenge yourself for this letter with fresh insults if you like. I fully expect you to do so, and I am quite indifferent in the matter.

"ALFRED DE MUSSET."

So that it had come to this : that, within a few months of Rachel's first appearance, the greatest of the French dramatic critics and one of the greatest of the French poets were ready to fly at each other's throats—and would actually have flown at each other's throats if they had not both been men of peace, more skilled with the pen than with the sword—over the question whether she was, or was not, at her best in a particular part. Even when we have made every allowance for the seriousness of the French in matters of art—they are at least as serious about art as we are about theology—the fact remains a striking proof of the suddenness of her rise to the sublime heights of glory.

Rachel

Naturally, too, she was anxious to pursue the further acquaintance of the chivalrous young man of letters who had come forward, uninvited, as her champion; and it was an easy thing for her to do, as he was a young man who haunted theatres. So she asked him to call—or perhaps it was he who asked permission to call—and he went to see her; and then she swept him up, one evening, in the galleries of the Palais Royal, and carried him off to supper; and his description of that improvised supper-party, published in the volume of his *Œuvres Posthumes*, is the best and most intimate picture which has been preserved of Rachel in the days when, in spite of her celebrity, she still lived a simple life because, though her salary was large, her father drew it for her, and only allowed her a small share of it as pocket-money.

CHAPTER VI

THE revellers were quite young people—recent recruits at the theatre and the Conservatoire, and competitors for the privilege of admiring them. Alfred de Musset, who was eight-and-twenty, was distinctly the patriarch of the party. They streamed gaily up the staircase of the house in the Passage Véro-Dodat in which the Tribe of Félix lived on Rachel's salary. Jacob Félix had gone to the opera to see the début of a co-religionist of the Tribe of Nathan, and Madame Félix was taken by surprise.

She was an excellent person for an old-clothes woman, with a certain measured dignity in her demeanour even when she tripped and sprawled over the rules of grammar; but she had the figure of a mother of sixteen, and she could not be hustled in her old age to wait on her daughter's friends. Since Rachel insisted on sending the servant to the theatre to fetch a handful of rings which she had left on her dressing-table, she must get the supper herself. There were steaks in the kitchen. If Rachel liked to grill them, her guests were quite welcome to eat them.

So Rachel put on " a dressing-gown and a night-cap," and, looking " as beautiful as an angel,"

Rachel in Phèdre

Rachel

brought in a dish of three beef-steaks which she had grilled with her own hands. " Help yourselves," she said, laying the dish down; and then she retired again, and presently reappeared carrying a tureen of soup in one hand and a saucepan full of spinach in the other. Next, she dived into a cupboard and found a bowl of salad there; and finally she informed her friends that, as the servant had the keys of the plate cupboard in her pocket, they must be satisfied to eat with the kitchen forks.

They were young and light-hearted, and had not the least objection. The only objection came from Rachel's elder sister Sarah, who tiptilted a disdainful nose, and sniffed. For Sarah was an actress, like Rachel, but a different kind of actress; not the sort of actress who acts, but the sort of actress who seeks invitations to supper—*une soupeuse* is the scornful French name for such. She wasn't used to that sort of thing, she said—she really couldn't. But the others only laughed at her, and the meal proceeded merrily, Rachel, in spite of the protests which Sarah mumbled in German—or perhaps it was in Yiddish —recalling memories of the days of her early struggles.

" Imagine it ! When I began to play at the House of Molière I had only two pairs of stockings, and——"

" Rachel ! Rachel ! Really, Rachel ! " interrupted Sarah.

" And I had to wash a pair every morning, and hang them over the back of a chair to dry, so that I might be able to play in the evening."

" And the house-keeping ? " asked Musset.

" Yes, I did that too. Every morning I was up

E   49

at six. By eight I had made all the beds, and then I went to the market to buy the dinner."

"And were you an honest marketer?"

"Generally; but once I cheated, and saved up until I had got three francs together?"

"And what did you do with those three francs, miss?"

"Sir," broke in Madame Félix, with grammatical eccentricities which it is impossible to render, "she squandered her money on the works of Molière."

At this stage the servant returned with the lost bracelets and rings—hundreds of pounds' worth of them—the gifts, no doubt, of admirers of the actress's genius. Rachel scattered them carelessly about the table, as if they were gauds of no importance, and called for kirsch, and set to work to mix a bowl of punch. The punch was set alight, and the candles were put under the table, so that the lurid blue flames might produce their full effect; Madame Félix keeping a watchful eye on Musset—so Musset says—for fear lest he should seize the opportunity of pocketing the jewels in the darkness. Then the candles were replaced and the punch was distributed. Rachel drank her share of it with a spoon from a soup-plate, and, afterwards, borrowed Musset's sword-stick to use as a tooth-pick.

That was the first phase. The second began when the other guests departed, and Sarah went to bed, and Madame Félix fell asleep in her chair. Then the actress, finding herself alone, or practically alone, with the poet, ceased her nonsense and became serious. She leaned for-

Rachel

ward, gazed eloquently into his eyes, and asked
the inevitable question—

" Why don't you write a play with a really good
part for me in it ? "

Already! She was only eighteen, and she had
only been acting for a few months; but she had
reached the point at which she was persuaded that
the greatest of the French poets could undertake
no nobler task than to write a play with a really
good part in it for her. And the poet was quite
of her opinion as to the essential nobility of such
an undertaking; and then the talk turned on the
iniquities of the dramatic critics whose notices had
been unkind, and on Rachel's ambition to show
what she could do in the difficult part of Phèdre—
the part which really tests the powers of a French
tragic actress. As for those critics—

" They attack me in vain—I will not be put down
by them. Instead of helping me and encouraging
me, they are always trying to damage me; but I'll
play, if I must, like four women rolled into one.
Oh yes, I've had some very nice notices—candid
and conscientious—they have been most useful to
me. But there are so many writers who use their
pens to lie, and destroy reputations. They are worse
then thieves and cut-throats. They try to kill
your soul with pin-pricks. How I should like to
poison them ! "

Already, though so young, she had grasped the
theatrical doctrine that the *raison d'être* of the public
press is to praise actresses; but she did not dwell

on it. Having said what she had to say, she proposed that she and the poet should read *Phèdre*
together; and of course the proposal delighted him;
so she went to fetch the book.

" Her manner and her gait have something solemn
and sacramental about them. She reminded me
of an officiating priest on his way to the altar, carrying the sacred vessels. She sat down close to me
and snuffed the candle. Her mother smiled and
went off to sleep again."

The scene, Musset says, was like an illustration
by Rembrandt of a chapter from *Wilhelm Meister*.
It was, at any rate, an impression of the artistic
life never to be effaced from his recollection. But
it was an impression which was very soon disturbed. At half-past twelve there was " noise
without," quickly followed by a noise within·
Jacob Félix was back from the opera, and in a surly
temper. He wanted to know what Rachel meant
by sitting up so late. He told her to stop reading
and go to bed at once. He gave her guest to understand that it was high time for him to take his leave;
and Musset departed, " melted to tenderness, and
full of admiration and respect," not, of course, for
Jacob Félix, but for his daughter.

Presumably the Head of the Tribe surmised that
here was a suitor for his daughter's heart who came
wooing without any pieces of silver in his hand. If
so, he surmised correctly. Instead of pieces of silver
Alfred de Musset offered a play—albeit a play which

Rachel

he had not yet written and would never write; and the play—though only a fragment—served his purpose. As soon as Rachel had quitted the parental roof to draw her salary for herself she invited her poet-playwright to visit her in a villa which she had acquired at Montmorency. He accepted the invitation, and, for a few days, he was very happy. " How charming she was ! " he exclaimed in a letter to Mme. Jaubert, " running about *her* garden with her feet in *my* slippers ! "

But she was only charming for a little while, and then the inevitable quarrel occurred. What they quarrelled about no deponent has related; but many causes can be conjectured. The flock of other suitors trying to unlock the door with golden keys may account for a good deal; and the poet's potations may account for the rest. He was not only addicted to beer, to brandy, and to absinthe. It was his unpleasant habit to mix the three stimulants in a single tumbler; and a poet who does that sort of thing cannot hope to retain any lady's favour permanently. So presently there was a wrangle as to which of them had thrown the other over; and the poet addressed the actress in pathetic verse—

> Si ta bouche ne doit rien dire
> De ces vers désormais sans prix ;
> Si je n'ai, pour être compris,
> Ni tes larmes, ni ton sourire;
>
> Si dans ta voix, si dans tes traits,
> Ne vit plus le feu qui m'anime;
> Si le noble coeur de Monime
> Ne doit plus savoir mes secrets;

Rachel

Si la triste lettre est signée;
Si les gardiens d'un vieux tombeau
Laissent leur prêtresse indignée
Sortir, emportant son flambeau;

Cette langue de ma pensée,
Que tu connais, que tu soutiens,
Ne sera jamais prononcée
Par d'autres accents que les tiens.

Périssent plutôt ma mémoire
Et mon beau rêve ambitieux !
Mon génie était dans ta gloire ;
Mon courage était dans tes yeux.

In a romance, of course, the curtain would have fallen on those lines in which the poet resigns his ambitions because the actress has ceased to smile. In real life, equally of course, it did not. There was an interval of three years during which the poet and the actress did not speak when they passed by; but the poet did not consecrate the time to tears. He devoted most of it to making love to Princess Belgiojoso,—a story which, having been related in *The Passions of the French Romantics*, need not be repeated here. At the end of the three years he met Rachel again at a dinner-party given by Buloz of the *Revue*, and she came up to him, with an outstretched hand, and a pretty air of coquetry, asking—

" Well, are you still cross ? "

" Why didn't you ask me that question three years ago ? " he replied. " I bore you no malice. We should have been friends again at the end of four-and-twenty hours."

" What a lot of time we have lost ! " she rejoined. And then they made it up like two children; and,

Rachel

after that, we read again of appointments in the dressing-room for the indulgence of caprices; and finally there comes a story of another supper-party, of a very different character from the one described above.

There was none of the simplicity of the improvised picnic this time. Instead of the kitchen forks, solid silver adorned the table; instead of steaks and salad, the masterpieces of a chef were served, and champagne was circulated in place of punch. Nor did any dozing mother superintend propriety with sympathetic somnolence, for Rachel had long since passed into the world in which chaperons are not. All the guests were men of fashion, and most of them were men of wealth—those gay and festive persons whom the French call *noceurs*. One of them, sitting next to Rachel, admired one of her rings, and a happy thought occurred to her. She took the ring off.

" Very well, gentlemen," she said. " Since the ring pleases you, it is for sale. I put it up to auction. Please to bid; " and the bidding began at once—

" Five hundred francs ! "

" A thousand ! "

" Fifteen hundred ! "

" Two thousand ! "

" Three thousand ! "

" And you, poet ? " said Rachel, turning to Musset, who, having no pieces of silver, but only genius, had kept silence. " I do not hear you bidding. What is your offer ? "

" I offer you my heart."

" The ring is yours."

Rachel

Not that she really wanted his heart any more than he wanted her ring; but the gesture seemed noble, and the temptation to it was not to be resisted. So she placed the ring on his finger in the presence of the company, saying that his acceptance of it was a promise that he would write a play for her.

He promised, and wrote the play—or, at any rate, began to write it—but she never played in it, for fresh quarrels quickly intervened. She heard him praise the acting of her colleague, Rose Chéri, and she considered that he had no right to praise any one but herself. That was the beginning of the second rift; and Musset seized the opportunity of returning the ring before Rachel could ask for it. She forgave him for that, however—more or less—and asked him a third time for a play, which she seems really to have wanted. The success of his *Caprice*, in which Madame Allan had won golden opinions, seemed to mark him out as the man to work for her. He was quite willing to do so, and began a piece called *Faustine*; but he had reckoned without her caprices.

It came to her ears that he was also working for Rose Chéri. Very well, she said. Of course he must write for Rose Chéri, if he wanted to, but, if he did, he could not write for her. It was an ultimatum, and he accepted it, and this time they quarrelled for good.

"Farewell, Rachel! It is you whom I bury in this drawer for ever," said the poet, as he locked up his manuscript; and Rachel applied to another author for the light comedy in which she desired to appear

Rachel

as a relief from the perpetual recitation of Alexandrine verse.

" Gozlan," she wrote to the friend who was to act as her intermediary, " can knock me off what I want, in a day or two, better than any one, now that Musset is dead—to literature."

For it had actually come to that. Literature, in Rachel's view, meant dramatic literature. There was no other kind of literature; and the author whom she would not allow to write plays for her was dead to the only sort of literature that she recognized. So potent may be the effect of flattery on the minds of young women who achieve glory on the stage.

And that was really the end; and there was no subsequent reconciliation. It seemed worth while to depart from chronological order for the purpose of telling a story which so clearly marks the contrast between Rachel's simplicity in the days when art was all in all to her, and the haughty airs and affectations of the time when her head was turned by the homage of the illustrious and her fibre coarsened by her great possessions. Now it is necessary to turn back and observe how, having first won renown on the stage, she became, almost as suddenly, a personage in society, yet comported herself as she chose, without much regard to the accepted code either of morals or of manners.

CHAPTER VII

IT has been mentioned that Dr. Véron claimed
to be one of Rachel's "discoverers." It must
be added that she entered upon the period of her
splendour and grandeur under his "protection,"
and that may possibly have been one of the reasons
why Jules Janin was not permitted to encourage
her by putting his arm round her waist.

The doctor was middle-aged and unprepossessing;
but he was rich. He had made a fortune in phar-
macy by exploiting a proprietary cough-drop, and
was to make another in journalism by exploiting
Eugène Sue's sensational stories. Moreover he was
a *boulevardier*, and he had "influence"; and it is
said that there is nothing like "influence" for
furrowing the way to the favours of an actress
in the morning hours of her career. An actress
is tempted to lay sentiment as an oblation on the
altar of professional ambition, and her heart, in
consequence, cannot always be taken seriously.

Rachel's certainly cannot—at all events at this
period of her life. She was passionately eager to
succeed, and it seemed to her that the end justified
any means; so she first accepted protection and then
indulged caprices, as her cynical admirer quite
expected her to do. He did not love her as

Rachel

Alfred de Vigny loved Marie Dorval—blind passions of that sort were quite out of his line; nor did he require her to love him in that grand, disinterested style—for he had lived long enough in the world to know that December (or even November or October, for that matter) must not expect too much of May. He was quite willing to shut his eyes from time to time, provided that there were no too shocking surprises for him when he re-opened them. But he did demand that he should not be made ridiculous; and it is precisely because that demand was not honoured that there is a story to be told.

Even Sainte-Beuve, who had very few relations with the theatre, was impressed by Rachel's proceedings, and commented on them in a letter to his friends, the Oliviers of Lausanne.

"Between ourselves," he wrote to them, "Rachel is behaving very badly. She is not, by any means, living the simple life, but has any number of lovers, and, with an income of £4,000 a year or more, finds herself hard up. Still, her status in the world of fashion is not affected by her conduct."

And what Sainte-Beuve observed Dr. Véron could not help suspecting; and presently his suspicions were strong enough to induce him to make inquiries. His position in Paris was such that he could apply to the police for help; and he therefore requested that detectives might be set to shadow Rachel, and that the results of their inquiries might be reported to him.

The police were accustomed to commissions of

the kind—reports on the private lives of actresses abounded in their archives—and they did what the doctor asked them. Their report was to the effect that his *protégée*, while writing him ardently affectionate letters, was regularly making, and keeping, assignations with several other men, in various houses in various parts of Paris. The doctor was not exactly heart-broken by the discovery; but he was annoyed, and determined to avenge himself. So he invited several of his friends to lunch, saying that he had an interesting communication to make to them; and, having thus collected an audience, he first showed them Rachel's love-letters, and then read them her *dossier*, as compiled by the detectives.

It would be superfluous to interrupt the narrative in order to point out that his behaviour was ungentlemanly. Dr. Véron might have replied to that charge by pleading that he did not claim to be a gentleman. But in so far as his purpose was to make things unpleasant for Rachel he succeeded. The position which she had made for herself in the world of fashion became untenable, and she fled before the storm. A letter to Samson mirrors her feelings :—

" I am going away," she wrote to her old teacher. " A cowardly wretch has insulted me. I have not the courage to take my own life, and yet despair is in my soul. There is no God—I do not believe in Him any longer. The world is killing me. Presently, it may be, God will know my heart. I have been silly, but I have never belonged to any man."

Thus she cried aloud under the stroke, expressing

Rachel

disbelief in God in one sentence and appealing to Him in the next; and though her triumphs at the theatre soon restored her courage and her self-esteem, the Faubourg Saint-Germain cast her out, and never again took her to its bosom.

It was a wonder, indeed, that the Faubourg Saint-Germain had ever been gracious to her, for that is not the Faubourg's usual way with actresses. The Faubourg, as a rule, draws a sharp line of demarcation between the society in which men seek their wives, and the society from which they select their mistresses. It does not, like Mayfair, believe that actresses are virtuous, and it does not desire them to be so. Consequently while, on the one hand, it does not suffer its own daughters to seek a career on the boards, on the other hand it only invites actresses to its receptions as hired entertainers, not as guests and equals. One or two social " mixers," like Madame de Girardin, whom we shall meet again, might, for one reason or another, open their houses to them; but the Faubourg as a whole viewed them as brazen creatures, and was only distantly polite.

But though that is, and always has been, the rule, the case of Rachel furnished an exception to it. She was so young; she looked so innocent; she had done so much for the rehabilitation of tragedy. Moreover, ill-educated though she was, she concealed her ignorance with a woman's cunning. Crémieux, the brilliant barrister who had represented her in her suit against the theatre, was privileged to re-write her drafts of her letters, correcting her many errors of punctuation, orthography and syntax. So the Faubourg viewed her as a vestal virgin, the High Priestess of her Art, and accepted her in its salons, treating her as a friend, even when it paid her a fee. It " adopted " her, writes Alfred de Musset's friend, Alton Shee, and " titled champions guaranteed her virtue "—those champions including the Ducs de Noailles, de Fitz-James, de Richelieu, and de Guiche, as well as Comte Walewski, who was afterwards to acknowledge himself the father of one of her children.

The accounts preserved of her behaviour in these great circles and grand circumstances differ. According to some chroniclers she moved among duchesses with dignity, as if she were a duchess herself—Théophile Gautier in particular was much impressed by the aristocratic air with which she held a fan. Others record acts of *gaminerie*, more vivacious than refined. The truth seems to be that she could behave perfectly when she chose, but that she did not always choose, being a creature of many moods, as good an actress off the stage as on, and somewhat prone to what anthropologists call " reversion to type."

She reverted to type, for instance, after her appearance before Queen Victoria at Windsor Castle. " Such a nice, modest girl," was her Majesty's verdict on her deportment on that occasion; but she had scarcely left the royal presence when she kicked her heels into the air, exclaiming, " O, mes amis, que j'ai besoin de m'encanailler ! "

She reverted to type again when Ernest Legouvé found her dancing in her dressing-room at the theatre—and not dancing merely, but dancing the cancan—in the classical costume of Virginie. She reverted a third time in her relations with Count Walewski, Napoleon's natural son, subsequently French Ambassador at the Court of Saint James's, and already mentioned as the admitted father of one of her children. He admired and respected her so much that he was prepared to marry her, at whatever risk to his career in the diplomatic service; but he heard presently that she had said behind his back, " Le comte m'embête avec son comme-il-faut;" and then he did not respect her, or admire her, or feel inclined to marry her any longer.

A fourth reversion to type is the subject of one of the best stories in Legouvé's *Soixante Ans de Souvenirs* :—

" Her fair fame " (Legouvé writes) " was, as it were, a sacred fire tended by the greatest ladies in France. One of these—and she neither the least illustrious nor the least intelligent—wishing to demonstrate her respect for the great artist to the community at large, took her for a drive to the Champs Elysées, in broad daylight, in an open carriage, with her own daughter sitting with her back to the horses. On their return from the drive, Mlle. Rachel, on re-entering the drawing-room, curtseyed to the duchess, and said to her, in a voice broken by tears : ' Madame, this proof of your regard is more precious to me than my talent.'

" The emotion of the mother and the daughter may be guessed. They raised the actress to her feet, and embraced her, and, after a few more moments had been consecrated to emotion, she took her leave. The drawing-room, which was very large, was entered by way of two much smaller ante-chambers. Mlle. Rachel, as she retired, passed through these two rooms, without perceiving that the girl was attending her, a few paces behind, to show her deference and sympathy. Arriving at the last door, she opened it, turned round, and believing that she was alone, placed her thumb to her nose and extended her four fingers, making the gesture with which small children express their contempt for things and persons.

" Unhappily this last door had glass panels. The artist's gesture was reflected by them on to a mirror in the other ante-chamber in which her hostess's daughter was still waiting. She saw it, and ran back, amazed, and threw herself into her mother's arms, sobbing with indignation."

It is a queer story, and one which may well have done quite as much to shake Rachel's position in the Faubourg as Dr. Véron's exposure of her promiscuous caprices. The Faubourg felt that the gesture was equally unbecoming in a social débutante and in a High Priestess. The Faubourg felt, most justly, that Rachel might have chosen a more graceful way of indicating her unworthiness of the honours showered upon her. It was no wonder, the Faubourg thought, that a young woman capable of such gestures was " bored " by the " correctitude " of her well-bred admirers; and therefore the Faubourg, for this reason among others, dropped Rachel like a hot potato.

Rachel

That did not happen immediately, however, and, in the meantime, she enjoyed many splendid moments.

It was a splendid moment when the Duchesse de Noailles said to her : " Mademoiselle, before you came to us we could neither read nor listen patiently, but you have taught us both accomplishments." And when the Duchesse d'Abrantès said, " Mademoiselle, when one plays as you do, it is one's mission to regenerate the French stage." And when the Comte de Molé, of the French Academy, said, "Madame, you have saved the French language from destruction." Whereto Rachel replied : " Sir, my credit is the greater in view of the fact that I have never learnt it."

It was a splendid moment again when Chateaubriand gave Rachel his arm, and spoke to her of his approaching death, so that she was able to respond : " Ah, but there are some men who are immortal." There were splendid moments, too, when the presents began to pour in : bracelets, and brooches, and a jewelled flask of attar of roses from the seraglio of the Sultan of Turkey, and a complete library, especially bound, of the masterpieces of French literature. Arsène Houssaye, who was a poet, as well as a theatrical manager, supplied yet another splendid moment by dedicating to her the quatrain :

Champmeslé, Lecouvreur, et Clairon se sont tues,
Mais tu règnes, Rachel, coeur qui bat, front savant ;
Ta grande âme domine un peuple de statues,
Muse des passions, coeur d'or, marbre vivant.

But the most splendid moment of all occurred in Madame Récamier's salon in the Abbaye-aux-Bois.

Rachel

Rachel had come there to recite, not for a fee, for Madame Récamier was poor, but as a friend. Chateaubriand sat on his special chair as on a throne; his court of devout women had disposed themselves at his feet ; representatives of the rising literary generation were grouped about the room. It had been whispered that perhaps—perhaps—the illustrious sentimentalist who had restored religion to France while Napoleon was restoring order would convert the most illustrious of the daughters of Israel to the Christian faith. There were those who already pictured the magnificent scene in the dim Gothic aisles of Notre-Dame on the occasion of her reception into the bosom of the Mother of the Churches; and meanwhile Rachel declaimed appropriate lines from the part of Pauline in *Polyeucte* :—

> Mon époux, en mourant, m'a laissé ses lumières ;
> Mon sang dont ses bourreaux viennent de me couvrir,
> M'a dessillé les yeux et me les vient d'ouvrir :
> JE VOIS, JE SAIS, JE CROIS.

She had got so far when the door opened, and the servant announced :—

" Monseigneur the Archbishop of Paris."

There was " movement " and keen expectation as Madame Récamier rose and presented the actress to the prelate—

"Mademoiselle Rachel, monseigneur, who has been so kind as to render a scene from *Polyeucte*."

And the prelate replied as a man of the world—

" It would be very painful to me to think that I had interrupted Corneille's masterpiece. Pray permit me to be included in the audience."

" If I might recite some lines from *Esther* instead ? "

Rachel

Rachel proposed. " I feel that that rôle suits me better."

It was her way of intimating that even the author of *Le Génie du Christianisme* had not persuaded her to become a Christian, and that those who pictured the ceremony of her conversion at Notre-Dame imagined a vain thing. But the Archbishop was far too good a man of the world to touch upon that point. He merely paid a compliment with the proper ecclesiastical turn to it :—

" It is not often the privilege of the ministers of the Most High to see and hear the great artists of the stage; but I myself have twice enjoyed that good fortune. In a drawing-room at Florence I heard Madame Malibran, and now I have to thank Madame Récamier for the pleasure of hearing Mademoiselle Rachel. The lips which recite those magnificent lines with so much eloquence must indeed be inspired by a heart filled with the sentiment which they render."

Whereupon Rachel, like a true daughter of the theatre, bowed profoundly, saying " Monseigneur, je crois," and leaving her archiepiscopal flatterer to find out for himself how much or how little she meant by it. And of course she meant nothing in particular.

That moment, however, may fairly be viewed as the climax of what Legouvé calls Rachel's " prehistoric period." In spite of her irresistible disposition to " revert to type " she indisputably enjoyed her social triumphs; and she sometimes even philosophized about them. We find her doing so in a remarkable letter to her brother Raphael.

Rachel

Raphael, she surmises, will wish to become an actor, and she proceeds to offer him some good advice on that hypothesis. He must, she tells him, be conscientious, and work at his art in the spirit of an artist. He must be inspired, not merely by a desire to get on in the world, but by " passionate love for the works which nourish the intelligence and guide the heart." Above all, he must educate himself; for a man needs education much more than a woman does.

" A woman, no doubt, may attain an honourable and respected position in society without that varnish which the world rightly calls education. The reason is that a woman does not lose her charm, but adds to it, by being very reserved in her behaviour and conversation. Her business is to reply, instead of leading the conversation; to listen, instead of starting subjects. Her natural coquetry makes her desirous of self-improvement; she remembers what she is told; and so she can often acquire the varnish without the solid foundation. But a man's case is very different. A man needs to know, every day of his life, the things which a woman is permitted to be ignorant of. The knowledge of them increases his pleasures and diminishes his difficulties. It enables him to vary his enjoyments and pass for a wit. Think of that; and if the work seems hard at first, remember that you have a sister whom your success will make proud and happy."

Sound sentiments, as the men and women who have risen must often have realized from their several points of view. It was all very well for Rachel,

Rachel

when reading poetry, to stop to ask the meaning of difficult words; but if Raphael did so he would make himself a laughing-stock. Moreover, it was unlikely that Raphael, albeit a personable young man, would be able to find educated persons eager to write his letters for him for the sake of his beautiful eyes. That is the privilege of actresses, but not of actors. Rachel had no need to study spelling, because she could get her letters written for her, in accordance with the specifications which she supplied, by her excellent friend Crémieux.

CHAPTER VIII

ADOLPHE CREMIEUX has already been mentioned as the Hebrew advocate who represented Rachel in her suit for the rescission of her contract with the Théâtre Français. He was forty and serious, a patron of the arts, but not a haunter of the *coulisses*. So he invited his client to his house, with the full approval of his wife, and tried to watch over her welfare in a paternal way.

Rachel declared, in later life, that he was the only man of her acquaintance who had never made love to her. Instead of doing that he coached her in ancient history and mythology, so that she might understand the classical dramas in which she shone, and read the Book of Genesis with her, and told her the meaning of the word " firmament," and rendered her a still greater service by writing her letters for her at the time when she was on probation, and on her best behaviour, in the Faubourg, and very much afraid lest her ignorance of grammar should impede her social progress. Her correspondence with him is a faithful mirror of as much of her life as she chose to submit to his inspection.

" My dear and tender M. Crémieux," is the nearest approach to affection in her style of address. More

Rachel

often she writes to him as "Dear papa Crémieux,"
and subscribes herself "Your child." The diction
is playful, ungrammatical, and only partially punctuated; but it draws a pleasant picture of a dazzled
girl, delighted at the multitudinous proofs that she
is getting on, but steering her course timorously
through the strange social waters and very glad of
the advice of a social pilot.

One finds an interesting illustration of the motherly
attitude of the Faubourg towards her in her account
of a party given for her by the Duchesse de Berwick.
Her mother, she says, took her to the house and left
her there; the duchess herself drove her home in her
own carriage. She asked the duchess to set her
down at M. Crémieux's door, but the duchess refused
to do anything of the kind. "No, my dear," she
said, "your good mother entrusted you to my care,
and it would not do for me to resign you into any
hands but hers." Which, of course, is just what she
would have said, in similar circumstances, to a girl
of her own social rank, though it may also have
implied a fear that actresses would be actresses if
left to themselves, and that no barrister could safely
be regarded as above suspicion where they were
concerned.

"So don't be angry with me, but pity me," is
the conclusion of the letter in which Rachel tells
the story and there follow some letters which may
be allowed to speak for themselves:—

"People are bombarding me with invitations and
it is quite impossible for me to come to see you even
for a moment that is very unfortunate isn't it but I

am going to ask you another favour. Mademoiselle
Déjazet has just sent me a charming letter which I
enclose and please write me an answer to it a very
polite answer please for I want to refuse her invitation so tell her I'm very sorry but it doesn't matter
as I'll come another day. It must be a very nice
letter please because she's sure to show it round."

"My dear and amiable M. Crémieux I forgot to
tell you that I have received a present from M.
Duchâtel and I want to thank him the sum is a thousand francs, and there is the Duchesse de Berwick too
whom I haven't seen for several months but as she
hasn't been to see me in the country as she promised
I'm afraid she's angry with me and as I don't hear a
word from her I thought perhaps she thought my
visits a nuisance, so send me a little letter to tell her
all that, and send both letters at once if you possibly
can as I am going away at mid-day and I want to
write from Paris."

That is a fair reproduction of her prose style in the
days of her novitiate; but she took pains to improve
it, as if she knew that she would not always have
Crémieux to depend upon; and presently we find her
writing to him to report her progress :—

"I expect you think me an awful nuisance but in a
few months time I shall be able to write all that sort
of thing for myself only my studies aren't finished
yet and I hope you won't drop me before they
are. I know now how to accept an invitation
to dinner and I shall soon know how to accept

Rachel

invitations to evening parties and then my course
will be complete."

Queer letters truly for a Queen of Tragedy who was
being congratulated on having saved the French
language from destruction at the hands of " Victor
Hugo and the Vandals and the Ostrogoths "; but then
the standing marvel about Rachel is that she accomplished so much with such a poor equipment. Her
method was to reveal the nakedness of the land to the
few in order that it might not be detected by the
many; and the few, fascinated by the thought that
genius leaned on them, guarded her secret jealously
as though they rejoiced in being parties to a pious
fraud. That was the state of things, at any rate,
when, having astonished Paris, she set out, in 1841,
to astonish London.

It was on that occasion that Queen Victoria
invited her to " declaim " at Windsor, and found her,
as she told the King of the Belgians, " such a nice
modest girl." The Duchess of Kent was equally
enthusiastic. An Indian shawl and a golden bracelet
with Queen Victoria's name on it in diamonds were
among the royal gifts to her.[1] Society, following
the royal lead, overwhelmed her with bouquets,
compliments and invitations. The receipts, she
writes, on the night on which she played *Marie
Stuart*, " amounted to thirty thousand francs and
a few guineas"—coins which she apparently confounded with pence; and she noticed what seemed
to her a remarkable habit of the English journalists.

[1] Rachel gave out that the inscription was " Victoria à Rachel." It
really ran " Victoria R. à Mademoiselle Rachel"—which is different.

73

Rachel

They flattered her to the skies, "*sans cartes de visites*"; which means, of course, that they sought no reward for their praise, and did not, like Jules Janin, presume to encourage her by putting their arms round her waist—a tribute to the disinterestedness of our dramatic critics which must on no account be left unrecorded.

An English witness to her triumphs in society as well as on the stage may be quoted first :—

"Everybody here is now raving about her. . . . Her appearance is very striking; she is of a very good height, too thin for beauty but not for dignity or grace; her want of chest and breadth indeed almost suggest a tendency to pulmonary disease, coupled with her pallor and her youth. . . .

"I was very much pleased with the quiet grace and dignity, the excellent *bon ton* of her manners. . . .

"She is completely the rage in London now; all the fine ladies and gentlemen crazy after her, the Queen throwing her roses on the stage out of her own bouquet, and viscountesses and marchionesses driving her about *à l'envie l'une de l'autre*, to show her all the lions of the town."

So Fanny Kemble writes, recalling one of those scenes of glory and enthusiasm which, for a brief moment, appear to mean so much, but are found to mean so little, and leave so evanescent a trace when once the curtain has rung down on them. And the triumph, like all her triumphs, meant an immense deal to Rachel. She enjoyed as one can enjoy at one-and-twenty. "Glory! Glory! Glory is the best thing in the world next to God," she

Rachel

exclaimed in one of her letters to Crémieux; and it is from that correspondence that we can derive our most vivid pictures of the visit.

Let a picture of the reception at Windsor have priority :—

" Yes ! Yes ! My triumph ! At nine o'clock her Majesty the Queen sent a beautiful carriage to convey me to the ancient and magnificent Castle of Windsor. As we drove from the hotel to the Castle I thought I was in a dream, but no, it was all true. I was actually getting out of an equipage belonging to Queen Victoria, and, in another instant, I found myself in the halls of the Thousand-and-One Nights.

" The Queen had a dinner-party of a hundred guests that night, so that I was left alone, for some time, in the galleries which, in spite of the brilliant illumination, still recall the tragic scenes which have passed there. At ten the Queen is announced. What a sudden change of expression on every countenance—one person forcing a smile, another trying to remember the compliment which he composed a week before ! All rising, the Queen enters slowly, smiles charmingly on all, bows to the company and takes her place in the midst of the mute assemblage which watches her least gesture. At last all are seated, and I await the Queen's orders. Presently a tall thin man came up to me. It was the Lord Chamberlain, who told me, in bad French, that the Queen was waiting. I was terribly frightened, but I felt that I must conquer or die. Besides, as I was to begin with the second act of *Bazajet*, I perceived that, happen what might, I must collect myself and behave like the majority of those about me.

" One of my company had eagerly accepted the honour of going to the English court and proving his gratitude to me by giving me my cues. Roxane and the scene of irony between Pyrrhus and Hermione obtained unanimous applause—a thing forbidden by etiquette, only her Majesty was kind enough to give the signal for it.

" I finished this brilliant evening with the third act of *Marie Stuart*, which pleased the young queen immensely. She told me so herself. She sent for me, and said that she had had even greater pleasure in hearing me recite at Windsor than at the house of the Duchess of Kent, though she had been delighted then, and she wound up by giving me a very pretty bracelet with her name and the date on it. That pleased me even more than the gift. Then, it being past midnight, the Queen withdrew with the same ceremony with which she had entered.

" And that was the end of this brilliant evening, so full of honour for my professional career. They had set out a splendid supper for me, but I was too tired to touch it. . . . And so you see, my dear friend, at what a pinnacle I have now arrived."

A picture of the triumphs in English society may come next :—

" To-morrow I have promised to go to the Derby with Lord Normanby. I dined with him on the 23rd. He is the Minister of the Interior, and he is married, and his wife has been extremely kind

Rachel

to me. Next Saturday she is going to take me for a drive and introduce me to her mother.

" I have given recitations at the houses of Lady Jersey, the Marchioness of Ailesbury, and Countess Cadogan. As for dinners, I am refusing them right and left. Ah, I forgot. I am to dine with Lord Palmerston, Lord Clarendon, and Lord Lovelace— I forget who else has invited me. The Duke of Wellington paid me many compliments at Lady Jersey's party, and came to call on me the next day. That is not the least of my London successes."

The Duke, indeed, not only called on Rachel, but wrote her a letter which must on no account be withheld, for the light which it throws on the intimacy of his knowledge of the idioms of the French language is lurid :—

" Le maréchal duc de Wellington présente ses hommages à Mlle. Rachel; il a fait prévenir au théâtre qu'il désirait y retenir sa loge enfin de pouvoir y assister à la representation pour le benefice de Mlle. Rachel.

" Il y assistera certainement si il lui devient possible de s'absenter ce jour là de l'assemblée du Parlement dont il est membre.

" Il regrettera beaucoup si il se trouve impossible ainsi d'avoir la satisfaction de la voir et l'entendre encore une fois avant son départ de Londres."

Thus the victor of Waterloo to the *protégée* of the proprietor of the cough-drop. It is a pretty picture of the effect of limelight in distorting the

world's scale of values. One cannot wonder that
Rachel basked in her glory, and began to feel that,
daughter of an old clothes-woman though she was,
a great gulf, social no less than artistic, was opening
between her and ordinary theatrical people. As for
the members of her company, who had no such
social pretensions—

"I have taken my precautions, and only allow
them to come and see me in the evening, about nine
o'clock, when no one in good society is likely to
call."

A happy instinct, too, told Rachel that her glory
would be greater if she refused to accept fees for
her appearances in the drawing-rooms of the leaders
of fashion. Her father, who was with her, though
he was not invited to accompany her into society,
thought the policy mistaken. *Non olet* was always
his motto where pieces of silver were concerned.
Rachel, however, wiser in her generation, knew what
she was about, and followed her own course with
a fine air of high-minded grandeur, drawing dis-
tinctions between her own position and that of
meaner artists who could not be expected to be so
magnanimous.

"I am making friends in the world of fashion,
not clients, as the singers do. Not that I am at
all surprised at the singers, but as for myself I think
that sort of thing is beneath the dignity of a Princess
of Tragedy. Don't you agree with me, my dear
M. Crémieux ?"

Rachel

Even Rachel's prose style appears to have improved under the stimulating influence of her renown. The letters which she wrote to Crémieux from London are much more grammatical than those which she wrote to him in Paris; but still she did not trust herself. She seems to have provided herself with formulæ for accepting and declining invitations; but when more difficult letters were required she still sent to Paris for them. We find her, for instance, appealing to Crémieux to tell her how to thank Lord Normanby for giving her a ring —" you may breathe freely, for he is old and ugly," she adds, to reassure him. We also find her appealing to him for a letter to Lady Normanby—a letter for which Lady Normanby has asked Mme. Félix— to thank her for her kindness and hospitality. We find her finally soliciting his assistance on a still more important occasion :—

" Her Majesty the Queen has told Lord Normanby that she would like to have my signature in her album. I have asked several persons in the highest position what I ought to do, and their advice is that I should write her Majesty a letter on the morning after the entertainment at Windsor. So, my dear Crémieux, in spite of the great progress which I am making in French composition, I must once more throw myself upon your kindness."

So that if there is, in fact, any letter from Rachel to Queen Victoria preserved in the royal collection of autographs, the secret is now out that not Rachel but her legal adviser composed it.

Rachel

That is the end of the story of Rachel's first triumphant excursion to London : a story to which it only remains to be added that, in the midst of her triumphs, she received her first serious warning that her glory, though brilliant, would be brief, and that she could only pursue fame at the peril of her health.

Samson had already cautioned her, begging her to reserve her strength for the theatre instead of dissipating it in society whenever the theatre did not claim her. She had laughed at his warning, partly because she was young and eager to enjoy, and partly because the gifts which society poured into her lap were welcome. A fainting-fit in her dressing-room, after a trying performance, had proved that there was reason in what Samson said; but she had recovered from it and continued to live as recklessly as before. From London, however, she wrote to Crémieux that she had spent four days in bed, and felt very weak.

" The name of the disease," she explained, " is hemorrhage"; and we all know that hemorrhage is generally the prelude of pulmonary consumption.

CHAPTER IX

RACHEL recovered from her hemorrhage, making little more ado about it than if it had been a cold in the head, and hurried on to fulfil an engagement at Bordeaux. There also she was received with as much honour as if she had been a princess, and thence also she wrote to Crémieux, rejoicing in her glory, and demanding drafts of letters suitable for various occasions.

She had no sooner arrived, she told him, than musicians appeared beneath her balcony to serenade her. Whenever she descended into the streets she found a crowd of cavaliers waiting to escort her. A Paris deputy, Vicomte Jacqueminot—Rachel spells the name Jacmino—happening to be staying in the same hotel, had at once waited on her. A M. Aguado, whoever he may have been, had driven her out to his château, and insisted upon her carrying off a case of the best wine in his cellar. It had been impressed upon her, in short, not only that she was the most important of the actresses, but also that actresses were the most important members of the community.

And that, it may be remarked in passing, was the general attitude of the French provinces towards her. " The Girondins," she wrote to Dr. Véron, " overwhelm me with verses, odes and sonnets." The hotel-keepers of Marseilles competed for the

G 81

privilege of entertaining her gratuitously. Rouen, which boasted that, in its independence, it had once hissed Talma, overwhelmed her with acclamations. The magnificence of her gesture in declaring that it was her " sacred duty " to give her first performance on the birthday of Corneille stirred an enthusiasm which swept the Rouennais off their feet. A magnificent medallion of Corneille was at once presented to her; and we must hope that there is no truth in the story that she at once took it to a jeweller and exchanged it for pieces of silver. At Lyon the police had to take special measures to keep order at the pit door. The receipts amounted to £292; and the members of the Lyon Academy subscribed to offer Rachel a golden crown.

" And now I am wondering," she wrote to Samson, " how I ought to comport myself when I receive these gentlemen, and what will be the proper reply to make to their address. If only I could induce you to compose a little speech for me—but you never write, not even to ask how I am getting on ; and now I have to get out of this business with honour and dignity as best I can."

The speech which occurred to Rachel's unaided imagination was to the effect that she wished she were already on the road to Paris with the Academicians' golden crown safely packed among her baggage. Decidedly it was a remark to be classed with the things which one would rather have expressed differently; but the dazzled provincials, being quite sure that she meant well, forgave her, and left

Rachel

her happy in the knowledge that they placed actresses on a loftier pedestal than any other artists. She was only twenty, and it was not to be expected that she would dispute, or even doubt, the propriety of their adoration.

In the midst of the homage, however, her trouble about her health continued. A letter in which she boasts of £328 in the house, " an unheard of figure," is quickly followed by a letter in which she complains of " pain between the shoulders."

" I cannot use my left arm without feeling it. The damp, I think, makes it worse; and it has not stopped raining since I have been here. It affects my spirits and makes me melancholy. . . . When I think that I have still eleven performances to give, I am appalled by the fatigue in store for me. I have to keep quiet between the performances. It is a great effort to write to you, for, as I said, writing makes me worse."

Thus she writes to her father in a letter in which she also says that at Lyon she has passed all the sorrows of her childhood in review. It is one of our first glimpses at the gloom which gradually settled down upon her in spite of her determination to experience every kind of delight and drain the chalice of pleasure to the lees. The source of the melancholy beyond a doubt was the consciousness of failing strength, and the perpetual conflict between the passion for activity and the need for rest—the strain of packing the achievements of a long life into a few short and feeble years. A picture of that strain

Rachel

and stress, which was to aggravate the melancholy in the end though, at the time, it might seem to offer an escape from it, may be taken from Edmond Got's[1] recently published *Diary*.

" Here," Got writes, " is Mlle. Rachel off again to tour the provinces. It is to be a tour, they tell me, of three months' duration, just as it was last year, when she played ninety-one times in ninety days, whereas in Paris we have all the difficulty in the world to get her to play twice a week.

" How she sticks to it, though, and how terribly it must tire her ! Starting off with a company composed partly of members of her family and partly of the youngest pensionnaires of the Comédie Française, whom she thus diverts from their proper and natural career—crowding them all into a diligence, in the *coupé* of which she herself sleeps, occasionally, it is said, inviting a male member of the troupe to share the compartment with her—packing and unpacking the costumes at every stage of the journey—and never a moment's respite ! Sometimes they give two performances a day in towns two leagues apart."

And Got proceeds to relate how, when members of the company suffered from fatigue, or indigestion, or caught cold, Rachel and her sister Sarah used to doctor them in the diligence, dosing them with homely remedies, and even applying blisters, poultices and leeches with their own hands. The entry belongs to a date somewhat later than

[1] Ultimately the *doyen* of the Comédie Française, but in Rachel's time a very junior member of the company.

that under review, when Rachel was still more tired
and still more strenuous. Already in the early
forties, however, Rachel was weary, and nevertheless
was rushing through life as if a gadfly spurred her
on.

Already, too, she was beginning to shock and
surprise her serious friends, and she more particularly
shocked and surprised him whom she called " papa "
Crémieux. He had supposed himself to be completely in her confidence; but there were certain
secrets as to her way of life which she was trying
to keep from him, and he found them out.

Apparently he knew that the Marquis de Custine
had courted her *pour le bon motif* and made her an
offer of marriage. Very likely he was the author
of the letter in which she declined the proposal—
she certainly cannot have written it herself, for it
is cold, correct and closely reasoned. He must,
at any rate, have been in sympathy with the refusal,
for Astolphe de Custine, the only son of Chateaubriand's friend Delphine de Custine, had blemishes
of character of the sort that neither men nor women
pardon. Chateaubriand himself had told him that
his only way of clearing his reputation would be to
fight duels right and left; but he had challenged none
of his calumniators, and the houses of his reputable
acquaintances had been closed to him in consequence.
The kindest thing which they could be got to say
of him was that a blow which he had received on
the head from a falling picture in an Italian gallery
might perhaps have made him unaccountable for
his actions. In spite of his title, therefore, he was
an " undesirable "; and Crémieux may well have

Rachel

patted Rachel on the back when he found that the title did not tempt her. His emotions were very different when he heard about Dr. Véron.

He had idealized Rachel as an innocent angel of spotless purity; but he had no disposition to idealize that fat Amphitryon with the double chin—the *boulevardier* whose chief boasts were that he had drunk champagne every night of his life for thirty years with impunity, and that no woman had ever resisted his advances. It was incredible to him that his little white dove could have let herself be entrapped by the unhealthy-looking proprietor of the cough-drop; but the evidence accumulated, and at last he felt that he really must take notice of it. So he and Madame Crémieux put their heads together, and it was decided that Madame Crémieux should write Rachel this letter :—

" MY DEAR CHILD,
   " I am heart-broken. My husband is just back from Paris, where he has spent the afternoon in visiting friends, and the sad certainty has been borne in upon him that the rumours about which we spoke to you are appallingly circumstantial. Rachel, my child, you must not hesitate any longer. You must break with him publicly—the rumour can be silenced in no other way—or else you will fall from your pedestal. But, no. One who has climbed so high as you have cannot endure degradation while there is still time to avoid it, and cannot afford to lose so fair a fame in a day."

M. Crémieux, the letter continues, has spent three

Rachel

hours in discussing the matter with "honourable journalists," a fact which shows to what a degree the affairs of actresses may be regarded as the affairs of all the world. He has asked them why Rachel was coldly received on her last appearance at the theatre. They have answered, with one accord, that it was on account of Dr. Véron.

" Do not look for any other reason, for there is none. Many great ladies had come from their country houses, with flowers in their hands, to welcome you on your return. But the talk of the whole house was of your disgrace. They discussed it in all its details, and they retained their bouquets rather than give you any proof of esteem and interest."

So Rachel must drop the doctor. Madame Crémieux implores her to do so " with hands joined in prayer." Better that she should get married to some honest man, and that " this poetical name of Rachel " should be exchanged for a bourgeois appellation, than that it should be profaned by opprobrious epithets. For every one was talking. Every one was saying : " She has been to see M. V. She spent whole hours alone with him. Only last Sunday she took him to Montmorency, and drove back to Paris with him in his carriage at the dead of night." A terrible future was in store for Rachel if she went on like that. She would have to shed " bitter tears," and therefore—

" Rachel, my dear child, if my entreaties still have any influence over you, answer this letter and

87

Rachel

tell me that you are going to do as I ask you. If you do not answer, I shall understand the meaning of your silence, and, though my heart will be broken, I shall say no more. . . . But no. You do not want to be merely the actress whom people go to see at the theatre on account of her talents—you who have hitherto been so pure and so charming that the highest in the land have invited you to their palaces and their drawing-rooms. You do not want girls of good family to avoid you—you whom the girls of the best families like to call their sister.

" Rachel, my child, you are on the edge of the abyss. Step back from it. There is still time to-day. Do not wait until to-morrow.

" I thought it better to write to you myself than to leave my husband to do so. He never expected this general outcry, and it has thrown him into a state of consternation. On Monday at one he will call for your answer. May it then be possible to us to announce that you are still, as we know that you are, the Rachel whom we love with all the tenderness of our hearts."

A letter truly of a deep and moving pathos. Madame Crémieux was one of those who saw no reason why the daughters of the theatre should not cultivate precisely the same virtues as the daughters of the *bourgeoisie*. If she knew, as she must have known, that some actresses did not, she believed that Rachel was an exception to the rule. Or, at any rate, she believed that Rachel, having been lured into error, would return, a repentant Magdalen, in tears, holding a candle, attired in a white sheet,

88

and promising never to offend again. Which is to say that she did not understand how the theatrical point of view of these matters differs from that of the professional classes, and also that she did not know Rachel. A *bourgeoise* had indeed died young in Rachel; but it was dead, and was not to come to life again for some years to come.

The servant who delivered the letter inquired whether there was any answer to it, and was told that there was none. A few days afterwards Crémieux sent his messenger again. Perhaps, he thought, Rachel had desired a little time to think the letter over before replying to it. Surely now, after reflection, she had a word to say. But no.

" Mademoiselle Rachel has already said that there is no answer to the letter," was the only response that he got.

That was the end of what Legouvé calls Rachel's " prehistoric epoch "—her definite announcement that, having crossed the Rubicon without the knowledge of her serious friends, she considered herself better off on the further side of it, and intended to remain there.

CHAPTER X

CRÉMIEUX'S reason for dropping Rachel may or may not have weighed with the Faubourg. The Faubourg, at any rate, had also other, and graver, grounds of quarrel with her. The vulgar gesture with which, as has already been related, she expressed her contempt for the Faubourg, was one of them. Another was the strange story of her relations with the Prince de Joinville.

He was Louis-Philippe's third son, thirty years of age, a handsome blond, very popular with women, and an admiral. His squadron had just brought the ashes of Napoleon back to France from Saint Helena; and he was a sailor who, as Arsène Houssaye writes, "made havoc of virtue—of the virtue, that is to say, which only demanded that havoc should be made of it." So, having admired Rachel at the theatre, he proceeded with nautical directness, sending up his card to her dressing-room, with a note scrawled on it; the note, which is famous, running as follows:—

"Où? Quand? Combien?"

And Rachel sent the card back with the reply—

"Chez Toi. Ce Soir. Pour Rien."

Rachel
From a portrait by Dévéria.

Rachel

That was one of the stories circulated. Another was to the effect that Rachel, meeting the Prince de Joinville for the first time at a dinner given by Molé, went home with him in his carriage. Either story, if believed, would have sufficed to convince the Faubourg that it had erred in distinguishing Rachel from other actresses; and though no one can vouch for the literal exactitude of either story, the fact on which both stories are founded does not admit of doubt. Rachel, it was quite clear, had invaded the Faubourg, and carried off its brightest ornament, not merely for a passing adventure, but for a romance of some duration—and that at the very time when her other male admirers in the salons vied with one another in guaranteeing her impeccable.

It is even said that the Prince de Joinville succeeded Crémieux as Rachel's letter-writer in ordinary. However that may have been, he was for a season passionately in love with her, as is proved by one of his letters, discovered in the Tuileries on the day when the mob sacked that Palace and sent Louis Philippe and his family about their business :—

"So you are ill," he wrote, "and God knows what will be the end of it. I await to-morrow with impatience, in the hope that my anxiety may be relieved, for I have had no letter from you to-day. Can it be that you are worse ? The thought pains me. I cannot keep quiet any longer, and I have just told my aunt that I shall start to-morrow. I am leaving all my business and getting away as best I can. I was in a state of fever all night long. After

reading your letters, I could think of nothing else, so
great is my love for you."

That seems to have been written in 1843, when
Rachel was "curing" at Ems, "coughing," she
wrote, "as if I should bring the house down."
Whether the Prince de Joinville joined her there is
not known. He had, at any rate, long since passed
out of her life at the time when the letter was found
and read by eyes for which it was not intended,
and one only quotes it to show under what brilliant
auspices Rachel broke with the Faubourg and crossed
the Rubicon, and how splendid were the hosts who
delighted to entertain her after the Rubicon was
crossed.

The Prince de Joinville, though the first, was not
by any means the last. His bust, together with a
specimen of his handwriting—one does not know
whether it was the famous "Où ? Quand ? Combien ? " or not—was long one of the most admired
ornaments of her library in her mansion in the
Rue Trudon; but the rest of the furniture and
decorations of that mansion were provided, not
by any member of the House of Orleans, but by a
member of the House of Bonaparte.

One has named, of course, Count Walewski, the
son of Napoleon and his Polish mistress, Madame
Walewska. He was rich, and a widower, and
sufficiently an amateur of the arts to write a comedy
—*L'Ecole du Monde*—which was hissed at the
Théâtre Français : a circumstance which inspired the
ironical condolences of Thiers : "My dear friend,
why on earth did you do it ? It is so difficult to

Rachel

write a comedy in five acts, and it is so easy not to write one." According to Arsène Houssaye, Rachel won his heart by inviting him to supper, and flattering him with the following Napoleonic menu :—

SAUCISSON A L'AIL DE TOULON

OMELETTE AU JAMBON DE MAYENCE

ANDOUILLES A LA BONAPARTE

POULET A LA MARENGO

BOMBE GLACEE A LA MOSKOWA.

Whether that story is true or only well invented matters little. The woman who had to ask Crémieux the meaning of " firmament " was certainly incapable of the historical allusions; but her friends, or even her cook, may have been capable of them on her behalf. In any case Rachel pleased Walewski, whether by this device or by another; and he was a lover who did things in a much grander style than any of his predecessors.

We need not, indeed, assume that the Prince de Joinville took Rachel at her word when in reply to his "How much?" she answered that she would make no charge. Princes cannot, and actresses know that they cannot, afford to take advantage of such magnanimity. But Joinville, in view of the exigencies of his position, had been discreet. Though he had loved Rachel, he had not called the world to witness that he loved her; he had not provided her with an establishment. Walewski did so. He set her up in a magnificently furnished mansion—the Hôtel of the Rue Trudon—with a large staff of servants. She settled down there, and bore him a child. " It

Rachel

was only a theatrical marriage," writes Arsène
Houssaye, " but it was a marriage all the same."
Which means apparently that, when the son was
born, Walewski took the necessary legal steps to
recognize him publicly as his. And, as has been
already mentioned—M. Léon Séché being the authority for the story—he would have gone further and
actually made Rachel his wife if he had not heard
that she had said of him behind his back : " Le
comte m'embête avec son comme-il-faut."

Merely as his mistress, however, she was at the
apogee of her social splendour. Having the public
as well as her lover on her side, she could snap her
fingers at the boycott of the Faubourg; and we find
her, for a season, comporting herself with dignity,
as though recognizing that she had been raised to
an exalted rank only to be occupied by actresses
who were sedate in their demeanour and exclusive
in their affections. That was particularly the case
when the elder Dumas presumed, with characteristic swagger, to make love to her. The story was
told, with documents in support, in the *Gaulois*,
about a year ago.

She was on tour, it seems, with Walewski in attend-
ance, and at Marseilles she met the ebullient mulatto
at dinner. On her departure he wrote her a letter—
not a brief business-like communication like that of
the Prince de Joinville, but a verbose effusion of seven
amorous pages. He addressed her as " My beautiful
Queen." Though he had only been two days
in her company, he said, those two days had set an
ineffaceable mark upon his life. Perhaps she had
not given him a second thought, but she was never-

theless hidden in a fold of his heart. He loved her; he felt that he had always been predestined to love her. Every look that she had given him had alternately inspired him with hope and fear. She was one of those queens whom one adored, and before whom one trembled. Writing from a distance he dared to tell his love. He doubted whether he would have the courage to tell it in her presence.

And so forth, through seven pages; and when there was no answer, Dumas despatched seven other pages, all in the same passionate tone. " I love you, Rachel," the ventripotent one declared. " I love you to distraction. So passionately do I love you that I am repeating the words aloud to myself as I write." And he continued—

" Listen to me, I implore you. A look may deceive one—it may be that one intercepts a look intended for another. A pressure of the hand may deceive one—a pressure of the hand may be nothing more than the expression of a condescending friendship. One may be deceived even as to the signs of such emotion as seemed to me to thrill through you when you leant against me on that beautiful evening on this beautiful beach. It may, in truth, have been my own heart, and not yours, that was beating. But a word, a line—these things do not deceive."

So he begged Rachel to write to him. She did write, but her letter was not at all the sort of letter which he had expected. Rachel wrote that she had hoped that her silence would have been sufficiently a clear hint that Dumas' letters were unwelcome to

Rachel

her. As it was, she must request him, in plain words, to cease his annoying correspondence; and she added two stinging sentences:—

" You tell me, sir, that you would not venture to say in my presence the things which you write to me. I can only express my regret that I do not inspire you with as much respect when you are at a distance as when you are near at hand. . . .
" I knew that, when one had to do with a fool, it was necessary to weigh and consider the meaning of his most casual words. I did not know that there were some men of intelligence with whom the same precautions were necessary."

But the mulatto was not beaten yet. He wrote, for the third time, thus:—

" MADAME,
Since you absolutely insist upon it, let matters rest where they are. At least we have accomplished a part of the journey which we may complete hereafter.
Your admirer and, above all, your friend,
" AL. DUMAS."

To which piece of insolence Rachel rejoined—

" SIR,
I return you the brief note which you were not ashamed to address to me. When a woman has made up her mind not to appeal to any one for help, that is her only way of replying to an

insult. If I have misapprehended your meaning, and if you wrote these few lines through a slip of the pen in the midst of your innumerable occupations, I am quite sure that you will be glad to recover them.

" RACHEL."

Whereupon the mulatto, whose chief desire was now to cover his retreat, took up his pen yet again, and wrote, this time, to Walewski.

" MY DEAR COUNT,

"I have attempted the siege of a town of which you are the governor, and I have been badly beaten. Receive my compliments.

"I would rather that you received the news of your victory from me than from any one else. Doing so, you will have no right to bear me malice for my defeat.

"Pray tell Mademoiselle Rachel that I am not contented to continue to be the admirer of her talents, but that I desire also to remain her friend.

"Always yours,
"A. DUMAS."

Whereto Walewski, who knew his Dumas and had no confidence in him, responded by enjoining him to keep silence under pain of consequences:—

"I should be obliged, to my great regret," (he wrote, continuing the military metaphor) "to take the field if the enemy, after raising the siege, should change his tactics, and should either try to penetrate into the citadel by surprise or to diminish the merit of the defence by circulating rumours of its capitulation."

That was all. Dumas was beaten to his knees and slunk away. More than ten years afterwards, in circumstances which we shall come to, he avenged himself by a scurrilous newspaper attack; but for the moment he had nothing more to say; and the Rachel who rebuffed him cuts a figure of quite unusual dignity—even though one feels quite sure that the letters in which she put Dumas in his place were not of her own, but of Walewski's composition.

All through her relations with Walewski, indeed, her proceedings strike one as comparatively simple and sincere. She liked him, and he did things in style; and the latter consideration was as important to her as the former.

Perhaps that is not seldom the case with actresses. They certainly give one the impression, far more than any other women, when one reads their biographies, of being less in love with their lovers, or even with love itself, than with the splendid trappings and accessories of love—the bijou villas, the champagne suppers, the priceless furs, and the diamonds. They have an air of looking upon love as a vain thing unless it leads to the acquisition of such trophies. There are indications that it is a maxim with them—based, perhaps, upon a sort of self-respect—that great passions should be

Rachel

reserved for men with great possessions; and great passions thus discreetly regulated cannot, of course, be regarded as of high sentimental value.

There have, no doubt, been exceptions to the rule: Marie Dorval, for instance, who loved first Alfred de Vigny and then Jules Sandeau without fee or reward, but threw a flat iron at the head of an elderly admirer who approached her on the assumption that she put a price upon her favours; and also Déjazet. But Rachel was not an exception. She occasionally indulged caprices; and there are letters of hers in collections of autographs in which we seem to detect the genuine, though ungrammatical, exclamation of the heart. An unknown admirer at Rouen drew such an exclamation from her.

" Pray for poor Rachel," she cried. " You should not blame but pity her."

But that was quite exceptional. In the main Rachel, even while indulging her caprices, trampled on feelings which threatened to seduce her from the path of glory—just as the wise young man tramples on the passion for the barmaid or the ballet-girl which threatens to compromise his career. If her left-handed alliances were to be enduring, they must be splendid. Splendour, she seems to have felt, was due to her position, her art, and the national theatre of which she was the ornament. Only, as was natural, she preferred that the splendour should be provided by an admirer who had also the qualities of a lover; and Count Walewski fulfilled that condition.

He was no double-chinned debauchee, like Dr.

Rachel

Véron, but a dashing and attractive suitor. Instead of a double chin and a protuberant stomach,
he had a tender and sympathetic heart. His proceedings were respectful as well as romantic. He
paid the bill without assuming the airs of the
man who concludes a purchase. He did the
thing in style because that was how he liked to do
it—because Aristotle's " magnificent man " was
his model. It seems that he really tried to screw
his courage to the point of promoting Rachel from
left-handed to right-handed status.

In the end, as we know, his correctitude jarred
upon her, and she so acted as to divert him from his
intention. In the meantime, however, he loved
her, and she let herself be loved, and repulsed his
mulatto rival with a correctitude equal to his own,
because inspired by it, and basked, if not in sentiment, at all events in a luxury which she had never
previously dreamed of.

CHAPTER XI

RACHEL had already quitted the parental roof in order to "live her own life." Her flat, rented at £200 a year, was in the Rue de Rivoli. She was often to be seen, it is said, in the basement, gossiping with the concierge, and even helping her to make a salad or a stew. In that manner, and to that extent, she kept herself in touch with the homely habits of her early years. Now, as if she had suddenly found Aladdin's lamp, she was transferred, in the twinkling of an eye, to such a palace as one reads of in the *Arabian Nights*.

The hall was paved with mosaic; the grand staircase was of white marble. The visitor ascended it through an avenue of flower-pots, beneath a dome embellished with arabesques in the style of the Alhambra, and passed through an ante-chamber panelled with white oak and hung with green and gold brocade. He entered a dining-room with four lofty windows, decorated with frescoes in the style of those discovered at Pompeii, and admired Etruscan vases on the marble mantelpiece. His dinner, if he stayed to dine, was served partly on solid silver plates, and partly on Sèvres porcelain, with a large "R" marked in gold on every piece.

Adjoining the dining-room was a boudoir, hung

Rachel

with Persian drapings, and crowded with divans, and low chairs, and whatnots, and cabinets, one of ebony and one of tortoise-shell, richly stored with treasures and curiosities. On a table lay thirteen daggers with dazzling jewelled hilts, and on the walls hung valuable pictures—by Dévéria, Meissonier, Diaz, and other masters. Beyond the boudoir was a library, with six book-cases of carved oak, containing four or five thousand volumes, including a graphically illustrated quarto edition of *La Pucelle*. The principal ornament of the room was the bust of the Prince de Joinville— Rachel's memento of the correspondence quoted in the last chapter.

On the first floor was the drawing-room. A procession of the Nine Muses defiled along its walls in white and gold; the chandelier was of bronze, with little Cupids in silver; the doors and windows were draped with Chinese silks. The arm-chairs were of gilded wood, and covered with cherry-coloured damask; the ottomans had lace antimacassars. On the mantelpiece two enormous blue Sèvres vases flanked a gold clock designed like a terrestrial globe. Close by was the bedroom, where the bed, of carved and gilded wood, with a coverlet of silk embroidered with gold, was overhung by a baldaquin with purple curtains. On the wall hung a portrait of Adrienne Lecouvreur in Beauvais tapestry; and in a corner stood a piano with a carved oak case, so that Rachel might be played to sleep when she was restless.

The total cost of the furniture and decorations is said to have been £12,000; and that estimate is,

102

of course, exclusive of the cost of innumerable offerings in kind. To such magnificence had genius, combined with a certain readiness to let herself be loved, brought the daughter of the pedlar and the old clothes-woman at the age of twenty-three. One can quite understand that Rachel, for a while, felt the need of living up to the unaccustomed grandeur, and developed, under its influence, not only a kind of self-respect, but even a kind of prudery. The tone of her dismissal of Dumas, whose circumstances were humble in comparison with hers—for the days of the Villa Monte Cristo were still to come—was only in keeping with her surroundings; and so was the tone of her refusal of a valuable picture—a study in the nude—offered to her by one of her theatrical colleagues.

The picture, she wrote, was " too undraped " to be admitted to her establishment. " I am no prude," she protested. " But why," she asked, " should I deprive you of a picture which I should be obliged to hide ? " Whereto the colleague, addressing her as " dear and great comrade," replied that she had been " silly, and indeed almost impious," to have deemed her little picture worthy of hanging-room in such a house, and continued : " But, at any rate, my foolishness has supplied me with really precious information concerning the sincerity of your claim to modesty."

One seems to see, too, the effect of magnificent surroundings on an ill-balanced mind in Rachel's haughty treatment of Mademoiselle George.

George had had a brilliant past. She had been at once a queen of tragedy and the mistress of an

Rachel

emperor.[1] Constant, Napoleon's valet, had been sent to the theatre to fetch her, and had driven her to the Tuileries amid the plaudits of the populace. But she had come to poverty, losing her vogue together with her lovers, and needed a benefit. She called on Rachel, to ask her to play at her benefit, and Rachel declined to receive her, sending down a message to the effect that George had better put her request in writing. But George put something else in writing—

" No, thank you. I have not quite come to that. I am as much a queen of the theatre as she is. I, like her, have been a beautiful light o' love, and the day will come when she will be a poor old woman like me. No, I shall not write to her. I shall not ask her for alms."

Thus George poured out her harrowed soul in a letter to Victor Hugo, published in *Choses vues*, continuing—

" She forgets that she was once a beggar, and she doesn't dream that, some day, she will be a beggar again. Yes, M. Hugo, she was actually a beggar in the cafés. People threw coppers to her; and now she plays lansquenet at Véron's for louis points, and wins or loses ten thousand francs in a night. In thirty years' time she won't have six farthings,

---

[1] Of two Emperors in fact. After Napoleon had tired of her she went to Russia and was for a brief season the left-handed consort of the Tsar, introduced to him by courtiers for the purpose of seducing his affections from Madame Narishkine.

Rachel

and will be in the gutter, with her boots down at heel. In thirty years' time the name of Rachel won't be worth as much as the name of George. Some other girl, gifted with talent—and youth—will come up and walk over her head, and we shall see her prostrating herself humbly. One knows she will be humble then, because one sees how insolent she is now."

It was not a true prediction; for Rachel was of the race which is business-like as well as artistic, and her supersession by a younger rival was to find her with plenty of money in the bank; but the display of insolence is a shadow by no means to be left out of the portrait. It shows us the living picture trying to live up to the gorgeous frame in which it has been placed, yet reverting to type in the very act of doing so—the queen of the theatre trying to be grander than the grandest, yet unwittingly introducing the manners of the gutter into her palace.

We must let that story pass, however, for it was only an episode, and carried no consequences. The reversion to type which did carry consequences lay in that impatient exclamation: "Le comte m'embête avec son comme-il-faut." That was the really symbolical and fatal utterance. Much as Walewski loved Rachel, he loved correctitude more. A wife thus liable to revert to type and relapse from the stars to the gutter would clearly be fatal to his prospects in the diplomatic service; so he broke off his relations with Rachel and married Anne-Alexandrine-Catherine de Ricci, a Florentine lady, instead. The news of his decision reached Rachel

Rachel

at a time when she was touring in Holland; and a spectator of the comedy commented sardonically—

" Comte Walewski has left her to marry a lady. It is a very ordinary incident, but the actress takes it seriously. She threatens to leave the stage. It it said that she means to go and live in Italy. But you may make your mind easy about that. She will not die; she will not go away. She will remain at the service of French playgoers, and will continue to attract crowds and restore the popularity of Corneille and Racine by her splendid talents."

The spectator was right in his prophecies, and right also in his affirmation that Rachel was seriously afflicted by the rupture. Her distress appears in her correspondence alike with Madame de Girardin, and with Madame Saigneville—a lady who sometimes acted as her secretary and helped her to keep her theatrical accounts. " The news which I found awaiting me at Amsterdam," she wrote to the former, " was such a trial to me that I forgot all about my successes every evening as soon as the curtain fell;" and she further spoke of an illness which nearly carried her off in punishment for her faults, and continued : " A strange muddle this, you will think, reading my letter, but not understanding what it means." To Madame Saigneville she was more explicit—

" I have been so overwhelmed and dazed by the blow of the news of W.'s marriage that I cannot keep calm enough to write to you at any length. You will understand the depth of your poor Rachel's trouble too well to be angry with her. Your letter helped me, but I am not to be consoled. All the fault is on my side. It was my own conduct which brought about the calamity which overtakes me to-day, so that I can find no peace in a clear conscience. No, no. Weep for me, but do not pity me. It was all my own doing, and God has punished me for it.

"It is all over with me. But if I can no longer live for myself and my own future, I must not forget that I can still be useful to my poor child and my numerous relatives. So I must put up with life for their sakes. Little did I think when I took my mourning with me on my tour that it was the colour which I should have to wear for the remainder of my existence.

"You are right to congratulate me on having my brother with me. I cannot describe the devotion of this boy, whom the spectacle of my trouble has transformed into a man. Doubtless God sent him to me to arrest the despair in my heart. God bless him! May all my friends bless him as I do.

"It is to-morrow that I am to make my first appearance at the Amsterdam theatre. What courage I shall need to hide my trouble from the public!

"I can hold my pen no longer. My tears choke me. All my friends declare that I ought to write to W. For three days I have been trying in vain to do so. Whatever I write is obliterated by a flood of tears. It seems to me that I am speaking to him, and I fall in a fainting fit before him, as poor Phèdre before Minos. Tell him, if you see him, the things which I cannot bring myself to write. . . .

"Farewell! Pity me! You can never pity me enough.

"RACHEL."

It is an eloquent letter, especially if one reads between the lines. Two things are clear from it : that Rachel had indeed hoped for and expected elevation to right-handed status; and that she was very conscious that her prospects had been blasted by her own misconduct. One may fairly assume that her expression of impatience at her lover's correctitude was not her only fault, and that she had reverted to type in other ways as well. She had thought her position so secure that she could afford to be capricious, and she had found that she was mistaken. Hence those tears, which seem to have been inspired by baffled ambition rather than a stricken heart.

One might have expected, indeed, from the eloquence of the letter to see the tears accompanied by magnificent gestures of tragic indignation, and a scornful return of the presents bestowed by a faithless *fiancé*; but, on the other hand, it is only just to admit that the very number and bulk of the presents interposed a difficulty. It is a simple matter to return an engagement ring and a bundle of faded letters, tear-stained, and tied up with blue ribbon. When it is a question of returning pianos and dining-room tables, and drawing-room and bedroom suites, to say nothing of pictures, and carpets, and sideboards, and stair-rods, and crockery, and cutlery, and plate and linen, the case assumes a very different aspect. No one desires to see an announcement that a marriage which has been arranged will not take place followed by the arrival of a long procession of furniture vans at the front door of a faithless swain.

Least of all, we may be sure, did Count Walewski desire to see his liaison thus dramatically terminated. Such a gesture would have been like the bursting of a bomb-shell in the midst of the trim garden of his admired correctitude. He much preferred that the recollection of having paid nobly for his entertainment should stand between him and any haunting fear that he might have behaved ill, assuring him that he had as good a right to change the object of his affections as to change his coachman or his secretary, or his legal or medical adviser; and that was how the situation was resolved.

Walewski, having married, prospered, becoming French Ambassador, under the third empire, at the Court of Saint James's. Rachel's son was sent to school at Geneva, and grew up to be a credit to his country and his parents, holding posts in the consular service successively at Salonica, Valentia, Carthagena and Palermo. Rachel herself remained in the lordly pleasure-house which Walewski had built for her, and entertained other guests there in his place. Notably, she entertained young Arthur Bertrand, whom she was presently to lure, supposing that she had not already done so, from his allegiance to the audacious and delightful Déjazet.

CHAPTER XII

DÉJAZET shone in farce—outrageous ultra-modern Palais Royal farce—as brilliantly as Rachel in tragedy. It is related by Fanny Kemble that, when she performed in London, Whewell, the Master of Trinity College, Cambridge, rose in his seat and stalked out of the theatre, with Mrs. Whewell on his arm, because it shocked and pained him to behold her brazen face. It is also related that the Duc d'Orléans took her as his lady companion to the French military manœuvres. A few more such *cantinières*, commented Arséne Houssaye, and —*on referait la grande armée.* She appears, too, in the annals of the Romantic Movement, as the lady companion of Musset's friend Alfred Tattet, stockbroker and man about town.

Tattet took Déjazet to Italy at the time of Musset's Venetian honeymoon with George Sand, and he wrote Musset a remarkable letter on the subject, pointing out the particulars in which Musset's case differed from his own. Stockbrokers, he argued, belonged to a different amorous category from poets; and actresses did not, like woman novelists, expect to be taken seriously. Musset and George Sand, in short, were in love and were doomed to suffer;

Mme Déjazet

whereas he and Déjazet were merely " indulging a caprice," and would part, the best of friends, after the caprice had been indulged.

It was a true prediction. The actress as well as the stockbroker felt the need of indulging a series of caprices as the years rolled by; but the only one of her caprices which concerns us here is that for Arthur Bertrand.[1]

He was the son of Napoleon's Bertrand—the faithful companion of the emperor's last years at Longwood; and he went the way of many of the scions of the great imperial families, squandering his substance riotously in the *coulisses* and at the gaming table; a spoiled child, dashing and handsome, but selfish and weak, winning in his ways and capable of meaning well, but without backbone or conscience. Déjazet's tenderness for him shines out as a streak of sincerity in a miscellaneously amorous career.

She was many years his senior. Her age, when they first met, was thirty-six, and his was only seventeen. She loved him, she said, for his " pretty face," and she threw another lover over for him; but her affection was as much that of a mother as of a mistress. His own mother recognized that fact, and blessed the illicit union, not, of course, as an ideal, or an end in itself, but as an alternative to more perilous possibilities. Déjazet was presented to her, at her request, and she was captivated. She welcomed Déjazet, just as Madame de Musset had welcomed Madame Allan-Despréaux, as an ally who might help her to keep her son out of mischief.

[1] See *Un Amour de Déjazet*, by Henry Lecomte.

Rachel

She even presented her, as a pledge of her regard, with a lock of Napoleon's hair—

"I have the greatest pleasure, madame, in sending you the precious lock of hair which you desire to possess. I shall always be glad to do anything to oblige you. I am grateful to you. I am attached to you. I have already told you so. Receive the assurance of my sentiments.

" FANNY BERTRAND."

Thus the young rake's mother wrote to the queen of farce; and the actress, whose face the severe Master of Trinity had found so brazen, justified the confidence reposed in her—or, at all events, she did her best to do so. If she did not keep the boy out of mischief—all other mischief than his relations with her, smiled on by his mother, might be held to imply—it was not for want of trying. A maiden aunt, entrenched behind virginal innocence, could not have given him better advice or more of it. Perhaps she chiefly differed from such a maiden aunt in her more indulgent readiness to forgive the prodigal when he returned.

" Your life, my dear Arthur, for a whole month, has not been what it ought to be. You are slipping down the same slope as Germain, de Boigne, and that set. I am the only person who can sometimes check your course, and when I am no longer with you, you will come to grief. You are going on like a man with an income of £4,000 a year. Over and over again, when you have money in your pocket,

Rachel

you talk of losing fifty louis as if it were only a question of a five franc piece. A few weeks ago you were borrowing four thousand, or perhaps it was six thousand, francs from your notary; to-day you are borrowing another three thousand. Can your fortune stand that ? Would your father approve of it if he knew ? And, even now I have said nothing about the twelve thousand francs which you proposed to spend on travelling—another piece of foolishness which compels me to repeat the question : Can you afford it ?

" Tedious moralizing, isn't it ? But now that we are about to part, Arthur, I want to open your eyes to your future, and leave you at least one proof that your first love was worthy of your first sacrifices. When you read this letter over again, many years hence it may be, you will shed a few tears over a memory of gratitude and death. . . .

" I renounce you, Arthur, because you do not love me exclusively. I have seen that for the last month, and your choice of this evening proves it. I am no longer any more to you than an ordinary mistress."

So she pleaded with him; and when he came back to her, saying he was sorry, she forgave him—for she also sometimes needed forgiveness for not loving exclusively; and so things went on for years. Decidedly, there was more of tenderness and sincerity beneath the mask of that brazen face than the Master of Trinity suspected. And Déjazet, it must be remembered, was not trying to introduce order into the finances of a lover who might enrich her. On

Rachel

the contrary, she was trying to protect from the consequences of his own folly a lover who was not ashamed to borrow from her and was in no hurry to repay the loan.

" My sweet little Nini, you must really be so very kind as to send me a thousand francs. The notary with whom I have an appointment in two days' time in Paris seems to think that I can do without the money I have asked him for until then. Happy as I am to be able to apply to you, my Nini, you can understand how I blush to do so."

He would repay the money, he said, in two days' time; but a later letter of hers shows that, eighteen months afterwards, he had not yet acquitted himself of the obligation.

" Tell me, dear ! Couldn't you manage to let me have 500 francs of the small sum you owe me ? There are the heavy expenses connected with the New Year, and I have my rent to pay, and, if you do not help me a little, I really don't know how I shall get over my embarrassments. I am so hard up that I could not meet a bill of 300 francs, and so had to incur 80 francs costs."

But Arthur did not pay; and nine months later, after some unsuccessful appearances at the Limoges theatre, Déjazet wrote again—

" I am furious. I haven't made a penny in this confounded town. All the people have gone to the

Rachel

country on account of the heat. On two evenings
the takings were only 270 francs. Nice, isn't it?
It upsets me the more because I have two bills to
meet to-day. So, my dear boy, if you can manage
to let me have a few hundred francs on account of
our little debt, I shall be infinitely obliged to you.
It is very painful to me to mention the matter again;
but the fact is that you forget all about it, and it
cuts me to the heart to hear you talk lightly of your
losses at play while you are so indifferent to my
embarrassments. To think that you have nothing
for me who would sell my very soul to get you out
of trouble! Come, Arthur! Leave that green
cloth which is absorbing the best years of your life,
and spare me a few parcels of that accursed metal
which, alas! in spite of all my contempt for it, I
cannot do without."

A pathetic letter truly. In spite of the Master of
Trinity, one feels more and more sure as one proceeds that the woman with the brazen face was a
woman with a heart of gold. If she had a multitude
of sins, she had also the virtue which covers them,
and there was really no need for Mrs. Whewell to
pass away from her with a lifted skirt. Madame
Bertrand, who perceived the good in her, and
appealed to it, and did not appeal in vain, had the
truer insight, as well as the greater charity. As for
Arthur . . .

But further comment on Arthur would be superfluous. The letters quoted are his sufficient con-
demnation. It only remains to be added that he
took to drink, and that Virginie Déjazet reproved

Rachel

him for that fault also. "You seem to be proud
of your drunken habits," she wrote with a touch of
scorn. Poor Virginie! For she was willing to
forgive Arthur for his inebriety, as she had forgiven
him for his infidelity; and almost before she could
do so, Rachel swooped down on him and swept him
off.

She and Déjazet had been friends. Déjazet had
made generous advances at the time of her début.
We have seen her appealing to Crémieux, in the
days before the Rubicon was crossed, for a suitable
reply to Déjazet's "charming letter"—a reply which
would not make her look ridiculous by its ortho-
graphical irregularities if Déjazet should show it
to her friends. The help was the more necessary
in that, before providing herself with a secretary, she
had addressed Déjazet as "la meilleur des femmes."
There had been an interchange, not only of compliments, but of hospitalities. But that made no
difference when there was a caprice to be indulged.

It may be that Rachel regarded her successful
raid as a fair triumph of tragedy over farce—of
the nobler over the less noble art—though it was
more truly a triumph of youth over middle age.
Both Rachel and Arthur were still in the twenties,
while Déjazet was getting on for fifty. Moreover,
Rachel was just then the special heroine of gilded
youth, living such a life and supported by such a
retinue that George could write of her: "If she
became a respectable woman and lived quietly, no
one, after a month or two, would pay any further
attention to her." But that was unjust and untrue.
Rachel's renown rested upon a more solid basis than a

Rachel

reputation for loose living; and she was, apparently, more in love with Arthur Bertrand than she had been with Walewski.

Arthur, at any rate, did not bore her with correctitude. The trouble was rather that he wanted her money, just as he had wanted Déjazet's money, to support him in lapses from correctitude. Whether he got any of it is doubtful; but there is a letter in which we see Rachel on her guard against his proclivities. She reproaches him for not having come to kiss her, whether in her house or in her dressing-room. She signs herself " your loving little wife." But she concludes with a significant postscript : " If you want to play lansquenet, you must provide yourself with the necessary funds. My brother has cleaned me out and my purse is empty."

On the whole, that looks as though Rachel were shy because she had been bitten; for it was only where members of her family were concerned that she esteemed it more blessed to give than to receive. She generously furnished a flat for Rebecca, and she repeatedly paid the debts of Sarah—" the valiant heroine of the supper parties," as she is called by Arsène Houssaye; but it was no part of her programme that lovers should live at her expense. The wonder is that Arthur's ideas and hers on that branch of the subject did not conflict sooner. There can be little question that they conflicted in the end.

For a while, indeed, his devotion was so conspicuous that the newspapers remarked it. They drew the attention of playgoers to Arthur admiring from his box and Rachel playing up to him. They even went so far as to announce an engagement of marriage between the admirer and the admired. But there was no foundation for their rumour. Arthur, whatever his reasons, loved and rode away, without even recognizing the son whom Rachel had borne him.

A son who, be it remarked here, became, like his elder brother, a credit to his country. Gabriel Félix entered the French navy in 1864, fought in the Franco-German war, had a part of his nose carried off by a fragment of a shell at the battle of Beaune-la-Rolande, was rewarded with the ribbon of the Legion of Honour, and died, in 1889, as French Resident at Brazzaville, in the Congo. His father, who seems to have taken no further notice of him after his birth, had already died, a bachelor, in 1871. On the whole, perhaps, it was better for Gabriel to be his mother's than his father's child— sealed of the Tribe of Félix, and therefore sure of her affection, even though she doubted, for a moment, as one of her letters shows, whether he was worthy of any higher position in the world than that of his brother's coachman.

As for the circumstances of her rupture with Arthur, these are not known, and do not matter. All that one does know is that it did not take place without tears and dramatic gestures, and that the Press took notice of the gestures, as it may be relied upon to do when an actress strikes an attitude, and attributed them to their true cause.

Mademoiselle Rachel, the newspapers wrote, was quitting the stage, was leaving Paris, had some thought of leaving France. The climate of Pisa

Rachel

had suddenly become necessary to her and she was
going there—

" Wounded affections are conducting Melpomene
and her frenzies at full gallop. . . . Look out
for the ruts ! Nothing can arrest her progress—
neither the tear-stained shirt-front of the respectable author of her being, nor her sister's creditors,
nor her brother's interests, nor the lamentations of
the cashier in his box-office, nor the entreaties of the
sociétaires, nor the humiliation of Mlle. Judith, nor
the tears of M. Lockroy."

With a good deal more in the same strain of false,
and presumably assumed, alarm. For the gestures,
after all, were only gestures, and carried but few of
the consequences which they threatened. An actress
of genius does not retire from the stage because there
has been a crisis in her emotional affairs. She goes
on acting and acts better than before—the emotional
crisis being a part of her education. Nor does she
cease from travelling to Cythera because, on one of
her voyages thither, she has found the weather
stormy. On the contrary. Such a passenger can
always find a captain, and therefore. . . .

And therefore Rachel not only soon returned to
the scene of her artistic glory, but also resumed her
journeys to Cythera, captained this time by Prince
Napoleon: Plon Plon, the son of King Jerome of
Westphalia, and the father of the present Bonapartist
claimant.

His is the last name which it is necessary to
mention in this particular connection; and, as for

Rachel

the story, there is none to tell. The importance of the new union was not sentimental but social. It was a left-handed alliance of a splendour suitable to Rachel's dignity. It introduced her to the Tuileries in circumstances to be related in their place; but it had no romantic significance, and there is no evidence that its vicissitudes either exalted Rachel or depressed her. She viewed it, so far as one can judge, as a matter of course, and all in the day's work—an interchange of civilities meaning no more to her than a good-morning or a good-night. So true is it that even the voyage to Cythera, if undertaken too frequently, may end by becoming as unexciting and uneventful as a week-end trip to the seaside.

So that we are now free to quit the theme and turn to other topics, reviewing Rachel's progress in her art, and remarking alike her loyalty to the Tribe of Félix and her thorough methods of spoiling the Egyptians.

CHAPTER XIII

The failure of *Judith* and the discomfiture of Mlle. Maxime.

IT would be easy to fill a volume with the elaborated record of Rachel's professional successes; but to what end? Old dramatic criticism, though by Jules Janin, or even by Théophile Gautier, is insipid and flavourless stuff. One cannot check it, as one can check literary criticism, by turning to the thing criticized; and one soon tires alike of reading and relating that the house "rose," that the box-office rejoiced, that bouquets abounded, and that the tributes offered in the way of precious stones were rich and rare.

Nor is it worth while to dwell upon the statement that Rachel (or any other actress or actor for that matter) "created" such and such a part. Statements of that nature sparkle through the pages of *Who's Who?* and similar works of reference; but they are inspired by vanity, and there is no other foundation for them. To create means to make out of nothing, and that is the author's business. The player's function is the humbler one of seizing the author's meaning and interpreting it. That fact is not the less a fact because the interpretation is very far from being a mechanical process, and affords scope for genius as well as talent, and even for the expression, within assigned limits, of a personality.

Rachel

For the limits are always there, and the expression of the personality on the stage can only be imperfect. The personality over which the public waxes enthusiastic is often an entirely illusory personality, or, at all events, a composite one into which the actual individuality of the player enters for very little. The real individual is only to be discovered after the curtain has fallen and the applause has ceased. So with Rachel. She imposed her glory, but she did not impose her personality. Our quest is for the personality behind the glory. It is because of the glory that we turn to look for it; but it is not in the detailed relation of the achievements which earned the glory that we shall find it, so that that relation must be got over as quickly as possible.

The first modern part which Rachel set herself to " create " was that of the heroine of Madame de Girardin's *Judith ;* and she got but little glory out of that. Indeed, one would wonder how so bad a play ever managed to get itself produced if one were not able to see the " influences " at work.

The fact of the matter was that Madame de Girardin was a great lady with a salon and an influential husband. As Delphine Gay, she had been a Muse of the Romantic Movement, remarked as the cleverest and most beautiful of her sex at Nodier's receptions at the Arsenal, though unhappily undowered and not of aristocratic birth. But for those drawbacks, Alfred de Vigny would have married her. Unable to secure him, though

Rachel

she tried hard, with her mother's help, to do so, she married, instead, Emile de Girardin, the founder and editor of *La Presse*, a newspaper as " live " as the *Pall Mall Gazette* in the days when Mr. Stead was in his prime. She sometimes wrote the dramatic criticism; and she " received."

Her social function—a far rarer one in France than in England—was that of a " mixer "; the representatives of Bohemia and of the Faubourg meeting in her drawing-room. She took up Rachel at the time of her début, telling Lamartine that she was " charming," and had " very grand manners," and that no one would ever have guessed her to be " the daughter of wandering pedlars." It was through her introduction that Rachel met Chateaubriand and the Archbishop of Paris in Madame Récamier's apartment. She still stuck to Rachel after her passage of the Rubicon. She flattered Rachel, humbled herself before her—and made use of her. She appealed to Rachel to " encourage " her in dramatic composition; and Rachel replied that her " dreams were of *Judith* and the author of *Judith*." Pulling those wires, and pulling other wires simultaneously, she got *Judith* accepted and staged at the national theatre.

But *Judith* was rank rubbish, full of long and tedious speeches; and neither Rachel's talents nor those of the advertising department could save it. It was given out that Rachel would appear covered from head to foot with precious jewels, valued at many millions of francs, lent to her by the Baroness de Rothschild and other great Israelitish ladies; that it would be necessary to fill the house with

Rachel

policemen in order to protect her from possible thieves. The announcement, as might have been expected, filled the house from floor to ceiling; but an inopportune and unlooked-for occurrence spoiled the magnificent effect.

In the midst of one of the wearisome monologues a stray cat strolled on to the stage, looked up at the speaker, and began to miauw, as if in pained protest against the tedium. It would not take a quiet hint to go, but had to be chased away. Driven behind the wings, it ran round them and reappeared before the footlights, leaping over the furniture with armed pursuers on its track. The spectators naturally withdrew their interest from the tragedy and concentrated it on the chase, some shouting encouragement to the pursuers and others to the cat; with the result that *Judith* perished amid inextinguishable laughter.

It was a case in which the " creation " of a part would indeed have meant making something out of nothing; and Rachel discovered that that was a thing which even she could not do. Her true task was to interpret the creations of the classical masters. In that she was supreme; and many years were still to pass before the competition of any rival would be formidable to her.

One rival, indeed, did appear in the person of Mademoiselle Maxime; and the duel between the two claimants for artistic primacy was more dramatic than the piece in which they met.

Mademoiselle Maxime had come to the front during Rachel's absence on one of her long tours. The

Rachel

public were disposed to favour her because they were annoyed at Rachel's frequent quests of gold and glory at a distance from the capital. It was a quest which Talma and Mademoiselle Mars had disdained, declaring that their connection with the Théâtre Français was more to them than wealth; and Rachel was reproached for not taking the same high disinterested line. Jules Janin, too, had loudly sounded the praises of the newcomer—whether because she had allowed him to encourage her by putting his arm round her waist or for other reasons.

Rachel, returning from her travels, learnt what had happened, and what was expected to happen. It was as if an insult had been offered and a gauntlet flung at her feet. The affront seemed personal rather than artistic. She was very angry; but she knew her power, and she was full of fight. Though she was of frail health, living on her nerves, yet she could trust her nerves to carry her through this ordeal to yet another triumph. Wait, she said to herself and to her friends, till she and Maxime appeared together in the same piece! Then it should also be seen which of them, in our modern parlance, could play the other's head off.

Her chance came when the bills announced *Marie Stuart*, with Rachel as Marie and Maxime as Queen Elizabeth. All Paris had been advised that this was to be the night of the great duel; all Paris had fought for the chance of witnessing it; all Paris, with the true Parisian earnestness in matters of art—especially dramatic art—had come to the theatre prepared to take a side, and back a winner.

Rachel

Maxime had lately shown herself sublime in
Phèdre; at all events Jules Janin had said so:—

" The very sight of her reveals the woman who
is courageous, energetic, passionate beyond measure. . . . She comes on the stage like a desperate
creature; nothing dazzles, nothing stops her. . . .
Her head is full of energy, her look, of animation;
she has a fine voice that no exertion wearies, ready
tears, simple and natural gestures. *She* does not
play with Racine's verses as a child with a hoop. . . .
She does not declaim, she acts. . . . We have found
a Phèdre at last. Go and see her; go and applaud
her; go and defend her. She is alone, without
support, without coterie, without protection, left
to her own true instincts."

And so on in that remarkable prose style
which flowed interminably like a bubbling brook.
Decidedly, when such things could be written
of a débutante, Rachel must look to her laurels.
Jules Janin's word carried so much weight that
many of his readers believed, as, indeed, many of
them wished to believe, that Rachel would look to
those laurels in vain, and that her star was destined
to set almost before it had fairly risen. Others,
not seeing the theatre through the great critic's
glasses but preferring to judge for themselves, were
not so certain. But all were eager to see the contest.
" Amateurs," wrote Jules Janin, " imagined themselves back in the days of the memorable struggle
between the beauty of Mademoiselle George and
the talents of Mademoiselle Duchesnois."

Rachel

So the curtain rose; and the house was a riotous tribunal of divided sentiment, applauding, or withholding its applause, in support not of the performance, but of its own preconceived opinions. At first it seemed that Maxime was having everything her own way; and her supporters roared themselves hoarse; but old playgoers knew that the test was yet to come. In the earlier acts the opportunities which the two parts offered were not equal; Maxime had many opportunities and Rachel very few. Rachel's great chance would not come until the Third Act, in which the two queens, Marie Stuart and Elizabeth, stand face to face and pour the full vials of their hatred on each other's heads. Rachel was waiting for that scene; she could be seen waiting for it.

It came amid a deadly silence; and Maxime entered, pale, embarrassed, with insults in her mouth. She was not merely the queen of England insulting her Scottish rival. She was the débutante of the Comédie Française in revolt against its sovereign, committed to the task of sweeping her from her path.

" Venom and scorn were on her lips and in her look; and then it was Rachel's turn. Marie Stuart, exposed to the contempt of this insolent queen, had listened with quivering emotion to all her insults. She had borne her disdain in silence. She had stood there, with bowed head and folded hands; she was waiting. But when her turn came—when she was free at last to utter all the bitterness of her soul—ah ! then, ye gods and goddesses, she was superb. It seemed as though she were saying to us—and saying

Rachel

infinitely well : ' Ah, so you have set up a rival to me in my absence. So you want to build altar against altar; Maxime's and Rachel's altars in the same high place. And you think that I shall take that quietly, without any show of emotion, without any attempt at revolt. You think that I am going to put up with those comparisons. No, no! You shall see that I know how to defend myself, that I need the support of no foreign favour, that the great heart of the people is on my side, that I mean to be queen of the theatre, and that no rival shall divide my sovereignty with me.' "

So Jules Janin writes, won back to Rachel's side, by the spirit and energy of her genius. He speaks of her passion as almost delirious in its violence; " it gripped one, and was superb; " and he goes on to describe how Maxime was, and showed herself to be, crushed by it :—

" She recoiled in terror, astounded and abashed; she gazed at this display of power with haggard eyes. It seemed to her that she now had to do with a different woman. But no, it was the same woman; and when Elizabeth, at last, baffled, humiliated, panting for breath, hardly dares any longer lift her head, ah! then it was a sight to see Mademoiselle Rachel turn, with a queenly gesture, towards the enthusiasts who had been supporting Mademoiselle Maxime, and exclaim, with contempt in her voice, and fire in her eyes—

" J'enfonce le poignard au sein de ma rivale."

Rachel

And that, in truth, was the end of Mademoiselle Maxime. Rachel had not only played her head off, but had practically played her out of the theatre. Jules Janin, now completely converted, writes that she " disappeared from the scene for evermore." The actual fact is that, after struggling on obscurely as an actress for some years, she retired from the stage, and took to letting furnished apartments—with or without board.

So that the path was once more clear. There was no longer any obstacle to hinder Rachel from going on from one success to another, or any grave danger that the triumphs of her provincial and foreign tours would imperil her place in the hearts of Parisian playgoers.

CHAPTER XIV

Rachel and Charlotte Brontë—Relations with Viennet and with Lamartine.

" La province, Rachel, c'est quelque chose aussi."

THUS a well-meaning Norman poet hailed Rachel's first performance at Rouen; and though only moderately inspired, he spoke the truth. There was abundance of gold and glory to be gathered in the provinces; and still more could be amassed in England, Scotland, Belgium and Holland. Writing from Holland, Rachel boasted that she had paid more than £2,000 into her bank in a fortnight. In London the receipts at a single performance were £1,200. The report of one of her French successes was crowned by the statement that she had " taken more money than Talma." One perceives from the letters to Madame de Girardin that, when things went wrong with her love affairs—when Walewski, for instance, proved untrue—she derived an equal comfort from the thunders of applause and from the reports of the money in the house. She was received, too, wherever she went, with such honours as are now reserved for the President of the Republic.

The chronicle of these matters is in her letters to her parents, to Dr. Véron, and to Madame de Girardin. Reference has already been made to them, and there is no need to go over that ground again; but there is one report of the impression

made by her acting which must be given, because
it is the report of a woman whose genius was equal
to her own, albeit manifested in very different ways.

The place was Brussels. All that Brussels possessed of rank, fashion, culture and intellect
was in the house to salute the rising of the new
star; but the most important of the spectators was
a governess, who seemed of no particular account—
a plain and prim little body from a Yorkshire parsonage, striving to improve her French in the hope
of obtaining a more profitable position as a teacher.
She, too, though no one knew it, was consumed by
sacred fire—albeit not the kind of fire which blazes
up suddenly, making a spectacular display. She
had not the least idea that, for her also, a time
would come; and she sat humble, abashed, and
even a little frightened by the audacity of a sister
woman who dared to display passions which she
hardly dared to feel.

One has named, of course, Charlotte Brontë.
She had no knowledge of theatrical technique, and
very little knowledge of the French language; she
was the last person in the house to offer a competent
criticism of the actress. But she could criticize
the woman, and she could recreate her own emotions; so that no one of the dramatic reviews
printed in the Brussels papers has half the vitality
of hers. It is in *Villette*, and Rachel is there
spoken of, not as Rachel, but as Vashti—

" The theatre was full—crammed to its roof :
royal and noble were there : palace and hotel had
emptied their inmates into those tiers so thronged

and so hushed. Deeply did I feel myself privileged in having a place before that stage; I longed to see a being of whose powers I had heard reports which made me conceive peculiar anticipations. I wondered if she would justify her renown: with strange curiosity, with feelings, yet of riveted interest, I waited. She was a study of such nature as had not encountered my eyes yet : a great and new planet she was : but in what shape ? I waited her rising. . .

"I had heard this woman termed 'plain,' and I expected bony harshness and grimness—something large, angular, sallow. What I saw was the shadow of a royal Vashti : a queen, fair as the day once, turned pale now like twilight, and wasted like wax in flame.

"For a while—a long while—I thought it was only a woman, though an unique woman, who moved in might and grace before this multitude. By and by I recognized my mistake. Behold ! I found upon her something neither of woman nor of man : in each of her eyes sat a devil. These evil forces bore her through the tragedy, kept up her feeble strength—for she was but a frail creature; and as the action rose and the stir deepened, how wildly they shook her with their passions of the pit ! They wrote HELL on her straight, haughty brow. They tuned her voice to the note of torment. They writhed her regal face to a demoniac mask. Hate and Murder and Madness incarnate she stood.

"It was a marvellous sight : a mighty revelation.

"It was a spectacle low, horrible, immoral. . . .

"Suffering had struck that stage empress; and she stood before her audience neither yielding to,

Rachel

nor enduring, nor, in finite measure, resenting it : she stood locked in struggle, rigid in resistance. She stood, not dressed, but draped in pale antique folds, long and regular like sculpture. A background and flooring of deepest crimson threw her out, white like alabaster—like silver : rather, be it said, like Death. . . .

"Vashti was not good, I was told; and I have said she did not look good : though a spirit, she was a spirit out of Tophet. Well, if so much of unholy force can arise from below, may not an equal efflux of sacred essence descend one day from above?

" The strong magnetism of genius drew my heart out of its wonted orbit; the sunflower turned from the south to a fierce light not solar—a rushing, red, cometary light—hot on vision and to sensation. I had seen acting before, but never anything like this : never anything which astonished Hope and hushed Desire; which outstripped Impulse and paled Conception; which, instead of merely irritating imagination with the thought of what *might* be done, at the same time fevering the nerves because it was *not* done, disclosed power like a deep, swollen winter river, thundering in cataract, and bearing the soul, like a leaf, on the steep and steel sweep of its descent."

Decidedly there is something in that piece of criticism which we seek in vain in the prattling prose of Jules Janin, and even in the flowing, decorated periods of Théophile Gautier.[1] It makes no

---

[1] Dramatic critic for many years of *La Presse*.

presumptuous attempt to show the reader how the thing was done—it was for the professional critics to do that; but it makes the reader realize, as the writings of the professional critics fail to do, the nature of the feeling which "got over the footlights" when Rachel played; and, in doing that, it also helps to explain how actresses, strutting their little hour upon the stage, have, one after the other, come to be acclaimed as only a little lower—if at all lower —than the angels.

Their art is to express, as if they were their own, the emotions and thoughts of the great masters of thought and emotion. They have (or they would not be actresses) the natural gift of expression ; and they are encouraged, drilled, and trained to make the most of it. So that presently there disengages itself, and floats over the footlights, and pervades the theatre, and comes to pervade the town, the country, and even the continent, an impression of a wonderful woman living on a higher emotional plane than other women : a woman who is "sweeter," or nobler, or more intense, or more passionate, or more long-suffering—or, perhaps, in extreme cases, all these things at once—than her sisters. All this because the germ of emotion which is in her is, by art, brought to a fine flower in her rendering of it.

It is an impression which is perpetually being recreated. Consequently it is an impression which even those who know it to be unfounded find it very difficult to escape from. It conquers and reconquers men; it arouses the jealous enmity of women. Especially does it stir the envious hostility of women who are conscious that their own hearts hold feelings too deep for such spectacular display. To such women it is apt to seem that the impression which the actress produces is an effect without a cause; whereas their own emotions are causes which fail to produce their due effect. It is a resentment of that sort which one reads between the lines of the eloquence of the pathetically proper little governess from the Yorkshire parsonage.

Perhaps, too, Charlotte Bronté divined—as most women indubitably divine—that the qualities which actresses express so admirably on the stage are not, as a rule, qualities which they personally possess in any pre-eminent degree. For though there are stage-struck women just as there are stage-struck men, whom the actress's art of expression convinces of the virtue of her sentiments and the sublimity of her character, the clever woman, knowing her own heart and the tendencies and temptations of her sex, looks cunningly beneath the make-believe for quite other attributes, and discovers, or imagines that she discovers, vanity and greed, engendered by indiscriminate and excessive homage.

It may be that Rachel was rather proud than vain; but to say that is only to say that, as a rule, she displayed her vanity on great, in preference to small, occasions. She was not in the least sensitive about her humble origin. On the contrary, as has already been related, she recalled the days of her early struggles while trailing her sleeves in the sauces at supper-parties, and got great conversational effects out of the recollection. But she liked sometimes to demonstrate her grandeur by making the great feel small; and she generally reverted to type in the act of doing so. " Je ne jouerai pas cette—" she said to Ernest Legouvé when he submitted a play to her; and she used a word which Legouvé, in telling the story, declines to print on the ground that it is "outside the classical repertory."

Still more deliberately and elaborately insolent was her treatment of M. Viennet, who also wished to write for her.

Viennet was hardly a great man; but he was in a great position, being a member of the French Academy—the member whom the Academicians had, for reasons of their own, preferred to Benjamin Constant. He waited upon Rachel in her dressing-room, and proposed to read his piece to her. She said that she was only too proud to think that so great a poet had desired so humble an artist as his interpreter. He begged for an appointment, and was requested to call at two o'clock on the following afternoon; and then the fun began.

"Madame is out," he was told when he rang Rachel's bell. "Madame is ill," was the message when he returned on the following day. On the third day he called yet again, with results which Legouvé relates :—

"He rang the bell in a furious passion. A man-servant opened the door.

" ' Is Mademoiselle Rachel at home ? '

" ' Please come in, sir.'

" ' At last,' thought Viennet.

Rachel

" He was shown into a small room in which a very handsome young man, wearing a decoration, was also waiting.

" ' Will Monsieur be so kind as to give me his card ? ' asked the servant.

" ' You have only to mention my name : Viennet.'

" ' I will inquire whether Madame can see you.'

" ' The servant opened the door of an adjoining room, and the poor poet heard Mademoiselle Rachel's voice replying to the question :

" ' M. Viennet ? Tell him—tell him he's a nuisance.'

" The poor poet's rage may be imagined. He felt capable of smashing the furniture. The young man began to smile.

" ' Are you laughing at me, sir ? ' said Viennet. ' Perhaps you don't know that this is the third time—"

" But the young man continued to smile.

" ' My dear M. Viennet,' he said. ' She'd play you far worse tricks than that if you were one of her lovers.' "

The story is quite of a piece with the haughty request that Mademoiselle George would " put in writing " her request for Rachel's assistance at her benefit. " Put a beggar on horseback," etc. One perceives how Rachel understood the obligation to maintain the dignity of a high artistic office. Perhaps her greed was also a perverted manifestation of her self-respect; but here it is necessary to distinguish.

" Rachel n'est pas Juive, elle est Juif," was a

character sketch of her, flashed out, under the influence of strong emotion, by her cousin, Mlle. Judith.

" Rachel était avide, mais elle n'était pas avare," was Dr. Véron's summary of her character.

The fact was that, in money matters, as in other matters, she exhibited perfect Jewish loyalty to her tribe. When she rose in life the entire Tribe of Félix rose with her, by her help, and at her expense. She demanded that all its members should be admitted to the Comédie Française, repeatedly threatening her resignation if she did not get her way, with the result that playgoers complained that going to the national theatre was as good, or as bad, as going to the Synagogue. She pushed her brother Raphael to the front as the business manager of her holiday engagements; she let her father drive her through her performances when she was really too ill to play. It is unnecessary to repeat that she enriched Rebecca and regularly paid the debts of Sarah of the Supper-parties. In these relations the qualities of her heart appeared. In her relations with men, however, it was her head rather than her heart that was in the right place; and she sailed through life like a true Israelitish queen, spoiling the Egyptians as she passed.

Her methods of doing so were twofold. When she saw anything which she thought she would like to possess, she asked for it. When it was given to her, she carried it away and stuck to it. On the other hand, whenever she gave a present (unless it were to a member of the Tribe) it was always with the mental reservation that the gift was in reality a loan which might be called in at any time. So

Rachel

when Beauvallet the actor received a gift from her, he announced his intention of chaining it to the wall of his apartment, in order that it might be impossible for her to resume possession of it; and when in a moment of effusion she presented Dumas *fils* with a ring, he instantly replaced it on her finger saying, " That is the better way, Madame. You will now be saved the trouble of asking me for it."

On the other hand, when she repented of having given Samson's daughter a parasol with a jewelled handle, she simply carried it off, declaring that she would send it to be re-covered, and Adèle Samson never saw it again.

Of the same stamp are the stories told of Rachel's address in extorting gifts from the reluctant. At a dinner-party given by Comte Duchâtel she danced round a silver centre-piece until her host felt that he had no choice but to lay it at her feet. He had hoped, being a married man, and aware that his wife valued the ornament, that Rachel would have forgotten all about his offer by the morrow ; but she did not wait until the morrow. Her host having proposed to send her home in his carriage, she accepted the suggestion, saying : " Thanks. Then there will be no fear of my being robbed of your present, which I will take in the carriage with me." Whereto Comte Duchâtel replied : " By all means, mademoiselle; but I trust that it is not too much to ask that you will return the carriage."

Very similar is the story told by the author of *An Englishman in Paris* of her method of plundering Dr. Véron :

Rachel

" Dr. Véron was despoiled with even less ceremony. Having taken a fancy to some silver saucers
or cups in which the proprietor of the *Constitu-
tionnel* offered ices to his visitors, she began by
pocketing one, and never rested until she had the
whole of the set."

And there is the story of the tickets for the charity
concert. Rachel refused to appear at it, but allowed
her name to be advertised on the understanding
that apologies should be made for her absence
at the last moment. She also stipulated that she
should be given ten tickets for herself. It was
assumed that she wished to give them away; but
not at all. She first sold the ten tickets to Walewski
for a thousand francs, declaring that she had paid
for them in the character of lady patroness. Then
she made Walewski give them back, and sold them
over again, repeating the same story, to various
other friends.

And, finally, there is the famous story of the
guitar.

Rachel first saw and admired the guitar in an
artist's studio. " Give it to me," she said. " I
want to pretend that it is the guitar on which I used
to strum in the days when I earned my pittance as a
street singer." The jest seemed a pleasant one,
and the artist handed over the instrument. Rachel
embellished it with ribbons, and hung it in her own
apartment, where it duly attracted the attention
of Achille Fould,[1] the banker. Hearing its story he

---

[1] The story is also told of Walewski, but it is probably of Achille
Fould that it is true.

expressed the wish to possess it. "Very well," said Rachel. "It is for sale. You can have it for a thousand louis." "Five hundred," proposed the banker, trying to bargain. "No, a thousand," repeated Rachel, expressing her disdain for those who haggled; and the banker actually paid a thousand louis for the worthless knick-knack. It is said that he learnt the truth when he tried to sell his treasure at the Hôtel Drouot, and that the discovery of the hoax nearly sent him into a fit on the floor.

Decidedly it is proper that these stories should succeed the spectacle of Charlotte Brontë dazzled by Rachel's tremendous power in the interpretation of sublime emotions. The contrast between the stage life and the real life is better marked by them than it could be in any other way. Yet, even while the stories were circulating, the view prevailed that the stage life represented the real woman; and the light which blinded the eyes of the little governess improving her French at Brussels had the same effect upon the vision of no less a man than Lamartine, who was then at the height of his renown.

He had made his first reputation long before by launching the Romantic Movement in verse. He had subsequently made a second reputation as one of the most brilliant orators in the Chamber of Deputies. He was shortly to make a third reputation as the Foreign Minister of the Republic of 1848. Both his personal and his political life were notoriously and conspicuously pure. He never sought either the favour of ministers or the favour of actresses. He was austere, though a sentimentalist, pompous

Rachel

and proud, and fifty-seven years of age. Yet he approached Rachel, who was thirty years his junior, as he might have approached a rival potentate. He took Madame Lamartine to call on her, and not finding her at home, he wrote her this letter :—

" MADEMOISELLE,

"Madame de Lamartine and I have ventured to present ourselves for the purpose of expressing our admiration, still aglow from our experience of the previous evening, and of thanking you for the opportunity of applauding the genius of poetry in its most sublime and touching incarnation.

" Again, this morning, I return to your door; but, in the fear that you may be unable to receive me, I take the liberty of leaving a visiting card in eight enormous volumes. It is a modern tragedy which thus approaches the tragedies of antiquity in indifferent prose. That tragedy will become both drama and poem in its turn, and, for that reason, it rightly appertains to you; for the drama is the popular history of nations and the theatre is the tribunal of the heart.

" Be so kind, mademoiselle, as to accept this feeble act of homage to the enthusiasm which you scatter broadcast, and recover wherever you go, and permit me to join therewith the expression of my respectful sentiments.

" LAMARTINE."

The " visiting card in eight volumes " was nothing less than Lamartine's *Histoire des Girondins*—

Rachel

the great work in which he strove to make the
Republican idea once more acceptable in France.
He probably expected Rachel to read it, and came
to believe, in due course, that she had done so—
she who practically never read anything except
plays, and "notices," and the poems addressed
to her by admirers. What else was so vain a
man to think when he heard that Rachel had
undertaken to recite, or chant, the *Marseillaise* on
the stage of the national theatre?

CHAPTER XV

The singing of the *Marseillaise*, and the republicanizing of the provinces.

IT made no real difference to Rachel whether the Chief of the State in France was a king, an emperor, or a president. That is a fair inference from the fact that her chanting of the *Marseillaise* was only an incident of an interlude between the attentions of Orleanist and Bonapartist admirers. And yet one must not infer that she was altogether insincere. There were certain memories. . . .

Rachel had known what it was to be poor. It may be an exaggeration to say, as Mademoiselle George said, that she had begged her bread. But she had, at any rate, strummed a guitar—though not the particular guitar which she sold to Achille Fould—for coppers; and baby brothers and sisters had been exposed beside her on a costermonger's barrow to appeal, whether dumbly or articulately, for the benefactions of the compassionate.

Those had been hungry days; she had not always had enough to eat. Or so she fancied, and it seemed a shame. It seemed a shame, too, that she should have been attired in rags while other women wore silks and satins, and that her mother should have had to tramp from door to door, dealing in old clothes, and have been splashed with mud by the equipages of the well-to-do. It had all happened too long

Rachel

ago to matter very much. She had long since arrived at splashing mud about with an equipage of her own. But still she remembered. There was the germ of an emotion there which might blossom into a fine, and even a terrible, flower when she expressed it.

She was so little in earnest, at first, that she asked the advice of a respectable man in high position. Everybody, she told him, was singing the *Marseillaise*. Lockroy, at that time Director of the Français, had suggested that it would " amuse people " if she were to sing it also. The fortunes of the theatre were, just then, very far from prosperous, and this demonstration might restore them by the magic of actuality. What did the respectable man in high position think ?

The respectable man in high position disapproved. The singing of the *Marseillaise*, it seemed to him, was an occupation fit only for the rabble. The song was charged with horrible menace not only to royalty, but also to property. He expected Rachel to be on the side of the respectable and the well-to-do. An actress in her position, he said—an actress who had performed under the patronage of crowned heads, and been embraced by the king's son—really ought not, should not, could not, etc., etc., etc. But he argued to deaf ears. Rachel " saw herself " in her new rôle, and began rehearsing it in her carriage while driving into Paris from the Porte Maillot with Louise Colet.[1] " One felt in the air," Madame Colet reported, " as it were a mighty breath of hope, bearing

[1] Known to the Romantics as Sappho, and as the Tenth Muse : the mistress successively of Victor Cousin, Flaubert, and Alfred de Musset. She wrote novels, now forgotten, but not without merit.

all youthful hearts along with it." That, and not the perusal of the eight volumes of Lamartine's History, was the origin of the astonishing performance.

Jules Janin was one of those who thought it objectionable. Just as it had seemed a shame to Rachel that she should have been poor while other people were rich, so it seemed a shame to Jules Janin that the comfort of the comfortable classes should be disturbed. He argued on the subject with his usual fluent plausibility. Nobody, so far as he could see, had any grievance. All was for the best in the best of all possible worlds. Some people, no doubt, were poor—but the poor we have always with us. It was a criminal act to pander to the rapacity of the populace, and so set class against class. Indeed it was worse than a crime to do such things; it was a blunder. A great artist like Rachel really ought to have known better.

So this moderate man argued, eloquently, voluminously, interminably; but Rachel, as has been said, " saw herself " in the rôle of political agitator, and that settled it. Jules Janin went to see her in it, and his sense of justice bade him give a true report. He described how she picked up the tricolour flag which had been left lying on a bench, stepped forward, with head erect and eyes glowing like coals of fire, and began, half to chant, and half to declaim, the inexorable hymn of vengeance—

" She was a Muse—a Fury. She came—from Helicon. She came from the Champ-de-Mars. A daughter of Pindar—and a daughter of Rouget de Lisle. She surpassed Erinnys the violent and

Rachel

implacable; and all this mob listened, gaping and amazed, to the curses uttered by the lips which, a moment before, had been divinely expressing the tenderness of Racine and the splendour of Corneille. . . .

" It was superb and awful. One shuddered; one trembled; the fever of heroism took possession of every heart. How beautiful and valiant she was at this moment of her terrible task! And how dangerous! War and peace were hidden in the folds of her mantle; this flag which she held in her grip was waved among the clouds. You would have said that she was the living and vehement statue of the heroic Muse, chanting miracles and lies to her audience. . . .

" One should have called to her, with the hero of the Odyssey: 'Stop! Stop! It is not true hospitality to terrify one's guests.' But neither the terrors of one half of the house nor the admiration of the other half, nor the rumours of the present, nor the echoes of the past availed to arrest this heroine in her course. One would have said, to hear her and to see her, that she was wreaking a personal vengeance, assuaging a personal hatred. One could imagine nothing more sincere or solemn than this Amazon intoning the chaunt of death. When one tells such a story of times so near to us, it is as if one were relating the figments of a dream, or inventing a dazzling drama without a name."

And Rachel, who produced this marvellous effect of breathless hostility to kings, was the same Rachel who had volunteered to be embraced, " pour rien,"

Rachel

by the Prince de Joinville, and was presently to
be embraced by the Emperor's cousin. The word
" cabotinage " inevitably comes to the point of one's
pen in the connection; but not, perhaps, quite justly,
unless it be " cabotinage " to bring the germ of
a real emotion to a fine flower in the expression of
it. The effect of the recitation, at any rate, was
immense. The fortunes of the national theatre were
restored by the national anthem; ·and Rachel's
father, observing what had happened, had a happy
thought—an inspiration related, it need hardly be
said, to the further amassing of pieces of silver.

For a heap of pieces of silver was the *summum
bonum* of Jacob Félix. As often as he perceived the
glint of a piece of silver, he was up and after it as a
terrier is after a rat. When one has related that of
him, one has already written his biography in brief.
He now realized that there were more pieces of silver
to be derived from Republicanism than from art.
It was merely a question of pulling the right strings.
Doing that, he might organize a great *battue* of
pieces of silver under official patronage, with the
Minister of Fine Arts for his beater. And this was
a thing which Jacob Félix, who was really a man of
genius in his way, contrived to do.

He, the ex-pedlar, contrived to be accorded an
audience by Ledru-Rollin, who was then Minister
of the Interior. He did not, of course, tell Ledru-
Rollin that there was money in Republicanism—
that was his secret which he kept at the back of
his brain. What he told Ledru-Rollin was that the
provinces wanted " republicanizing," that they could
be better and more thoroughly republicanized by

Rachel

his daughter's recitations than by any other means, and that the government had nothing to lose, but everything to gain, by giving Rachel's next provincial tour a semi-official character. He put his case so plausibly that a circular was actually addressed from the Ministry to the managers of all the provincial theatres in which she proposed to appear.

"CABINET OF THE MINISTER OF THE INTERIOR.

"*Paris, April* 23, 1848.

" CITIZEN MANAGER,

"Citizen Raphael Félix has formed a theatrical company with which he will visit several of the French Departments.

"It is his purpose to produce there the masterpieces of our dramatic literature with Citizeness Rachel in the leading parts. Citizeness Rachel had entered into several lucrative engagements with foreign countries; but she has cancelled them all in order to be able to remain in France. It is her wish to extend to the Departments the devotion to the Republic which she displayed in Paris in her admirable creation of the Marseillaise.

"The electrical effect produced here by her performances should have marvellous and salutary results in the provinces. In the name, therefore, of art, to which the Republic desires to accord its fruitful and powerful protection, I beg you to recognize the sacrifices which Citizeness Rachel has made, to give her your support, and to afford Citizen Raphael Félix every facility for organizing performances in your town.

"ELIAS RENAULT,

"*Provisional Director of Theatres and Literature.*"

Rachel

So that it had come to this : that the anthem of the Revolution itself was officially spoken of as having been " created " by the actress who declaimed it. In arranging that, Citizen Jacob Félix had truly proved himself a great man—a sort of Citizen Vincent Crummles raised to the nth. Like Citizen Vincent Crummles, Citizen Jacob Félix was *not* a Prussian—he was a patriot, for there was money in patriotism.

And not money merely, but, as the vulgar say, "pots of money." At Lyon, for example, the agreement was that Rachel should receive £176 a night; and she did only a little less well at Toulouse, Montpellier, Nîmes, Arles, Aix and Marseilles, and also visited, with more or less success, Strasburg, Metz, Besançon, Nancy, Dijon, Avignon, Toulon, Béziers, Cette, Orléans, Tours and Blois. In Paris she had been pleading ill-health and declining to play more than twice a week. In the provinces, with Citizen Jacob Félix standing over her, she had to play nearly every night. There might not be money in patriotism for very long, and Citizen Jacob Félix was determined to make his patriotic hay while the sun was shining.

Indeed the time soon came when there ceased to be money in this sort of patriotism; and then Citizen Jacob Félix and Citizeness Rachel dropped it. The *Marseillaise* came presently to be associated, not with the sublime sentiments of fraternity, but with the excesses of a blood-thirsty mob. Audiences came to be divided in their desire to hear it, and then the enthusiasts called for it in vain. The Citizen Actor Manager appeared before the curtain and announced that the Citizeness Leading Lady had a bad cold, and could not comply with the request. The pieces of silver being by this time safely in the bank, the republicanizing of the provinces ended in a diplomatic and imaginary catarrh.

Then, after a little while, occurred Napoleon's *coup d'état*; and it was no part of Rachel's function to resist it, or to join Victor Hugo in singing—

"S'il ne reste qu'un, je serai celui-là."

On the contrary. Rachel had, in Aristotelian phrase, purged herself of Republican emotions by means of pity and fear. She was ready, as were her audiences, for the expression of quite other emotions. There were those who expected, or said that they expected, to see her express them by declaiming *Partant pour la Syrie*. It did not quite come to that; but she found other means of proving her contentment with the new régime, as Arsène Houssaye relates.

Arsène Houssaye, as we read in his *Confessions*, received, one day, a mysterious summons to the Elysée. He had no idea why he was wanted there; but the summons was not one to be disobeyed.

" When I arrived," he writes, " I was shown into an ante-chamber. Thence I was passed on into a second, and then into a third apartment, where I saw Mademoiselle Rachel approaching me, wreathed in smiles. She seemed quite at home there—but she always seemed quite at home wherever one found her. Besides, she was, at that time, the ' mistress of the house.' "

Rachel

Which, is, of course, Arsène Houssaye's way of saying that Rachel, who had so lately aroused the frenzy of the populace by declaiming the imprecations of the *Marseillaise*, had now reconsidered her position, and improved it by responding to the advances of a Prince of the House of Bonaparte.

CHAPTER XVI

RACHEL had run to the Elysée because there had been trouble at the theatre.

Her colleagues wished to appoint their own committee of management, as they had been accustomed to do in the past, instead of being governed by a nominee of the Minister of the Interior. She preferred one-man government because it was easier for her to get her own way with an individual than with a committee. Moreover, she was aggrieved by the dismissal of Lockroy, at whose instance she had sung the *Marseillaise*. She had resigned, and withdrawn her resignation, and renewed it. The air was full of indignation and threats of litigation; and the upshot of the matter was that, when Arsène Houssaye kept the appointment made for him at the Elysée, he was received, not by the Prince President, but by the " mistress " of the house, who greeted him with the question—

" Would you like to be Director of the Théâtre Français ? "

Like it ? Of course he would ; and equally, of course, he displayed no surprise at being offered the appointment by an actress instead of a Cabinet Minister. Perhaps he was cynic enough to feel none. At all events he " knew his manners "—which

were those of an "arriviste." Though not a man
of genius, he was a humorist with a felicitous
instinct for the paths which lead to success in life.
So he took everything that happened for granted,
and clutched gratefully at the proffered petti-
coat. Presented, in due course, to the Prince
President, he thanked him for the nomination;
but the Prince President directed his gratitude to
the proper quarter.

"Don't thank me," he said. "Thank Mlle.
Rachel. The names of ten men of letters were
submitted to her, and she selected you. I'm sure
I don't know why;" and Arsène Houssaye still
showed no astonishment, but merely bowed.

Then the battle began. The news of what had
passed at the Elysée reached the sociétaires of the
Comédie Française. They at once called an extraordinary general meeting, as the result of which
they at once put on black coats and white ties, called
six cabs, jumped into them, drove in a procession
to the Ministry of the Interior, and demanded an
audience. They were admitted, and proceeded to
argue their case with glowing eloquence. This
interference with their rights, they said, was uncon-
stitutional—a violation of the Decree of Moscow.
The Prince President had no *locus standi* at their
theatre. A Prince President, who began by upsetting
the constitution of the House of Molière, would end
by upsetting the Republic. And so forth with such
persuasive vehemence that the Minister of the
Interior was bounced into promising to see justice
done, and the newspapers came out with this
interesting announcement—

Rachel

" M. Arsène Houssaye Director of the Comédie Française for five minutes."

So the sociétaires withdrew, reassured; and then it was Rachel's turn to renew the battle. She first threatened to leave France, taking Arsène Houssaye with her, in order that they might reap glory together in a foreign land. She next remembered that Dr. Véron had "influence," and besought him to pull the wires. She also, at the same time, set to work pulling wires with her own hands. It was pointed out, at her instance, to the Minister of the Interior, that the national theatre was steering a straight course for the shoals of insolvency. He was told of a terrible night on which there had only been £2 2s. 6d. in the house. Only the return of Rachel, he was assured, could avert disaster; and Rachel, it was intimated, would not return unless she were allowed to nominate the Director. It became clear to him, therefore, that to follow her was to follow the line of least resistance; and at last he took up his pen and wrote—

" MY DEAR MONSIEUR HOUSSAYE,
    " Your nomination, which was decided upon a month ago, is at last signed; but it will not be officially announced until to-morrow. Come and see me about six o'clock, that we may talk the matter over.
                          " FERDINAND BARROT."

Thus the appointment was settled; and the principal thing which the Minister of the Interior had to say at the interview was that he wished the new Director joy of his job, as the comedians were terrible fellows and fully resolved to make his position untenable.

And certainly the comedians tried very hard to do so.

Their first step was to serve their Director with a writ at the moment of his arrival in the theatre, charging him with trespass and demanding damages; but the Director waved the writ on one side as a document which must be left to lie on his table until he had leisure to attend to it.

Their second step was to appoint a Director of their own—M. Sevestre, of the Theatre of Montmartre. Arsène Houssaye, entering his office, found M. Sevestre installed there, sitting at the mahogany desk, and claiming, when questioned, that he had a right to sit at it. Whereupon Arsène Houssaye rang the bell. " Monsieur de la Chaume," he said to the attendant who responded, " this gentleman desires to do his work at this desk. Be so good as to carry it into some other room for him; " and M. Sevestre, being intimidated, glanced at his watch, and remarked that it was time for him to go out to dinner.

Their third step was to send the comedian Brindeau up to talk to the Director; for the comedian Brindeau had boasted loudly, and declared his intention of throwing the Director out of the window. But Arsène Houssaye rose, with a smile, and offered Brindeau his most comfortable arm-chair, and was so polite to him that the comedian who had proposed to throw him out of the window was won over, and ended by taking his part against his milder-mannered colleagues. And then it was Arsène Houssaye's turn to take the aggressive.

He boldly intimated that, if any comedian were so discontented that he desired to resign his position, the Director would, however regretfully, accept his resignation. He could depend upon Rachel, and upon Madame Plessy, who was on her way back from Russia. Among the pensionnaires, whom he could also depend upon, were included such excellent players as Got and Delaunay. Nor would the introduction of a little fresh blood do the theatre any harm. Bocage and Frédérick Lemaître were available, and could be engaged. So, if Samson and Provost really wished to retire, they had only to say so. Which of them would speak first?

But neither of them spoke first. They both still thought that they could remain and freeze the Director out. In order to remain, however, they had to do what they were told, even though they pretended that they were doing it of their own accord, as the result of decisions arrived at by their own committee, which still continued to meet. They did this, but did not cease to intrigue. There was a new Minister of the Interior—M. Baroche. They "got at" him, and induced him to depose Arsène Houssaye and appoint a certain M. Mazères in his place. This time their triumph seemed assured; but once more they had reckoned without Rachel.

They feared her persuasive tongue, indeed; but they had taken their precautions against its influence. Rachel presented herself at the Ministry, and was told to her astonishment that the Minister could not receive her. This happened not once only but three times. Arsène Houssaye himself believed that he was beaten, and prepared to evacuate his office; but Rachel bade him be of good courage. "Wait a bit," she said. "I have sworn that the Minister shall see me, and see me he shall." So she called yet again, not at the Ministry, but at the Minister's private house.

The Minister sent down word that he was dressing to go out to dinner, and could see no one—his carriage, in fact, was at the door, waiting for him. "Very well," said Rachel. "I too will wait"; and she got into the carriage, and made herself comfortable. The coachman recognized her, but said nothing. He knew his master, and jumped to the conclusion that he had arranged to take the actress for a drive. As a matter of fact the Minister did not even know the actress by sight; but she received him in his own carriage and introduced herself. "And now, M. le Ministre," she said, " we can talk about this little matter of business "; and she talked about it so efficaciously that the Minister was not only coaxed into consenting to cancel the nomination of M. Mazères, but also begged that Rachel and her Director would both dine with him on the following Saturday.

That was practically the end of the opposition to Arsène Houssaye's appointment. It only remained for him to overcome one or two elderly authors who fancied that they could browbeat the youthful Director into the production of unsuitable plays from their pens; and that was a comparatively simple matter. Empis, the Academician, for example, insisted that a piece of his should be staged on the ground that he was "one of the Forty." "Sir," replied Arsène Houssaye, "I am blond, but I am determined. It is true that you are one of the Forty. It is also true that Molière, who was nevertheless a playwright of some merit, was not. Moreover, it would be all the same to me if you were one of the Ten Thousand." "Sir," said Empis, "if I were not a man of great self-control I should throw you out of the window." "Sir," replied Arsène Houssaye, "as I am a man of great politeness I content myself with indicating the whereabouts of the door."

So that was over; and Arsène Houssaye, thanks partly to Rachel, and partly to his own resolute and radiant character, was firmly seated in the saddle, and remained in it for several years, with a free hand to follow his own policy.

That policy was, broadly speaking, to modernize the repertory. The classics were, of course, retained—a national theatre which ignored the classics would be unthinkable in France. On the other hand, the old-fashioned pieces of the day before yesterday were taboo; and the younger writers were given their chance, to whatever dramatic school they belonged, provided that they possessed that "don du théâtre" without which no theory of the dramatic art is of any avail. Victor Hugo, Dumas, Alfred de Musset, Ernest Legouvé—all these were included among the chosen. Madame de Girardin, who had failed so lamentably in tragedy, was given another chance, and succeeded in comedy with *Lady Tartufe*.

Not all the pieces produced, of course, were of

equal artistic value; but the new policy was, at any rate, pecuniarily successful. The day was not far behind when the national theatre had played, as has been stated, to a house of £2 2s. 6d., and its Director had not known where to turn to borrow ten thousand francs. The day soon came when it actually declared a dividend; and when that happened the comedians were conciliated. "We must make a night of it," said Samson when he heard the news; and they made a night of it. There was a supper; and after the supper there was a ball; and Samson, who had begun his relations with the new Director by serving him with a writ, now danced a gavotte in his honour : a sequence of proceedings which may be taken to demonstrate that even the greatest and gravest comedians are very much like children.

"The radiant period" is Arsène Houssaye's name for the epoch on which the theatre now entered —an epoch during which Rachel triumphed in the modern, as she had previously triumphed in the classical drama.

A good deal of its radiance may have been due to the sunniness of his own disposition. He was a disciplinarian, determined to have his own way; but he kept order with a pleasant smile, being determined to enjoy himself, and most anxious that others should enjoy themselves also. He was neither a prude nor a Pasha in his relations with the débutantes, but one who looked at the life of the theatre and found it very good, filled with perpetual hilarity by the amours of the *coulisses*—provided

Rachel

always that they did not interfere with business
—and resolutely maintaining that no one had the
right to expect the moral standards of the green-
room to correspond with those of a convent school.
He could enter into the feelings of Got, who wrote
in his diary, published the other day, that he went
on the stage because he desired " the proximity of
women," and felt his pulse stirred by the spectacle
of " the palpitating bosom of Madame Plessy."

The Comédie Française under Arsène Houssaye's
régime was the playground of Paris, and Paris was
the playground of Europe. The period was that of
the Third Empire—the period which the philosopher,
looking back on it after the lamentable crash of
Sedan, summed up in the phrase : " Au moins on
s'est diablement amusé." It will be proper to pause
and survey the amusements in so far as the intimate
life of the theatre served to provide them.

CHAPTER XVII

Life behind the scenes at the National Theatre.

THE first thing needful, according to Arsène Houssaye, was to get the mothers of the actresses out of the way.

They came to the theatre, he says, ostensibly to safeguard the virtue of their daughters, but in reality to boast of it. " My daughter," he heard one of them say, " is a vestal virgin "; and a moment later the vestal virgin entered. A false moustache was adhering to her lips—the obvious legacy of the embrace of a comedian in the wings. It was better that such a *contretemps* should occur off the stage than on, but still . . .

Moreover, the mothers of the actresses were a nuisance. They blocked gangways and interfered alike with business and with gaiety. The spectacle of a procession of elderly ladies going behind the scenes between the acts annoyed the audience; and when the ladies got behind the scenes, the actors, and the actresses—not to mention the admirers of the actresses—wished them further. So Arsène Houssaye first jestingly proposed that they should be killed and that a monument should be erected in the theatre to their memory, and then seriously issued a decree assigning rigid limits to their movements. They might go to their daughters' dressing-rooms, and stay there, or they might sit in the front of the house in an enclosure which should be appropriated to their use. But they must not pass to and fro from the one place to the other, and they must on no account be seen in the artists' *foyer*.

That was Arsène Houssaye's first great managerial reform; and it made matters much pleasanter alike for the players and for the privileged playgoers who enjoyed their *entrées*.

That privilege was accorded to almost any man of letters who cared to ask for it, and also to a limited number of men about town. These had nothing to pay, and were made equally welcome " in front " and " behind." Sometimes their business " behind " was to gossip and smoke cigars with the Director. More often their purpose was to enjoy the society of the actresses. Occasionally a man about town, if rich enough, took an actress—usually an actress of more beauty than talent—away from the theatre and installed her somewhere as his left-handed consort. The men of letters, unable to afford that extravagance, kissed them, and played with them, and promised each of them in turn the leading part in his next new piece.

Arsène Houssaye gives a picture of Alexandre Dumas, burly and boisterous, passing through a long avenue of actresses, picking each of them up and kissing them in turn. He also gives us this pretty picture of a scene in the *coulisses* after a performance of *Marion Delorme*, with Mademoiselle Judith in the rôle of the beautiful sinner—

" Victor Hugo pays her the great compliment of kissing her on the forehead, and she feels as if she had been sanctified. Alfred de Musset happens to be passing, and he kisses her on the arm. 'Who wants the other arm?' she asks; and the question does not fall upon deaf ears. Alfred de Vigny bows low, and takes her hand. Judith does not waste her time. 'You'll let me play Kitty Bell, won't you?' she demands; but Alfred de Vigny is a man who never makes promises."

Then there are pictures of certain supper-parties, and also of certain picnics. We read of one supper-party whereat a charming actress twined a wreath of roses and placed it on the brow of Alfred de Musset with "a resounding kiss." He drank her health so often, and so deeply, that he had to be assisted to his home. At another party, at an open-air restaurant in one of the parks, another actress, equally charming, saved the poet from a similar anti-climax. He had just mixed himself a tumbler of his favourite concoction of beer, brandy and absinthe, and was about to drink it, when she snatched it out of his hands and threw it away. He "dropped his walking-stick, threw himself at the actress's feet, and kissed her hand with tears." He believed, for the moment, that he loved her, and she, also for the moment, believed that she had saved him from himself; but nothing came of it. The poet soon relapsed into his old habits, and the actress diverted her affections into another channel.

Yet her endeavours were serious, and the blame for the failure did not rest upon her shoulders. She offered the poet the hospitality of her apartment, proposing to keep him at least moderately sober

Rachel

until he had written a play for her. He accepted the offer, and began to write the play; and all went well until, one evening, another actress came to visit his hostess. As she lived in the immediate neighbourhood, politeness required that Musset should offer to escort her home. Although, the distance being short and the weather fine, he went out without his hat, he did not return; and his hostess had no difficulty in guessing what had become of him. On the following morning, therefore, she sent both his hat and his unfinished manuscript to her friend's house, with an intimation that all was over between them.

That picture, perhaps, is more characteristic than proper. A picture which, while equally characteristic, approximates more nearly to correctitude, is that which Arsène Houssaye draws of the supper-party given in Rachel's mansion to celebrate the first night of *Lady Tartufe*.

The guests were hastily gathered in the *coulisses*, and the banquet was sent in from a restaurant. Madame de Girardin, of course, was there; and so was Emile de Girardin—" the husband of all the women in Paris except his wife." The only other lady present was a certain " soupeuse " of whom one knows nothing except that she was also a " grande amoureuse." The management was represented by Arsène Houssaye himself, and criticism by Jules Janin, Théophile Gautier, Paul de Saint-Victor, and Jules Lecomte—the Jules Lecomte who, of old, as a handsome tenor, had captivated the heart of the ex-Empress Marie-Louise. And the conversation !

It began with the inevitable congratulations on

the evening's successes, but soon drifted away from that. Emile de Girardin was anxious to hear about Jules Lecomte's successes with the Empress; and the ex-tenor, now a *chroniqueur*, was easily persuaded to tell the company all about them. He used to sup *tête-à-tête* with her. It was he who gave the orders and told the servants when to retire and leave him alone with their mistress. But he had no illusions. It was not the man of brilliant intelligence that she admired in him, but the tenor—she absolutely doted on tenors.

Whereupon Théophile Gautier, who was in a captious mood, proceeded to denounce tenors—"and all those who make a noise and call it singing"; and that gave Madame de Girardin her opportunity to chaff him in his turn : " Hush, Théo., hush ! In the days when you adored Julia Grisi you would have been willing to turn yourself into a nightingale to please her beautiful eyes." And then, apropos of nothing, there was "noise without," and in bounced Clésinger, the sculptor—the husband of George Sand's daughter Solange—and proceeded to lean over the back of Rachel's chair and talk about his wife. " A perfect angel," he said, " when her mother isn't there "; but then he discovered that there was no supper left for him and decided to bounce out again, leaving Rachel to confide to the company that when last he had called upon her he had declined to go, but had insisted upon spending the night on the sofa in the library. And so on till the party broke up, some time in the small hours, and Rachel's maid Rose was left exclaiming—

" God of Israel, what an orgy ! They call them-

selves wits, but Gargantua was an angel beside them
for gluttony. I don't dare look at the bill. A supper
at twelve francs a head! And twelve times twelve
is a hundred and forty-four; and they've got through
it all in an hour."

Such are our pictures—typical pictures which
could be multiplied indefinitely; and there are morals
to be drawn from them. The moralist, of course,
will draw one moral; but the historian and the critic
will draw another. To them the various pictures,
fused together, make one composite picture of the
collapse of the Romantic Movement, which, in
fact, perished at a time when its founders were still
alive and flourishing. Rachel's acting, as we have
seen and insisted, had arrested the Movement on
the stage. Viewed, as we have also seen reason to
view it, as a new attitude towards life, and personality, and love affairs, it seems to vanish like
smoke at Rachel's supper-parties.

The note of the Romantics, in these regards, had
been—to get back to our old formula—the substitu-
tion of sentiment for gallantry. The step was one
which even actresses—some actresses at all events
—had been taught to take. They had learnt to live
—a few of them, that is to say, had learnt to live—
as if they, as well as their lovers, had hearts, de-
vastated by passions of more than religious intensity.
Marie Dorval had learnt intensity from Alfred de
Vigny, and practised it on Jules Sandeau. Neither
of her lovers had enriched her, and yet, for the sake
of one of them, she had pretended to stab herself
with a paper-knife. The gesture had been magnificent, although no harm was done. The Romantic

idea had inspired it; and, in real life as on the stage, Marie Dorval had gone about tearing passions to rags. It had been easy for her to be fickle, but impossible for her to mock at sentiment. She had confused love with religion, and had died, a Catholic mystic, meditating among the tombs.

No one of the guests at Rachel's supper-party, one feels instinctively, was capable of that sort of thing, though there were eminent Romantics among them. Théophile Gautier's red waistcoat had been, as we know, the oriflamme of the Romantic revolt at the theatre of which Rachel was now the queen, and Madame de Girardin, as Delphine Gay, had been one of the Romantic Muses; but now Delphine could chaff Théo. about his passion for the singer—concerning whom he had said of old that he would gladly give all his worldly wealth for the privilege of seeing her emerge, undraped, from her bath; and Théo. and Delphine could combine to chaff the tenor whom an Empress had invited to supper and detained to breakfast. We are leagues removed there from the emotional expansiveness of the late twenties and early thirties, when divine approval was claimed for illicit love, and George Sand exhorted those about to profane their marriage vows to open the proceedings with prayer. Love, for these banqueters, was not a religious exercise but a diversion—they were out to enjoy themselves. The atmosphere of sentiment had evaporated, and the atmosphere of gallantry had reappeared.

These things being so, the members of the imperial household could, and did, bear a hand in the game; and there were conditions in the case which induced them to join in it more openly and with more spirit than the representatives of other dynasties.

Their house was not, like that of the Bourbons, of immemorial antiquity. They could not claim, as Louis XVIII did, even in exile, to be compounded of different clay from their subjects; nor had they, in the days of adversity, lived in pretentious pomp. They were only promoted *bourgeois*, and were regarded, at the other Courts of Europe, as upstarts. The Emperor himself had been one of the pillars of Lady Blessington's salon, and had borrowed money from a fashionable courtesan in order to defray his expenses as a Pretender. The Empress was more distinguished by her beauty than by her birth; and the old aristocracy of France showed no disposition to abase itself before her. It had slighted and snubbed her up to the day when her betrothal was announced; and her imperial husband was the emperor of men who had been accustomed to slap him on the back.

It was impossible for a Court so constituted to be, as vulgar people say, " stand-offish " or " stuck-up "; and it wisely made but few attempts in that direction. Its atmosphere was one of equalitarian, not to say Bohemian, *camaraderie*. The Emperor and the Empress were the playfellows as well as the rulers of their people. They not only took liberties, but allowed liberties to be taken. In particular, they encouraged men of letters and artists in general as these had never been encouraged at any other Court. That is to say, they did not patronise them with condescending *hauteur*, but made friends

of them, and even romped with them. "Ego et
Imperator meus"—"Ego et Imperatrix mea"—was
the order of thought which seemed natural to the
great entertainers of the time.

One has an example of this democratic tone in
the story of Alfred de Musset's conduct when
summoned to the Tuileries to read one of his un-
acted pieces to the Empress. At first he refused
to go—apparently on the ground that it was too
much trouble to keep sober. Arsène Houssaye,
however, over-persuaded him, and accompanied
him, in order, as one imagines, to make sure that he
did not drop into the Café de la Régence on the way.
He had avoided inebriety, and was well dressed
and well groomed; but his temper was the sullen
temper of a man who suffers from *mal de cheveux*.
It exploded when Baron James de Rothschild
strolled into the Empress's boudoir unannounced.
For Alfred de Musset, as for a later critic of life, it
was possible, and even easy, to have "too much
of Lord Rothschild."

"Who is that man?" he asked sharply; and
the banker was presented to him.

"Very well," he said, "I shan't read any more.
I did not invite M. de Rothschild."

"Pray continue, M. de Musset," said the Baron;
but the poet folded up his manuscript, and turned
to the Empress with flashing eyes.

"Madame," he said, "you are as charming as
you are beautiful. I am very pleased to read my
work in the presence of your Majesty, but no power
on earth shall induce me to read it in the presence
of M. de Rothschild"; and he stuck to his point

Rachel

so obstinately that the Emperor himself told the banker to go away.

There is no gallantry in that story, of course—it merely shows how boldly men of letters ventured to assert themselves in the imperial presence. Arsène Houssaye himself had not less self respect, though he was more ceremonious in the expression of it. He refused point blank, for instance, to walk backwards before the Emperor, holding a silver candlestick, on the occasion of a gala performance. The appeal to tradition, he said, left him unmoved; for Napoleon III did not "dance in ballets, dressed up as Apollo, like Louis XIV." And he continued—

"When the Emperor comes to the theatre he shakes me by the hand. If I were to hold the candle for him I should forfeit this mark of his sympathy. The Emperor often invites me to sit with him in his box. Do you think he would condescend to converse with one who carried a candle? Besides, I do not wish to feel that I am unworthy to converse with him or with myself."

He also refused point blank to take the beautiful Madeleine Brohan — the latest débutante at his theatre—to lunch with the Emperor at the palace of Saint-Cloud. He suspected, of course—what any other theatrical manager would have suspected in his place. He was not a man who pretended to specialize in virtue; but he had no intention of discharging the functions of—there is no need to print the word. So there was silence, until the Emperor begged the Director not to suppose that

Rachel

he ever invited an actress to visit him with any
" arrière-pensée." Whereto Arsène Houssaye replied that, of course, no such thought had ever
crossed his mind, but that he rather fancied that
this particular actress, if invited to lunch with the
Emperor, would prefer to be accompanied by her
mother.

And then there is yet another story which, while
exhibiting the Emperor and the Director on a footing
of democratic equality in their relations towards
the ladies of the theatre, brings us back to Rachel.

The hour of the *Marseillaise* being over, and the
emotions appertaining to it being extinct in her
breast, Rachel had proposed to habit herself as
the Muse of History and declaim some verses composed by Arsène Houssaye on the topical theme :
" L'Empire c'est la paix." This sort of thing—

> Grande ruche en travail, par les beaux-arts charmée,
> Paris, une autre Athène; Alger, une autre Tyr !
> Des landes à peupler, des villes à bâtir,
> Voilà les bulletins de notre Grande Armée !
>
> Sous le même drapeau, vainqueur des factions,
> Ramener les enfants de la mère patrie,
> Consoler tes douleurs, o Niobe meurtrie !
> Et convier le peuple aux grandes actions.
>
> Refaisons des tableaux dignes de la Genèse ;
> Que tout renaisse et vive, et que, de toute part,
> Les plus désherités puissent prendre leur part
> A ces amples festins que peignait Véronese.

It is poor stuff; but Rachel's rendering of it
impressed the Emperor so favourably that he sent for
the Director, fell upon his neck, and kissed him, and
bade him " pass the kiss on " to the actress. " I
rather fancy," Arsène Houssaye comments, " that

Rachel

he had long had the habit of kissing her without the help of an intermediary, and I myself certainly had not waited to kiss Rachel until I received the Emperor's instructions to do so."

And that is credible enough; for it appears to have been the engaging custom of Arsène Houssaye to kiss any actress to whom he took a fancy. His great grievance—in so far as that jovial man ever had a grievance—was that the faithful La Chaume was too prone to enter his office without knocking at the moments when he was doing so.

Such was the atmosphere in which Rachel flourished in the early fifties : an atmosphere in which Arsène Houssaye kissed all the girls, and the girls, on their part, distributed their kisses generously among all eligible applicants. " Sir," said one of them indignantly to Alfred de Musset, " I hear that you have boasted that you are my lover." " On the contrary, madame," was the poet's crushing reply, " I have always boasted that I was *not* your lover." " Your *fiancé*, dear," said another girl to a friend, " was formerly my lover." " I dared not hope, dear," was the rejoinder, " that I should ever discover a man whom you had not permitted to embrace you."

Et cetera, et cetera. Such stories flow from Arsène Houssaye's pen as from a fountain—a new fountain opened when that of Romanticism was sealed. Readers who have regarded the theatre as the scene of sincere and intense passion should go to his book and read it from cover to cover. It will instruct them; for they will find sincerity and intensity precisely the attributes most conspicuously lacking in the amours of the queens of his stage.

Rachel

They appear, rather, to have let themselves be loved, partly because it was " good fun " and partly because it was profitable to do so; and it was with Rachel as with the others.   Most of her love-affairs were either passing caprices or stepping-stones to social and professional advancement.   The note of sincerity is only heard—and is not heard very loudly even then—when the *bourgeoise* who had died young in her wakes up.

And that brings us to Hector B——.

CHAPTER XVIII

THE discovery of Hector B—— is due to Mlle. Valentine Thomson. Rachel's letters to him were communicated to her for publication; and a story arises out of them, though the details are left obscure and the name of the hero is kept secret.

He was a country gentleman, and the son of a country gentleman; not rich, one imagines, but comfortably well-to-do. The whole family seems to have been, not only provincial, but, as the French say, "de la bonne année" in its readiness to believe any beautiful article of faith. It was an article of faith with them, as it had once been with Crémieux, that Rachel could be tamed and domesticated—that it would be gratifying to her to escape from the glitter of the footlights and the frivolous round of supper-parties, and be established as the Lady Bountiful of a rural parish.

Rachel herself encouraged the belief, and, even for a short space, shared it. Frail health, overwork, and weariness of the vagrant life of a strolling player, were doubtless the chief factors in her feeling. Sickness of heart at the infidelity of Arthur Bertrand may have been another. She was tired, both physically and morally, and in a mood to long for the wings of a dove that she might fly away and be at rest. The dead *bourgeoise* coming to life in her bosom, she mistook that feeling for a desire to marry and settle down; and so she and Hector B——, who understood none of these things, became engaged to be married.

How long she had been acquainted with him one does not know; but the crisis occurred, and the correspondence began, in the course of her provincial tour in the summer of 1849. She was always more sincere and tender in the provinces than in Paris. The autograph hunters are perpetually bringing to light some fresh provincial *inconnu* whom she addressed, not as a princess claiming admiration, but as a weak woman sincerely longing for affection. They always vanished out of her life, having served their turn, when she got back to the excitements of the capital; but she was genuinely devoted to them for the time being, though they rewarded her devotion by offering her letters for sale. It was so with an *inconnu* of Rouen; it was so with an *inconnu* of London; and so it was with Hector B——, though this last case was the only one in which there was any question of marriage, or any recognition of the lover's family.

In this one case, however, everything happened —or at least began to happen—exactly as in bourgeois circles. Rachel wrote to M. B—— senior as "My dear and tender father," and signed herself "your very devoted daughter." Her letters to the son rain thickly, at least in the early days, and are— almost—the letters of a *jeune fille,* just affianced, and much fluttered by strange sensations of un- expected happiness. This is the first of them—

Rachel

" MY DEAR FRIEND,

" You asked me to write to you as soon as I arrived. Believe me, I made haste to do so, but my heart beats so violently at the recollection of the too short moments which I spent with you that my trembling hand cannot hold the pen. My heart is aching. I cannot live without you, and you are not here.

" All that I love is far away from me. I cannot describe to you to-day, dear friend, the joys and struggles of my poor heart. It is speaking so fast at this moment that my pen cannot follow it. I am crushed and overcome. I cannot bear the immense happiness which I have felt since you understood my weak and impressionable nature. No, the joy is too much for me. I laugh. I cry. I feel as if I were going mad. My God! My God! What will become of me ? I never knew what love was before.

" Since parting from you I have felt myself alone in the world. It seemed to me that I had lost you for ever. Torrents of tears flowed from my eyes. You were no longer with me, and yet—the strange effect of a delirious imagination—I fancied that I still saw you, and still held you pressed against my heart. I found my lips uttering tender words, and my heart beating as if I were still in your arms.

" I cannot go on. A terrible pain grips me in the breast. The excess of happiness which I owe to you makes me ill. Good-bye. Write to me every day, and tell me a hundred times that you love me. I need so much courage while I am away from you.

N   177

Rachel

"I thought I should be able to rest this evening, but the hope was vain. To-morrow at Bayonne I have another rehearsal. It is not till Thursday that I shall have a day and an evening to myself.

"Can I not consecrate all that time to you?

"On Sunday I shall be obliged to return to Mont-de-Marsan. This last little town promises well for the artist.

"You were quite poorly when I left you. Take care of yourself, dearest. Remember that you no longer belong to yourself. I, with more generosity, declare myself yours without restriction. Speak, give me your orders, I belong to you."

All this in a breathless, blundering, ungrammatical style, not to be reproduced in a translation, yet affording ample proof that Rachel employed no secretary in this correspondence, but wrote her letters with her own artless hand; the letters succeeding each other, as love-letters do in the early stages of romance, with only the interval of a day or two between them. It will be sufficient to quote scraps. For instance—

"I feel so strongly what I write so badly, but, then, one always appears brilliant to him to whom one says: 'I love you.'

"Ah, well! I repeat it a hundred times, and yet another hundred times, so that you can't fail to think me the most brilliant woman in France, or in Navarre.

"All my thoughts and all my being belong to

178

you. Never has God put more love in my heart than I now feel for you."

" I love you. Believe in me. Believe in your Rachel—in your wife, as I must not fail to be. Who will ever love you as I do? Who will ever prove it to you better? The future is all smiles for me. It delights me so much that I say to myself : It is only in this last week that I have known what it is to live."

" Yesterday evening, after L—— and his wife had left me alone in my room, I felt so clearly that you were with me, and that I was your wife, that I caught myself wishing good-night to your father. He was leaving us, and I was calling him my father too. I don't know how it was, but I was so overcome that I fell backwards, dazed and unconscious —of everything except the happiness which awaits us in the future."

" I will make you so happy when your Rachel joins you, never to leave you again. Once more I tell you, so emphatically that there shall be no need for me ever to tell you again, that my life is yours, and that my one and only thought to-day is of returning to your dear family, which I already love as if it were my own, and which, I am sure, will love me for the love which I shall give their darling child. . . . I want to be your companion, your wife."

" I want my love to rely on me as I rely on

him, and to know that I rely on him for the whole
of my life. . . .

"Observe, dear. Already I regard myself as so
completely yours that I talk business to you, just as
if we already had to think of the future of a dear
little Rachel, and a pretty and loving little Hector."

"Sir, when the time comes for me to belong to
you, and for me to make you as happy as I can, you
will feel very flattered to find yourself the possessor
of such a marvel as I am. It is not my fault if
my modesty is defective this morning. Everything
that I see, and everything that is said to me, makes
me conceited. Time enough to get back to the calm
pleasures of real life when I live under the same roof
as my country lover."

Such were the emotions of the first stage; and
Hector B—— —poor Hector *de la bonne année*—
doubtless believed that all the fairy tales were
coming true and would prove to be eternal verities.
It had not occurred to him that a great actress may
be a superwoman, not only in respect of genius, but
also in respect of mutability. So true is it that one
half of life is hidden from those who always live in
the country.

He knew, of course, that Rachel was already the
mother of two children—for she never made any
mystery about that; but perhaps he imagined that
they had been brought to her by the storks, or by
the doctor, or had been found among the cabbages
at the bottom of the garden. His whole conduct
impresses one as that of a man who would have been

likely to entertain that simple faith. He was to be awakened from his dreams, however, before very long—he was to begin to be awakened from them at the end of a few weeks when the passionate letters were succeeded by a letter which was not so passionate—

" To-morrow my vacation comes to an end. As soon as the performance is over I shall be off to Paris; but I do not wish to return before entreating you, my dear B——, not to join me in the capital until I write and tell you the day on which I shall have leisure to receive you without fear of interruption."

The change of tone is like the change from day to night; and it would be idle to accuse Rachel of insincerity either before the change or after it. She had really seen herself, for a moment, in this rôle of *jeune fille*, courted *pour le bon motif*; and she had played it charmingly; but she could not go on playing it for ever. Her view of Hector was coloured by the point of view from which she looked at him. Seen from Paris, through the smoke of supper-parties, Hector appeared bucolic. No doubt he was bucolic compared with Arsène Houssaye, and the Prince President, and Plon-Plon. His arrival would have been as irrelevant as that of a skeleton at the feast of promiscuous kisses. Hence the letter quoted.

Only Rachel was not hard-hearted, or intentionally cruel. Indeed it would even be an exaggeration to say that she was tired of Hector. The truth is rather that two sides of her character struggled for the mastery : on the one hand the longing for the wings of a dove that she might fly away and be at rest; on the other hand ambition, the *joie de vivre*, and the greed for gold. There was so much to be done, and so little time in which to do it. Whenever she exerted herself she felt tired and ill. As often as she recovered she found herself restless, impetuous, impatient. Hector seemed to be offering her an escape from life. At certain moments she thought she wanted it; but then the mood changed, and the feeling was that she would want it some day, but did not want it yet. To marry and settle down remained the goal—but a goal which constantly receded. Before reaching it she wanted more triumphs, more money—more embraces. So Hector was not dropped, but was put off.

" DEAR HECTOR,

" At last I am back with my family and my children, and getting a little rest. I should be perfectly happy if I could add that my dear friend was near me, but he isn't, and unhappily he can't be just yet. My reasons for not writing to you before are quickly told. Listen. On the 15th of next November I shall be free of my engagement with the Comédie Française, for it is settled (in spite of the magnificent offers made to me if I would reconsider my decision) that I am not to reappear on the stage in the Rue Richelieu until after a two years' vacation, during which I shall be able to secure the fortunes of those whom I love—that is to say you and yours."

Rachel

One is far removed there from the passionate effusiveness of the first six weeks. Hector now, it is clear, is only one among many objects of Rachel's interests and affections; but the engagement nevertheless continues. Rachel sends her " most tender respects " to Hector's " noble father," and expresses a desire for his " blessing." She promises to visit him, saying : " My mother, who is my best friend, will come with me "; and there remain a good many other letters, whether they are rightly to be called love-letters or not, to be reviewed.

CHAPTER XIX

The German tour—Quarrel with Hector B——.

RACHEL, as we have seen, having pulled wires and nominated the Director of her choice, made her peace with the Comédie Française. Consequently, instead of retiring for two years, as she had threatened to do, she contented herself with four months' leave of absence, which she did not take immediately, consenting, in the meanwhile, to appear in Dumas' *Mademoiselle de Belle-Isle* and Victor Hugo's *Angelo*. The former piece was a failure, for which the author held her to blame. The latter was only a *succès d'estime*, the author's royalties for fourteen performances amounting to no more than £144. After that came the famous and successful tour in Germany; and, in the meantime, the correspondence with Hector B—— ran its course, diminishing in ardour as it proceeded.

The first letter which catches the eye is one in which Rachel apologizes for having let ten days pass without writing, and pleads that she is too busy to give full particulars of the way in which she is spending her time. She will tell Hector all about that when she sees him. In the meantime she thanks Hector's father for having thought her worthy to " throw flowers on the grave of his children," and bids Hector himself " rely on me as I know that I can rely on you." The next letters are filled with

Rachel

dramatic gossip, accompanied by melancholy intimations of weakening health :—

" Yesterday I played *Mademoiselle de Belle-Isle.* My intelligence was up to the mark, but my physical force failed me. I must not be frightened. I ought to have rested a few days longer; but my great desire to reconquer my public caused me to presume on my strength. . . . Prince Louis was present on this solemn occasion, and I saw him applaud me over and over again."

Whether Prince Louis had yet acquired that habit, attributed to him by Arsène Houssaye, of kissing Rachel does not appear. If so, it was not a matter to be mentioned to Hector; so Rachel continues—

" To-day I feel quite exhausted, but I did not like to let the day pass without writing to you. My health causes me some anxiety. I cough a great deal, and I am getting thin, so you may imagine how bad I feel. If I am not better when the spring returns it will really be the end of everything for me. But life is so good, and God has made things so pleasant for me, that I do hope I shall soon be as well as ordinary people. . . . I expect I shall have four very profitable months in Germany, where I have never been, though they have long wanted to see me there. You, see, I am becoming quite a woman of business."

And then, evidently in reply to a letter exhorting her to take care of herself—

Rachel

" Yes, my health is in a very shaky state, and if I want my career to be worthy of me, to last, that is to say, a few years longer, I really must be very quiet and careful. Your good advice, my dear Hector, will complete my cure, though I think you push your melancholy predictions rather far. I forgive you, however, in view of your almost paternal interest in me."

She adds that she is now better than she has been—

" Since my last journey the pains in my chest have ceased. I think this improvement must be due to the warm weather which is now beginning. The winter is deadly to me, and the return of spring delights me, and enables me to thank God for all the joys of life and all the good fortune which makes life agreeable. I am going to create a new part. We are rehearsing every day."

The new part was that of Tisbé in Victor Hugo's play. Rachel, with professional exaggeration, speaks of her appearance in it as " a veritable triumph," adding that prose seems to lose its vulgarity when uttered by her lips. She is, she says, " the happiest of women in a world in which tears are more frequent than joys "—the happier because her sister Rebecca has appeared with her, in a part formerly taken by Marie Dorval, and acquitted herself " charmingly."

Then she went off, in a blaze of glory, to Vienna, and Berlin, and Potsdam.

Rachel

There is no question of the reality of her triumphs.
The record of it is in many letters, not only in those
to the *fiancé*. For instance—

" My successes in Austria surpass any that I have
achieved since I have been on the stage. The woman
and the tragédienne dispute the honours. When
I am not playing I am invited out and made much
of. The greatest personages and the noblest ladies
in the land take me for drives and make a fuss about
me. The day before yesterday I dined at one of
the Emperor's palaces. His Imperial Majesty's
carriages took us for a drive in the park, and Raphael
has received permission to fish in the Emperor's
private lake. . . . To-morrow the Grand Chamberlain
is going to show us the crown jewels.

" Apropos of crowns I believe the excellent Vien-
nese are having an elegant crown made for me, only
they tell me that it cannot be finished until after
my departure."

This from Vienna to Rebecca. For the chronicle
of the triumph in Prussia we must turn to a letter
to another correspondent. Rachel tells him of a
performance given at Potsdam at which only " the
august members of the royal family and their retinue "
were present. "Little Rachel " was treated " as
if she had really been the king's guest." The Crown
Prince and Prince Frederick of the Netherlands
showed her over the palace of Sans-Souci. The
Empress of Russia, who was on a visit to the Prussian
Court, referred to the Court etiquette, which forbade
applause, but added : " To applaud you, however,

mademoiselle, would have been impossible, for my emotion was too intense." The Tsar himself told Rachel that she was " even greater than her reputation," and begged that she would honour his country by visiting it. The letter proceeds—

" One needs a strong head to resist such ovations. All the flattering things that have been said to me, all the incense I have inhaled, all the compliments and bouquets I have received, and all the quaint names of the heads of royal houses who have clamoured to be presented to me—there has been enough of all this to fill the life of an ambitious artist. Talma and Mars, my illustrious predecessors, never enjoyed such ovations, and, in truth, I am very happy about it; only it ought to make me nice to people rather than proud, for, if I owe something to my own merits, circumstances have also favoured me. But, stay, I was forgetting the finest triumph of all; and that is the best proof that my head is not too swollen. Fancy that the Tsar, coming to speak to me, and observing that my exertions had tired me, stood while speaking, and compelled me to remain seated. Respect for his grandeur made me spring out of my chair, but the Emperor gallantly made me sit down again, taking hold of my two hands, and saying : ' Remain in your place, mademoiselle, I beg you, unless you desire me to withdraw. Sovereignties such as mine pass. The kingdom of art abides for ever.' "

" Fancy that ! "—those are the words which one seems to hear Rachel uttering. She, the daughter,

Rachel

as she exultantly exclaimed, of "father and mother Félix," the daughter of the pedlar and the old clothes-woman, acclaimed, in court circles, As a more sublime sovereign than the Tsar of all the Russias! Decidedly she had done well for herself on the other side of the Rubicon. She had not been educated to know that it is precisely by such exaggerated politeness that royalty sometimes marks its sense of its own immeasurable superiority to persons born outside the magic ring; and there was, at any rate, no room for doubt as to the value of the gifts which royalty bestowed. The Tsar's gift consisted of two magnificent opals set in brilliants. The King of Prussia gave twenty thousand francs. Rachel was indeed in a fair way to "secure the future" of those who depended on her.

And Hector?

Hector, it would seem, was still Hector *de la bonne année*, still supported by that faith which is the substance of things hoped for and the evidence of things not seen, still fondly hugging the belief that the fairy tales would come true, if not immediately, at least after the delay which caprices, disguised as necessities, imposed. Only that delay promised to be long. Rachel could not bring herself to assign a limit to it; and Hector could not help observing that her letters were both less frequent and less affectionate than of old.

It was a relief to him, no doubt, to learn that Rachel had temporarily ceased to be troubled by tightness of the chest. He may have been pleased to read that the Comte de Chambord had paid her compliments, and that the Grand Duchess Helène

Rachel

had given her a pair of earrings.   But what was he
to make of this ?

" I shall not draw you a picture of the capital of
Germany.   I have not yet left my apartment except
to go to the theatre or to dine in town.   You know
how lazy I am.   I am a veritable bear.   When once
I have settled down it is very difficult to get me out
of my retreat.   I shall not quit it, my friend, until
the day when I take my great and solemn resolution
to get married; and then I shall be the most melancholy, reserved and domesticated little creature
that I know.
" If you can write to me now and then and let
me know what you have to say about the long journey
which lies in front of me before my vacation will
be over, I shall be very glad to read what you write,
and will answer your letter as soon as possible.
Perhaps I shall be able to send you from here the
portrait which you asked for."

There was little indeed to be made of that except
that *tout passe, tout casse, tout lasse*—that the flame
of Rachel's passion, once so fierce, was now but a
poor flicker—that, in her real life, as in her stage
life, she must create a new part from time to time,
and that, in short—

> Souvent femme varie :
> Bien fol qui s'y fie.

Hector, it would appear, drew the moral reluct-
antly; but he had to draw it.   Exactly what passed
one does not know, but the following letter furnishes
certain indications :—

Rachel

" MY DEAR HECTOR,

" I hardly understand what N—— has just told me, but he says that you are furiously angry with me, and I want to see you in order to have an explanation with you about a certain ball at which you seem to think that I behaved in a manner in which I should not have behaved in view of your affectionate regard for me. I don't know what all this means, but I can assure you that balls are a matter of indifference to me. It is nearly three years since I last went to one; and, what is more, if I had been well enough to go last Thursday, and if I had been silly enough to seek my pleasure in such a place, it would not have been for the purpose of annoying you. You are the most loyal man whom I know, and I am sufficiently fond of you to be sorry that you should misunderstand me.

" Come and see me to-morrow morning. You ought to have been to see me two days ago.

" Alas ! my poor B——. Already you are becoming a Parisian. Already you are in a fair way to lose those illusions of the heart which are the best part of life."

And no doubt Hector was in a fair way to lose any illusions which he had not already lost; and no doubt the time was fast approaching when he would be no longer Hector *de la bonne année*, but a Hector who had passed through the fire and emerged from it, with his wings singed, but with his lesson learnt. The spectacle of Rachel rebuking him for having lost his faith in what she admits to have been illusion adds a moving touch of irony to the narrative.

Rachel

What happened next—whether Hector fought for the retention of his vanishing illusions or let them go without a struggle—is obscure; but there is another brief note which demonstrates that he did not retain them long.

" MY DEAR HECTOR,
    " I am sure I am quite as anxious to see you as you are to see me.
    " Come and call, then.   I shall be at home until two o'clock."

That is all.   We read between the lines that there has been a lovers' quarrel, which will not easily be made up for lack of any sincere desire to make it up. Evidently it was not made up; for this stiff note is the last of the series.   The dead *bourgeoise* which had come to life in Rachel's bosom had died its second death.   She had made her brief excursion into sincerity—a sort of vacation tour—and had returned from it.   The nervous life of Paris once more had her in its grip.   Poor Hector was altogether too provincial to be her partner.   He must suffer, and get over his suffering as best he could; the queens of the theatre being entitled to their victims.   Rachel wanted quite other admirers—a prince who, like Walewski, would do things in style for her, and an *amant de cœur*, who was not too naive, but understood theatrical love-making and its limitations. And that, of course, brings us back to Plon-Plon (of whom there is little to be said except that he made love to nearly all the actresses of his period in quick succession, being taken away by Rachel from Judith), and also brings us on to Ponsard.

CHAPTER XX

PONSARD, like Hector, had grown up in the provinces; but, unlike Hector, he had not stayed there. From Vienne in Dauphiné he had found his way to Paris and become a dramatic author; and it was in that capacity that he had first been blown about by the gusts of Rachel's caprices.

He had arranged for the production of his *Charlotte Corday* at the Odéon. Rachel heard of it. She either knew, or inquired, who Charlotte Corday was; and she demanded that the play should be at once withdrawn from the Odéon and submitted for her inspection, as she fancied that she "saw herself" in the title rôle. This after the manager of the Odéon had already distributed the parts among the members of his company!

The thing could only be done by permission of the Minister of the Interior; but obstacles of that sort were trifles to Rachel. Arsène Houssaye was "her man," willing humbly to do her bidding. He accepted her commission to wait upon the Minister of the Interior and inform him of her desire. The Minister of the Interior knew—what everybody in Paris knew—that Rachel had influence in even higher places than his office; so he not only submitted to her will, but arranged a dinner-party at the conclusion of which Ponsard was to read his play.

Rachel

Ponsard read it, as he supposed, amid enthusiastic approbation; but, before he had finished reading, Rachel had whispered to Arsène Houssaye that nothing on earth would induce her to appear in " that idiotic part." She not only said this but meant it, and the part was therefore given to Judith, who made a great success in it. That was not what Rachel had intended; so, after the third performance, she called upon Ponsard and demanded that the part which she had refused with scorn should now be taken away from her rival and given to her. That, however, was more than Ponsard could promise. He undertook, instead, to write a new piece expressly for Rachel. He duly wrote it ; she duly appeared in it; and then he underwent the charm.

But not, we may be sure, in the same way, or to the same degree as Hector *de la bonne année*; for a dramatic author's attitude towards actresses, however much they may charm him, can never be quite that of a young man from the country. Experience has taught him things which a young man from the country does not know. He does not credit the interpreter with all the virtues of the part which he has created for her to interpret, preferring to reserve some of the glory for himself. He knows that he must not ask an actress for more than she has to give. He even knows, as a rule, that it is over-sanguine to ask her for all that she has to give; for he is aware that there are likely to be other applications for her favours—*dona ferentes*—applicants whose applications she cannot afford to overlook if she desires to be more richly bejewelled than her rivals.

Rachel

So with Ponsard. He was a delightful stage lover
—one who well understood the limitations of the art.
He accepted the gifts of Heaven without allowing
jealousy to trouble him because he was not the sole
recipient of them. He was not blind, but there
were certain things which he refused to see, because
he knew that they would spoil the picture. It
was Rachel's whim that he should meet her from
time to time on her travels, and he fell in with it.
The letters which he wrote her from his country
retreat at Vienne are full of charm. Though the
story in them amounts to nothing, one cannot
refrain from giving extracts :—

" Dearest, here I am back again in my solitude.
They serenaded me delightfully. My friends have
shaken my hand, and my dogs have eaten me. I
have nothing left, except a heart to love you and
a hand to write to you.
" The first two days were delightful, but I wanted
you there to complete the charm. On the third
day I felt very lonely, and now I should be bored to
death if it were not for my memories. You have
stripped my poor trees and my dear old hills of their
enchantment. They are insipid companions now
that my dreams are of my dear comrade."

" Good and dearly loved Rachel, your letter
was charming and brought joy to my heart. I was
looking out of the window, like Sister Anne, and could
see nothing coming; but at last the postman came
with a ray of sunshine for me in his pocket—a
true ray of sunshine in the midst of unceasing rains.

Rachel

I am bored. I am bored to death. It rains on the fields and in my heart. The recollection of our happy time makes me so sad. . . .

". . .Yes, I believe in your affection, but I am not angry when people talk to me about it. When one loves, one also fears. It is quite natural that I should love you because you are infinitely lovable; but it is not at all natural to be loved by one of the good God's most charming creatures when one is cross and stupid as I too often am."

"Dear loved one, whom I love so tenderly, I received at Paris the kiss which you sent to Vienne, the mail having brought them to me here. I keep them in my heart and on my lips in imagination, alas! as a treasure; but I shall soon come and return them to you. I love you. It is not I who shall cease to love you, but you, madam, who will perceive, some day that your friend is not lovable at all, though very loving; and when that day comes there will be nothing left for me but to bury myself far away in a lonely place."

"Ah! the charming, the delightful, the ravishing pilgrimage which we are to make to Spa, to Aix, to Vienne. My mouth waters at the thought of it, and I dream of it day and night. 'See Naples and die,' says the proverb. I would gladly spend my whole life in this journey and then die when it was over. In the meantime I am dying—I am dead—and I await a kiss to bring me to life again."

Those, one feels sure, were the best love-letters that Rachel ever received—the best and the most appropriate. They are sentimental without being silly; they say a little more than the writer means—and yet not much more. Perhaps we may put it that they say what he would have been glad to mean if he had not known better. Ponsard could not have been reproached, like Hector, for having lost the "illusions of the heart." He knew very well that they were illusions, but he clung to them and enjoyed them, much in the spirit in which one enjoys the illusions of the theatre. The awakening from them, having been discounted, would be comparatively easy, but their charm, while they lasted, was great. We need not speculate whether those are happiest who take life in that temper. They run, at any rate, the least risk of making shipwreck of their lives.

Ponsard, at least, made no shipwreck of his life. He enjoyed what he could attain, without sighing for the unattainable—or, at all events, without screaming for it. It could not be helped—so one imagines him reflecting—that Rachel's affectionate regard for him ran concurrently with her tenderness for the Emperor's cousin. The relations of the stage to society were such that coincidences of the kind were not easily to be avoided; and the smiles of actresses were like the rain which falls equally on the just and on the unjust. So why make a fuss about it ? Why not enjoy while one could ? Even if love was only a game to Rachel, it was very pleasant to be privileged to play with her. So Ponsard wrote :—

" If you are free for ten days or a fortnight

towards the end of July, and if you would still like to see me, I might come and fetch you, and we could spend four days at Aix, which is quite near Vienne, and then you could come home with me. I should very much prefer, though, to take you to the Swiss valleys and the torrents of Mont Blanc. That, too, is only a matter of four days; and four days well spent are a treasure of keen emotion for the present and a charming recollection for the times to come.

"Farewell, dear Rachel! I love you more than you think, and I am longing to see you."

But the game was coming to an end, though without any audible lamentations. Rachel had made up her mind to accept the Tsar's invitation to play at Saint Petersburg. It was not Ponsard but Plon-Plon who showed sighs of agitation at her departure. Plon-Plon is said even to have pulled the wires of diplomacy in the hope of preventing it; but when it came to pulling wires Rachel was a match for the ablest.

The Crimean war was imminent—its premonitory rumblings were already in the air. It was easy to represent that Rachel was proposing to make sport for the enemies of France; and she was, in fact, accused, alike by journalists and by caricaturists, of unpatriotic greed. But the charges did not trouble her. There had been indications that the enthusiasm of the Parisian public for her was flagging. Jules Janin had accused her of playing Phèdre "as if she had had too much to drink." She might hope to reconquer France in

Rachel

Saint Petersburg, just as England had conquered France in Canada and the Indies. Moreover glory was more to her than patriotism—and so was money. So Plon-Plon pulled the wires in vain. Early in 1854 Rachel was off, in spite of him, for the Russian Eldorado.

Her first letter (to her mother) is from Warsaw. She rejoices in the weather—there has been no drop of rain to compel her to close the carriage window. She rejoices in the Polish *cuisine*—it reminds her of her mother's cooking. She complains of the prodigious charges of the Polish hotels—four francs for a cutlet, three francs for a plate of soup, fourteen francs for a bottle of table wine. She philosophizes concerning the sorrowful fate of the Poles—

"I have heard so much of this poor Poland—of its greatness and its fall. And then I am half Polish at heart on account of my little Alexandre.[1] So I have looked with both eyes at all that was to be seen from the windows of the railway carriage and the hotel; and I have listened, with both my ears, to all that I have heard; and with all my heart I pity this great people deprived of its chief good thing, its liberty."

Strange reflections, perhaps, for one about to make sport for the conquerors of Poland ; but Rachel's reflections on impersonal subjects are not, of course, to be taken seriously. She may have thought that it would gratify Polish patriots to see her plunder their oppressors, even though she

[1] Her son by Walewski.

kept the plunder for herself. It does not matter. At all events she did plunder them, and they let themselves be plundered gladly.

On the night of her first appearance in *Phèdre* the house held £480. The receipts of ten successive performances amounted to £3,920. Within a fortnight of her arrival she had sent home £3,200 to her father, with instructions to invest it in house property. At the end of five weeks her gains amounted to £8,000. Altogether she amassed about £12,000, and she wrote with scorn of the Comédie Française as " la grande boutique dégénérée."

The presents, too, were on the same scale of magnificence. The Tsar himself gave a ring of emeralds and brilliants, a pair of earrings of rubies, emeralds and brilliants, and a brooch with an opal pendant, surrounded by forty-five brilliants. From the Tsarina came a set of the most costly furs in the world. Other admirers bestowed every imaginable article of silver plate, from salad bowls to salt cellars. And then the Tsarina supplemented her original gifts with a casket of malachite and gilded bronze, and a she-ass, so that Rachel might sustain her health with asses' milk.

Ponsard, though, as has been said, the game which she played with him was practically over, was still in her confidence. She boasted to him of the benefactions showered upon her, and he applauded her determination thus to accumulate wealth. It was right, he said, that she should be rich. It was right that she should leave a great fortune to her children, so that she might never be brought to begging her bread miserably like poor George.

Rachel

And he made her a present of a precedent for her conduct :—

" My friend Voltaire, who was common sense incarnate, often used to say : ' I came early in life to the conclusion that a man of letters without money would have no real consideration paid to him. So I began by making my fortune, and, after I had made it, I wrote as I chose, and was able to impose my ideas on the world. My riches have given authority to my writings.'

" That is what Voltaire did. That is what I should have done if I had been able to. That is what Rachel is able to do, and Rachel is quite right to do it."

Ponsard was also informed that a swarm of admirers had arisen, as usual, and that several of them had offered marriage. Madame Félix was told of the crowds which followed her daughter through the streets, and—crowning glory—of the banquet given in her honour at the Imperial Palace : " Fancy that ! Me ! The daughter of father and mother Félix ! " And then the letter speaks of the plush and powder of the lackeys who took Rachel's cloak from her, and bawled out her name ; and it continues :—

" There were only thirty guests ! But what guests they were ! The imperial family, the grand dukes, the archdukes, the little dukes ! And all this medley of princes and princesses, inquisitive and attentive, devouring me with their eyes, watching my least movement, listening to my least word, observ-

ing my smiles, never taking their eyes off me. But
don't imagine that I felt embarrassed. Not the least
bit in the world. I behaved just as usual, at all events
until the middle of the banquet—every one seeming
to be much more interested in me than in the menu.
Presently they proceeded to drink my health, and
then there was a most extraordinary spectacle.
In order to get a nearer view of me the young
archdukes left their places, climbed on to their
chairs, and even put their feet on the table, and
almost in the dishes, without seeming to shock any
one, for even the princes in this country are still
rather like savages. Then they shouted their bravos
loud enough to deafen me, and called upon me to
respond. To respond to a toast by reciting a fragment of a tragedy was rather a strange idea, but I
was not to be disconcerted by such a trifle as that.
I rose and, pushing back my chair, assumed the
most tragic gesture in my repertory, and gave them
the great scene in *Phèdre*. Then there was a silence
like death—you could have heard a pin drop.
All my auditors listened religiously, leaning forward,
gaping at me, contenting themselves with stifled
cries and gestures of admiration. Then, when I
had finished, there were fresh cheers and fresh
toasts and clinking of glasses which, for an instant,
quite bewildered me. Presently I too got excited
by the wine and the flowers and the enthusiasm,
which was very pleasing to my pride, and I rose
again and chanted the Russian national anthem.
Then enthusiasm was no longer the word—it was
a case of delirium. They thronged round me, and
shook my hands, and thanked me. I was the

Rachel

greatest tragédienne in the world—the greatest
tragédienne of the present, the past and the
future—and so on for a whole quarter of an hour.

" But there comes an end even to the best of
things, and the hour for retiring had struck. I
withdrew with the same queenly dignity with which
I had arrived, escorted to the grand staircase by
the same grand duke, who was very gallant though
very ceremonious. Then there arrived gigantic
powdered valets, one of them carrying my cloak.
I put it on, and they escorted me to my carriage,
which was surrounded by other footmen, holding
torches to illuminate my departure."

So she rattled on, breathlessly and ungrammatic-
ally as usual, confusing archdukes and grand-dukes
with artless ignorance, and obviously intoxicated
with delight. Of all her triumphs this was unquestionably the most spectacular. One can imagine
her reflecting, if she had been capable of such
reflections, that art has no nationality and that
posterity begins at the frontier; for the men who
thus worshipped her as a goddess were the men
who were presently to be the enemies of her country,
and they knew it, and made no secret of their knowledge. They boasted to her that they expected
presently to be drinking the French champagne in
France. She had wit enough to reply that she
hardly thought the French Government was likely
to supply champagne to prisoners of war; but she
had not wit enough to perceive that the speech
was an affront which effectually cancelled all the
remarkable homage paid to her.

Rachel

France, at any rate, did not consider that her repartee redeemed her unpatriotic conduct in making sport for the enemies of France. Nor was France favourably impressed by her description of her profits as " spoils of war taken from the enemy." That sentiment had too Hebrew a ring to gain the applause of the French. It was counterbalanced by stories to the effect that Rachel was the last Frenchwoman to leave Russia before the war, and that she had been inclined to smile on the proposal that the Tsar should detain her as a hostage.

So that, at the very acme of her glory, Rachel's position was beginning to be undermined. She went back to a Paris which, if not yet hostile, was, at least, disposed to be hostile; and she awakened from her dream of fame and diamonds to find certain grave realities awaiting her—illness in her family, dramatic authors in a quarrelsome mood, and a young and formidable rival aspiring to supplant her.

CHAPTER XXI

Return to Paris—Death of Rachel's sister Rebecca—Relations with
Legouvé—*Adrienne Lecouvreur.*

REFERENCE has already been made, more than
once, to Rachel's undeviating loyalty to her Tribe;
and there can be no question that it was a loyalty
based upon affection. In her relations with her
family we always find her confidential and sincere,
dropping the artifices of the actress, and revealing
a woman who was really womanly. She was never
capricious with them, as with her lovers, her
colleagues, the dramatists and Samson.

No doubt there are one or two strange stories
afloat on this branch of the subject. It is related,
for instance, that, at times of embarrassment due to
extravagance, Rachel borrowed from her mother, and
that Madame Félix did not think it safe to lend to
her without requiring some valuable article of
jewellery to be deposited with her as a pledge; but
what of that? Old clothes-women, whether of the
Hebrew or any other race, are apt to acquire such
cautious habits; and the money which Rachel borrowed on these terms was, after all, money which she
herself had earned and given.

And she gave freely, quite falling in with
the view which her father, the ex-pedlar, had
expressed to Samson, that, as his daughter had talent,
he ought to make something out of her. There was

Rachel

no member of her family, indeed, who did not make something out of her. It was she who paid for the education which enabled her younger sisters to earn a living for themselves, and then pushed them into positions which their attainments hardly qualified them to occupy. Year after year she paid the debts of her elder sister, Sarah of the Supper-parties; and the necessity of doing so never estranged her from Sarah, who remained her confidential correspondent until the last; and we have seen her anticipating Arthur Bertrand's demands for help by the plea that her brother Raphael had " cleaned her out." But the one really deep and enduring affection of her life was for Rebecca. She had insisted, holding out the threat of her own resignation if she did not get her way, that Rebecca should be admitted to the Comédie Française; and we may borrow a story, illustrative of her playful fondness for her sister, from Madame Faucigny-Lucinge's *Rachel et son Temps—*

" One evening, when the two sisters had been playing in Victor Hugo's *Angelo*, and Rebecca had been received with enthusiasm in the part of Catarina Bragadini, Rachel said to her—

" ' My dear child, you played like an angel. I want to reward you. Take me to supper at your flat.'

" ' At my flat ! ' exclaimed the young actress, still in a flutter at her triumph and her ovations. ' You mean to say at home ! '

" ' Not at all ! At your flat ! Here is the key,' rejoined Rachel.

Rachel

"And Tisbe handed Catarina a key, which was not the key entrusted to her by Angelo in the play; and they started off—Rebecca immensely puzzled. Rachel's coupé set them down at the door of a pretty house in the Rue Mogador, a few yards from the tragédienne's magnificent mansion in the Rue Trudon, where she had surrounded herself with all the splendours and refinements of luxury. Rebecca thought she must be dreaming, or that this was some fantastic comedy in which she was being made to play a part. They went up the stairs to the second floor.

" ' Here we are,' said Rachel. ' Open the door ! '

" Rebecca was about to do so; but the door was already opening in answer to the bell, and there appeared a housekeeper of benevolent aspect, with a candle in her hand.

" ' What ! It is Marguerite ! ' exclaimed the young actress, astounded to meet an old friend of her childhood.

" ' Yes, come in,' said Rachel."

The flat, fully furnished, was her gift to her favourite sister, and she had sprung it on her as a happy theatrical surprise. Her life contains many scenes more splendid, but none more pleasing. Sincerity and theatricality meet in it. And now, at the hour of Rachel's acclamation by the grandest of the grand dukes of Russia, she heard bad news about Rebecca.

" Je vous laisse Rebecca," had been Rachel's last words to her comrades of the theatre when they reproached her for leaving them for so long. " C'est

Rachel

le trait des Parthes," had been their answer. It indicated, of course, a very poor opinion of Rebecca's acting; but that did not matter to Rachel. She had placed Rebecca at the Théâtre Français in the interest of the Tribe of Félix, not in the interest of dramatic art. But Rebecca had had typhus fever, and, in the course of her convalescence, the symptoms of consumption had declared themselves; and we find Rachel writing from Warsaw to Sarah—

"My mother writes to me that her health is quite re-established. You know how glad I am. But it seems that it is by no means the same with poor Rebec. and that is a terrible trouble to me. I shall certainly go and spend a week with her at Pau after the 13th of May, for I am sure my dear little sister will be glad to see me. I have told my mother that I am astounded that she should have been allowed to go alone with her maid. What is a family for it if does not show its devotion at such a time as that ? "

So Rachel hurried off to the Pyrenees, and found Rebecca fighting for her life. " I want to live," she said. " One does not die at twenty when one is the sister of the great Rachel "; and the delusive malady gave, as it so often does, the false promise of yielding to climate and treatment. Rachel set out to return to Paris, deceived by the apparent improvement; but the news of a relapse followed only a stage or two behind her, and when it overtook her she hurried south again. When next she came north it was to bring her sister's body for burial in

Rachel

a Paris cemetery. The principal speech over the grave was made by Jules Janin; and it was characteristic of that fluent, inadequate man that his long discourse was not a cry of grief for the dead, but an elaborate eulogy of Rachel's genius and devotion. Samson, who followed him, spoke from the heart; but Rachel, whom some theatrical quarrel had estranged from him, offered him no word of thanks. Let us hope that theatrical quarrels are not often so bitter, or so infected with false pride.

Such was the first of the grievous realities to which Rachel returned. The second was the dispute, ending in a fierce trial of strength, with Ernest Legouvé, whom success had made sensitive and arrogant, and who felt himself in a position to boast that, if he had not made Rachel's reputation, at all events he could do a good deal towards unmaking it.

His first relations with her had been due to Scribe. She had asked Scribe for a play, and Scribe had been alarmed by the commission. He dared not, he said, enter into competition with Corneille and Racine; but Legouvé laughed at his timidity. " Have you the courage, yourself," asked Scribe, " to write prose for the interpreter of Phèdre and Camille ? " " Most certainly I have," Legouvé answered. " Very well. Find me a subject, and we will collaborate." " Agreed."

The subject which Legouvé found was *Adrienne Lecouvreur*; and Scribe bounded out of his chair in his delight. " Good," he exclaimed. " That will run a hundred nights to houses of six thousand francs." "You think so?" "I don't think so. I am sure of it. Your subject is a veritable treasure-trove. You have discovered the only means of making Rachel speak in prose. We'll set to work to-morrow." So the appointment was kept, and the piece was written; and the next thing that happened was that Rachel capriciously decided that she did not want it. Some one had whispered to her that the interpreter of Racine must not stoop to be the interpreter of Eugène Scribe. When the play was read, therefore, she listened with a face as expressionless as marble, and announced that she did not think the part would suit her.

In private she expressed herself even more vigorously. She did not like, she said, to say "no" to M. Legouvé, but nothing should induce her to play that——. "I hesitate," Legouvé writes, "to print the word she used, for it was very energetic and quite outside the classical repertory." Scribe, in the circumstances, proposed to accept an offer which had been made to stage the piece at another theatre; but Legouvé, unwilling to admit himself beaten, undertook to talk Rachel over. He persuaded her to hear the piece read again. On the previous occasion Scribe had read it, and he read badly. This time Legouvé read it, and he read brilliantly. Rachel listened, at first with impatience, but soon with keen and eager interest. "What a fool I was!" she cried at last; and she threw her arms round the reader's neck, and embraced him in her best theatrical style.

So *Adrienne Lecouvreur* was produced, and made

the great success which Scribe had predicted for it; with the result that the creator and the interpreter were, for a long time, the best friends in the world. It was at one of the rehearsals that there occurred a certain pathetic scene to which reference has already been made. This is Legouvé's account of it—

" ' My dear,' I said to her, ' you played that fifth act as you will never again play it in your life.'

" ' I believe I did,' she answered. ' Do you know why ? '

" ' Yes, I know. Because there was no one there to applaud you. You were not thinking of the effect, and so you became, in your own eyes, the poor Adrienne herself, dying at midnight in the arms of her friends.'

" She was silent for a moment. Then she replied—

" ' No, you are quite wrong. A very strange thing happened. It was not for Adrienne that I wept, but for myself. I suddenly had a strange premonition that I should die young like her. It seemed to me that I was in my own room, at my last hour, a spectator of my own death. And so when I came to that phrase, ' Farewell to my triumphs at the theatre ! Farewell to the intoxications of the art which I have loved so well ! ' the tears which you saw me shed were real tears. I was thinking that time would soon carry away every trace of my talent, and that nothing would remain of what had once been Rachel.' "

That is the typical story which gives us our most

Rachel

vivid glimpse of Rachel's melancholy, and the
reason for it. Life was so good—but so short; and
the warnings had been so clear that it would be
shorter for her than for others. The thought was
always recurring, however hard she tried to subdue
it with work and pleasure; and she had neither a
religion nor a philosophy which could help her to
face the prospect without fear. With what gestures
she did sit down to wait for death, when its immi-
nence was obvious, we shall see very soon—there is
no need to anticipate.

Another confidence of which Legouvé was the
recipient related to her moral conduct. She gave
him half-a-dozen reasons why she had submitted
to be the mistress of a man whom she " hated
and despised "—meaning, as one supposes, that
unpleasant voluptuary, Véron. She seemed to
think that Legouvé would be surprised to learn
that Véron's " influence " had weighed with her;
for she prefaced the confession with the statement
that the heart of an actress was a riddle which
the wisest of men could not read. More than once,
she said, she had been tempted to shoot Véron from
the stage while he was applauding her from his box,
and had even gone so far as to make her entrance
with a loaded pistol in her pocket—a pistol which,
if fired, would probably have been a source of
danger to any one rather than the person aimed at.
" What a scene it would have been ! " she exclaimed,
with the inevitable professional touch; and she went
on—

" What would you say if I revealed my inner

Rachel

thoughts to you ?   You admire me, I believe.   You
are in ecstasies when I play.   Well, I assure you,
there is a Rachel in me ten times superior to the
Rachel whom you know.   I have not been one
quarter as great as I might have been.   I have talent,
but I might have had genius.   Ah, if only I had
been brought up differently !   If I had had different
friends around me !   If I had lived a better life !
What an artist I should have been in that case !
When I think of it such a regret steals over me . . ."

  She ceased, burying her face in her hands, to hide
her tears.   " There," she said, when she looked up,
" you know me better now than the people who
think they know me best."   Legouvé was cynic
enough to wonder whether she had deceived herself
or was consciously playing a comedy.   He could not
decide, and her biographer need not pretend to be
able to decide on his behalf.   Three days later,
however, she struck the first hard blow in the
quarrel with him which was not to end until he had
set up a rival to supersede her.

CHAPTER XXII

THE *causa teterrima belli* was Legouvé's new play.
Rachel had asked him to write a piece specially
for her. " If you will," she had said, " I'll promise
to write you a letter of thanks without a single
mistake in spelling." He had accepted the promise
as the " valuable consideration " of an agreement,
and had set to work upon *Médée*. Euripides had
dealt with the theme before him, but he was convinced that he could improve upon Euripides.
Where Euripides had contented himself with relating,
he would present. Medea should not kill her children
behind the scenes, but on the stage. There should be
other horrors of the sort which Horace deprecates but
modern taste accepts; and these should furnish
Rachel with unique opportunities for the display
of her intensity.

It seemed all right. Until she was brought right
up against the details of her part Rachel was most
amiable about it. Legouvé went to see her in a
villa which she had taken at Auteuil, and found her
in the garden, picking flowers, and in a mood to
entertain him with confessions. She was ready for
hard work, she said, because she felt so well. Health
was the best thing in the world. She had done with
the follies of her youth. They were amusing, but

Rachel

they had to be paid for, and the price exacted was too high. The pleasure of feeling well and strong was much better than any of the pleasures of dissipation.

But when Legouvé began to read his piece Rachel's mood changed, and she showed herself, first critical, and then dissatisfied. This, that and the other scene would not do, and must be cut out. The author had to argue, now giving way, and now insisting. He was a plausible and persuasive dialectician; Rachel, in that respect, was no match for him. He believed that Rachel's success in *Médée* would secure his election to the Academy ; and he therefore reasoned with her, insidiously and energetically. Rachel could only adopt an attitude of passive resistance, affecting to yield, but determined to get her own way, and making her plans accordingly.

All her objections being met, she could not prevent the piece from being put in rehearsal. The first rehearsal took place on September 2, 1853. There were eight rehearsals in all. "I was full of hope," writes Legouvé, "and believed that I was at the end of my troubles." But, in fact, he was only at the beginning of them. The rehearsals were suddenly suspended ; and on September 17 Legouvé received the explanation in a letter from Rachel's secretary—

"Do not be alarmed at seeing my handwriting. All is well; but I have to explain the adjournment of the rehearsals. Mlle. Rachel has been indisposed, and her doctor ordered her to spend four days in bed. Since then she has had other engagements, but she

instructs me to say that she will write to you as
soon as she feels able to resume."

Rachel's promised letter quickly followed. It
made some suggestions as to the distribution of the
parts in *Médée*, and continued—

" My health is still very shaky. I have just spent
four days in bed. To-day I am going back to the
country. I need the fresh air badly. I shall be
back on Tuesday to play *Cinna*.
                    Your invalided Medea."

Rachel was always ill enough, at this date, to have
the right to say that she was ill if she chose. Legouvé,
whether he believed the statement or not, had no
choice but to accept the excuse and wait. Instead
of the resumption of the rehearsals there was a bolt
from the blue, in the shape of another letter from
Rachel's secretary, dated October 5 :—

" You will have learnt from the papers, sir, the
fabulous offer which the Emperor of Russia has
caused to be made to our Rachel. The Government
has concluded that it ought not to deprive the great
artist of the opportunity of making a fortune in six
months.
" Rachel will return on May 15. She will arrive
with *Médée* in her head, and the piece will be put on
immediately. I enclose a letter which she instructs
me to forward to you as proof of her good will."

The letter enclosed told the same story, embroidered with the expression of the hope that Legouvé

Rachel

would not bear malice, but would keep his play for Rachel. " You have often," she wrote, "spoken of your friendship for me. Here is your opportunity of proving it."

She was playing with him, however, and he knew it. At the very time when she had pleaded that she was ill and unable to rehearse she had been engaged in negotiations for her Russian tour; and now she wanted to make sure that no one else should reap in her absence the laurels which she declined. It is not surprising that he was angry.

" I went at once to see her," he relates, " and was told that she was out. That was what I had expected. I called again in the evening and was told that she was ill. That also I had expected. On the following evening, however, she was playing *Polyeucte*. When she returned to her dressing-room, after the fall of the curtain, she found me installed there, waiting for her."

At last they were face to face, arguing, altercating —the author peremptory and the actress haughty. Their voices rose in anger. An ultimatum was presented and rejected—

" Will you or will you not resume the rehearsals of *Médée* ? "

" I most certainly will not."

"Very well. Henceforth it is war between us."

But the war, though declared, was not yet waged. Legouvé ran to his lawyer, but the lawyer counselled

Rachel

patience. Rachel, he urged, had changed her mind so often that she might change it yet again. In any case no effective steps could be taken until after her return from Russia. Better wait and see what happened then.

Legouvé agreed to wait, but ultimately wrote a letter which Rachel received at Warsaw on her way home. This time she was polite but determined. She said (untruly) that she was meaning to leave the Théâtre Français, and wished to appear, before retiring, in the whole of her classical repertory. To do so would take up all the time at her disposal. She did not care to imperil " seventeen years of success " by rash experiments; and she must therefore resign her part in *Médée* to some other actress.

The answer to that was a writ which was served on Rachel on the morning after her return to Paris. It caused her to assume the tone of one who had been injured, but would be magnanimous. She insisted upon addressing her persecutor as " My dear M. Legouvé." A pretty idea, she protested, that she should play *Médée* " by order of the court ! " The piece might fail, and then every one would say that she had wrecked it to avenge herself. Still, if he insisted, he should have his way. She would study her part while nursing Rebecca in the Pyrenees, and be ready to play it on her return.

She seems to have meant what she said—partly, if not altogether. At all events she took the tone of one who proposes a bargain with Omnipotence, speaking as if the Almighty were a playgoer and her particular admirer. If God would spare her sister, then she would consent to appear in Legouvé's piece. But that was not good enough for Legouvé, who tried, before making further application to the courts, to bring other influence to bear. He wrote to Madame Crémieux—the same Madame Crémieux who had broken off relations with Rachel when she crossed the Rubicon. The letter has been published in *L'Amateur d'autographes*.

Rebecca's illness, Legouvé represented in this letter, was no excuse for Rachel's conduct. It was not an acute but a chronic illness—it might last for months. Would Madame Crémieux be kind enough to tell her so, and to urge her to return to the path of duty? He would be very reluctant to " draw the sword against a lady at once so sublime and so capricious;" but what was he to do? She had tantalized him for fifteen months with procrastinations and excuses. He had asked her to see him on the subject, and she had refused. Might he, therefore, rely upon the kind offices of a common friend?

Apparently he might not. Whether Madame Crémieux intervened in the matter is uncertain; but, if she did, she intervened in vain. Rebecca's death released Rachel from the obligations of her vow. Most likely she resented Legouvé's lack of sympathy with Rebecca's illness, for her devotion to Rebecca was unquestionably the deepest sentiment of her life. At all events, she made up her mind at last beyond the possibility of changing it, and bade her secretary communicate her definite decision.

She dared not write herself, she said. She was afraid Legouvé would come banging at her door and making a scene; and she did not feel well enough to listen to his reproaches. In a sense, she knew, she was in the wrong. There was no denying that she had accepted the part, and even rehearsed it. But she could not bring herself to play it. She was convinced that it would not suit her, and it was too much to ask her to risk a failure at the moment of her retirement from the stage. She could only hope that Legouvé would not be very cross. She could not bear that. Her poor nerves were in such a shocking state. . . .

Legouvé, however, was much too angry to be moved by references to Rachel's nerves or appeals to his own better feelings. He bade his lawyer proceed, and Rachel called upon her old friend Crémieux to defend her.

Already, in 1848, she had tried to renew her friendship with him and his wife. Crémieux had been Minister of Justice during a part of that eventful year, and she had called upon him several times in his office and had been affably received. Perhaps it was not the best means she could have chosen to conciliate Madame Crémieux; and Madame Crémieux certainly had not been conciliated. Rachel had appealed to her to " open her arms " as a " tender mother "; but Madame Crémieux had replied that she believed neither in Rachel's penitence nor in her desire to alter her mode of life, and did not desire her company until she had altered it. Whereto Rachel had rejoined that, if only she had known how shamefully she had been calumniated, she would never have " lowered herself " by writing to Madame Crémieux, but that she still clung to the hope that, somewhere in the world, it might be her privilege to encounter "indulgent hearts and elevated souls."

That letter closed the door with a bang, and it remained closed for six years; but now, in 1854, it was once again thrown open. "Yes, she can come and see me," Crémieux said to Madame Félix, who had appealed to him. "A visit from her will make me feel ten years younger"; and Madame Crémieux said the same, and fell upon Rachel's neck and kissed her; and they all supped together after the play, and Crémieux undertook the case.

It was a *cause célèbre*; and the arguments, as usually happens in a French *cause celèbre*, travelled far away from the point nominally at issue. The question whether Rachel had broken her contract with Legouvé was quickly entangled with the question whether Rachel cared more for art or for gold, and then with the further question whether it was right and reasonable that the interests of French dramatic literature should lie at the mercy of an actress's caprice. Even the personal appearance of the advocate appears to have been regarded as relevant to the rights of the dispute. "The legendary ugliness of M. Crémieux," writes Legouvé, "caused the judges to shake with laughter on the bench." Their verdict for the plaintiff, he seems to have thought, was largely ascribable to their amusement at the grimaces of the defendant's advocate.

Very possibly he was right, for almost anything is possible in a French *cause célèbre*. Be that as it may, at any rate they gave judgment in his favour. Rachel was ordered by the court either to play the part or to pay damages. After appeals and rehearings, into the details of which we need not trouble to enter, the damages were assessed at 12,000 francs. Rachel paid, and Legouvé divided the money among various literary and theatrical charities.

'Twas well, 'twas something; but it was not enough for him. What he wanted was to see Rachel's legal defeat followed by her artistic humiliation; and circumstances were to favour him. Rachel was destined to fail in the play which she had preferred to his; and a rival was destined to triumph in the piece which she had rejected with contumely. Rachel's star, in short, was about to set, and that of Adelaide Ristori was already rising.

Mme Ristori

CHAPTER XXIII

THE piece which Rachel preferred to Legouvé's
Médée was *Rosemonde* by Latour Saint Ybars. It
was a tragedy in one act—a feast of horrors, as
it were, compressed into a tabloid, analogous to those
nerve-wracking melodramatic sketches which are
popular in our own music-halls at the present time.
It failed, and was withdrawn after a week's run,
helped to its end by an epigram launched anony-
mously, but attributed to Samson—

"Pourquoi nomme-t-on ce drame *Rosemonde* ?
Je n'y vois plus de rose et n'y vois pas de monde."

Rachel, disconcerted by the failure, went into
hysterics in her dressing-room, tearing the veil
which she had worn in her part to tatters, and
throwing the dagger which she had carried on to
the floor. There had been applause indeed; but
she had had to " work hard " for it. It was not
the sort of applause that she was used to; and she
felt the difference. It did not betoken enthusiasm,
but only courteous consideration for the feelings
of an old favourite. Her public, which had once
exalted her as a goddess, was now " letting her down
gently." Hence the painful scene which Jules

Rachel

Janin—that lively weathercock—now once more veering round to sympathy, describes—

" It was," he writes, " a sad and touching spectacle which I shall never forget as long as I live. She crouched in a corner of that historic dressing-room, still fragrantly reminiscent of Mademoiselle Mars. She was panting for breath, dazed, motionless and mute. No sight could have been more eloquent or more melancholy. Alas ! the daughter of the Muses was giving way beneath the burden of her task. She felt all its weight, and she was vanquished. Her spirit was restless, her mind was ill at ease, her health was broken. She had lost her courage and her hope. She pushed the bitter cup from her, weary of the pains due to her own past triumphs, which carried with them the imperious obligation to succeed.

" And so she began to cry. Her beautiful great eyes filled with tears; and when a rash friend tried to comfort her, she rent the drapery which wrapped her bosom, exclaiming : ' There ! Look at me ! You can see that my tears are the tears of a dying woman ! '

" We went out, despairing for her. It was the true beginning of her death agony—her first step on the straight road which was to lead her to the grave."

Truly there was more poignant tragedy in that scene than in all the emphatic violence of Latour's poor play—the peculiar tragedy of the calling in which achievement is evanescent as a perfume and

Rachel

failure seems painfully degrading because of its publicity. The failure was partially redeemed, after a rest, by a comparative success in Scribe's *La Czarine*. But only partially. Such vogue as the piece enjoyed was far more due to Rachel's costumes and jewels than to her acting. These, on one occasion, drew more money to the house than the house could nominally hold; but that, of course, was not the kind of success that Rachel sought or was accustomed to. She was even ashamed of it as a demonstration of her decline; and a dinner-party given to celebrate it by Dr. Véron, whom she still acknowledged as her friend in spite of the hard things she said of him, was a pathetic failure.

Sainte-Beuve, Prosper Mérimée, Aubert, Halévy, and Scribe were among the guests; but Rachel could not be cheered. She tried to enliven herself by drinking two glasses of that champagne which the doctor had drunk every night for thirty years without visible injury to his constitution; but it only gave her a headache. She said she must retire and lie down on the sofa. She dissolved on to the sofa in tears, and only rose from it to get into her carriage and drive home. A few nights afterwards *La Czarine* was withdrawn; and then, after a few appearances in her classical repertory, Rachel remembered a vow which she had made.

"If my popularity should ever diminish," she had once told Madame Samson, "I shall instantly retire from the stage"; and though she had never seriously anticipated that contingency, she now found herself face to face with it.

She had two rivals. Madame Arnould's successes

Rachel

in comedy were surpassing her own successes in tragedy; and on the horizon of tragedy itself the star of Madame Ristori had appeared.

Ristori has been styled " the Italian Siddons "; but designations of that sort are not very illuminating. Fanny Kemble, who had seen them both in their best days, declared, as has been already mentioned, that she could not hold a candle to Rachel; but, at the moment when comparison was challenged, Rachel was in her decadence and Ristori was in her prime. Moreover, she was sufficiently different from Rachel to make comparison interesting.

Rachel, as we have seen, was a child of the gutter, endowed with genius, admirably trained in the technique of her art, but, in all other respects, inadequately educated. She had lived as she liked, made herself notorious, squandered her own health and her admirers' substance in riotous living, and treated dramatic authors and her fellow-players with capricious contempt; but she had never, or hardly ever, posed as the possessor of an artistic soul. One might almost say that she had gone through life with the inevitable directness and simplicity which appertain to genius. Ristori, on the other hand, better born than Rachel, much better brought up, and thoroughly soaked in a kind of culture, had far less than Rachel's natural gifts, but went through life posing as if she had been a Fine Arts Ministry of All the Talents.

She was an actress who wrote, taking the public into her confidence, telling them what she thought about her parts and about the masterpieces of dramatic literature, affecting to know what the authors meant better than they knew themselves. She was an actress who studied with the limelight turned on her—before appearing as Marie-Antoinette, for instance, she let it be known that she had spent two days working up appropriate emotions in the cell which Marie-Antoinette had occupied in the Conciergerie prison. She was, finally, an actress who prayed—it was said that she always closed her eyes and offered up a silent petition for divine guidance while awaiting the cue for her entrance. Altogether she was a very original, and individual, though stagy, figure—stagy, one may say, with an intellectual kind of staginess. Madame Duse has been compared to her.

Like Madame Duse, at any rate, she first achieved fame in Italy, and then came to Paris to have the seal set upon her reputation; and Paris felt that it could not do her adequate honour without dethroning her rival. It is not thought necessary to pit poets or painters against each other as if they were competing for gold medals at exhibitions; but on the stage such jealousies and rivalries are normal, and playgoers are apt to back their respective favourites very much in the spirit of those who encourage dogs to fight.

So it happened now. The question was passed round: "Which is the greater, Rachel or Ristori?" Samson was almost the only man who declined to answer it, saying that he could judge Rachel, but could not judge Ristori because he did not know Italian. To the rest of Paris ignorance of Italian was no obstacle to the forming of an opinion; and all those who, for one reason or another, considered that they had grievances against Rachel made the rise of Ristori an occasion for humiliating, and even for insulting her.

Clésinger, the sculptor, affronted her with a dramatic gesture, which indicates that he had missed his vocation. He destroyed his statue of her, and made a statue of Ristori in place of it, declaring that the revelation of Ristori's acting had taught him that his statue of Rachel was not the image of drama, but only of melodrama. This without any visible motive beyond the desire of swimming theatrically with the tide. Alexandre Dumas was still more venomous.

He, unlike Clésinger, had grievances which rankled. Rachel had rejected some of his plays, and she had also rejected his admiration. If she had declined the former politely, she had declined the latter with scorn, in circumstances which have been related. He had neither forgotten nor forgiven; and now he saw his opportunity to punish. He was editing, at the time, his vivacious paper *Le Mousquetaire*, and he used its columns to praise Ristori at Rachel's expense, and to depreciate Rachel for Ristori's greater glory. This is how he apostrophized Rachel in a review of Ristori's performance of *Myrrha*—

"Go and see *Myrrha*. Go and study *Myrrha*. Try to add to the qualities which you possess one quarter of the qualities displayed by Madame Ristori, and, if a shower of gold then falls upon you, beautiful Danae, we will admit that justice has been done."

Rachel

A few days later, having heard the report that Rachel was about to leave Paris, he wrote as follows—

"Enough of all this to-do about Mlle. Rachel's departure! What does it matter whether Mlle. Rachel goes or stays—whether her requests for vacations are granted or refused. Like Ingres at the picture exhibition, she has the house to herself, —the house of the dead. Let her remain in it!"

And so on, day after day, until, at last, he delivered this sledge-hammer blow under the title of "A Dramatic Challenge"—

"We are authorized to make the following proposal for the performance which is to be given for the Benefit of the Authors' and Actors' Benevolent Fund.

" The Opera House to be hired for the occasion; the prices to be doubled; Mlle. Rachel to play *Phèdre* and Mme. Ristori to play *Myrrha*.

" Lots to be drawn to decide which of the two performances shall precede the other.

" The receipts will not amount to less than 20,000 francs.

"It is a matter of course that Mme. Ristori agrees.

"A. D."

It would indeed have been difficult, with this noise of battle in the air, for the two actresses to love each other, or for either of them to take an

Rachel

artist's delight in a fellow artist's success. Ristori, with the big battalions at her back, might indeed affect to do so. Rachel, deserted by her supporters, unnerved by the failure of her health, fighting with her back to the wall, could hardly even pretend.

And she did not pretend. In so far as the contest was one of politeness, Mme. Ristori certainly got the better of it, as indeed was natural, seeing that she had had a better early training in manners, had not been provoked, and knew that she was winning. " Lucky Rachel ! " she exclaimed. " The French can understand her "; and she invited Rachel, with many compliments, to come and see her play. But Rachel's manner of responding to these advances was ungracious, and savoured of "cabotinage."

It was what one would have expected, for the traditions of the stage, in her case, were grafted upon the traditions of the gutter, and not upon those of a finishing school for the daughters of gentlemen. We have seen her treating Mlle. George as a beggar on the occasion of her benefit, and exulting vindictively over the failure of Mlle. Maxime to supplant her—she was not likely, therefore, to be complacent towards Madame Ristori's usurpation of her popularity. What she did was to sit through her rival's performance with no more show of interest or emotion than if she had been listening to the recital of a lesson, and to leave the theatre before it was over; and, of course, Paris remarked her action and commented on it.

Dumas gloated over it as an admission of defeat. Others suggested that perhaps Rachel had been " applauding inwardly." Madame Ristori herself felt that she ought to make some dignified artistic observation. She said, therefore, that it had struck her as "curious" that Mlle. Rachel had refrained from applauding her. Whereupon Legouvé saw his opportunity. "Madame," he exclaimed, with that air of idolatrous deference which some clever men think it proper to adopt towards actresses whom they desire as their interpreters, "the jealousy of Mlle. Rachel was the one thing needful to set the coping-stone upon your fame."

Legouvé received his reward for his compliment. Madame Ristori consented to appear in an Italian version of *Médée*, which was specially translated for her ; and she triumphed in it, winning both renown and wealth, and wearing, as if they were her own, the laurels which her rival had disdained. It was the culminating blow; and Rachel had not waited for it, but had already made her plans. She feared the fate of Mlle. Maxime, who had fallen from the estate of a queen of the theatre to that of the landlady of a lodging-house; and she would not remain to be the witness of her own discomfiture. Elsewhere, if not in Paris, she could still trade upon her reputation. The proposals poured upon her from abroad were sufficient proof of that. The voice of America was inviting her. Like Canning (of whom there is no reason to suppose that she had ever heard), she could call the new world into being to redress the balance of the old.

The reputation of the United States as the land of dollars, almighty and innumerable, had already reached the ears of European entertainers. Dollars, like the sands of the sea for multitude, had been gathered in there by entertainers as diverse as Dickens, Fanny Elssler, and Jenny Lind; but the supply was inexhaustible, and another might still delve profitably in the same rich mine. Rachel's family, for whose profit, as well as for her own, she worked, emphatically urged the enterprise, dinning into her ears the eloquent fact that Jenny Lind had taken £68,000 in thirty-eight nights. The fact, she was assured, that the Americans were mostly ignorant of her language would make no difference. She had succeeded in London, though the English did not know French. Ristori had succeeded in Paris, though the French did not know Italian. So, in spite of the long voyage, and in spite of her weak health, she made up her mind to go.

Efforts were made in certain quarters to dissuade her. It was said that she was offered a piece of jewellery worth £4,000, on condition that she would promise to remain in France. It was said that she accepted the present, and gave the promise, and broke it. It is impossible to tell whether that piece of gossip was true or not. What is certain is that her enemies, having insulted her while she stayed, heaped fresh insults on her when she departed.

Dumas offered the genial prediction that she would die of fatigue in America, and that her brother, with his happy Hebrew instincts, would make a huge fortune by having her body embalmed and exhibiting it in a Dime Museum. Cayla wrote—

" If the artist carries out her designs she will have justified the reproaches of ingratitude and

Rachel

cupidity which tarnish her renown; and history, forgetting the artist, will only remember the Jewess."

Auguste Vacquerie expressed himself with even more spiteful virulence—

" So now she is in America," he wrote. " I hope she is going to stay there. I hope she will succeed there, and be overwhelmed with dollars, and enjoy herself, and fall in love with Racine, and marry him, and bear and bring up a large family of tragedies."

It was very brutal—the atmosphere of the theatre seems favourable to this kind of brutality. Rachel herself, as we have seen, was capable of it. But all our sympathies must, this time, be with her, if only because she was now a dying woman, awakening from illusion to reality, breaking her head against a fresh reality every day, and fighting her last fight in adverse circumstances. Whether she fought for gold or for glory, the fight itself was brave; and one is glad to think that the kindness of London did something to redeem the cruelty of Paris, and so to comfort her.

She played six times at the St. James's Theatre before embarking at Southampton. Her contract guaranteed her a minimum emolument of £200 a night, and on one of the nights the receipts amounted to £400. The English critics declared that she had lost nothing of her old powers, and the Duc d'Aumale, who was present at her first performance, paid her a compliment similar to one she had received from

Rachel

Molé at the very beginning of her career. " This beautiful language of Corneille," he said, " this language of my country, which I have just listened to, is to me like the fresh dew which falls on a scorching day in spring."

And so, at last, to New York, on board the *Pacific*, commanded by Captain Nye.

CHAPTER XXIV

The American fiasco—Serious illness of Rachel—Her last appearance at Charleston—Her departure for Havana.

RACHEL, it must be repeated, was, by this time, a dying woman.

Rest, perhaps, might still have saved her—rest, and pure air, and bright sunshine; but she was restless—the laurels of Madame Ristori did not suffer her to rest. Applause was as the breath of life to her—she felt that she could not live without it. She was avaricious, too, valuing money still more than she valued the good things which money could buy; and she was encouraged in her avarice by a family which desired to grow rich at her expense.

Her brother and sisters had begun by admiring her, and now they had arrived at exploiting her. Mrs. Pitt Byrne, in her *Gossip of the Century*, relates how she happened to sit in the midst of the Tribe of Félix at the theatre in the days when Rachel was still a dèbutante, and how she got into conversation with them, and how they boasted, saying: "C'est là notre jeune soeur; n'est-ce pas qu'elle sera la plus grande tragédienne du siècle ? " She had fulfilled their prediction to their great advantage, paying the debts of Sarah of the Supper-parties, procuring lucrative engagements for Dinah and Leah, and putting Raphael in the way of wealth as her business manager. It is hardly too much to speak of Raphael as a gadfly, driving her till she dropped.

He had computed his American gains with elaborate particularity. The takings were expected to amount to exactly £102,184. Rachel's share of them was to be £48,000. Each of her sisters was to receive £6,800. He himself was to keep whatever remained after expenses had been paid. His calculations were based upon the fact that Jenny Lind had taken nearly £4,000 at her first performance, and had garnered, as has been said, £68,000 from thirty-eight performances. Rachel, he argued, being more famous than Jenny Lind, would draw still larger houses. So he applied the spur, just as his father had applied it before him, and urged his sister on.

A note in Charles Greville's *Diary* is one of our indications of the state of health in which she started. " Rachel," he says, " when called on at the end of the piece, was so overcome that she nearly fainted, and would have fallen had not some one rushed on the stage to support her." Another indication is in a letter which she wrote to her mother, just before landing in New York. She speaks in it of " a pain in the side." It had disappeared, but, in its place, there had appeared " pains in the back and the chest," reminding her that her chest had always been weak. She made light of them, declining to give way to " blue devils "; but we can see under what difficulties she was engaging in her last fight for gain and glory.

During the greater part of the voyage she remained in her cabin, much depressed by the death of a fellow-passenger from her own malady, hardly emerging except to receive a magnificent box of perfumes, presented by Captain Nye on behalf of an American admirer who modestly withheld his name, and to lay the foundations of popularity by accepting the captain's invitation to dinner and begging him to distribute two thousand francs on her behalf among the crew. A proposal that she should make the occasion memorable by reciting poetry was met with a cold refusal; while an attempt on the part of her fellow-guests to distinguish it by singing the *Marseillaise* came ludicrously to grief through their inability to remember the words of that patriotic hymn.

It was not the best of omens; and another unfavourable omen was the fiasco of the arrangements which agents in advance had made for Rachel's reception. The band of the Lafayette company of the New York Militia, composed of American citizens of French birth, was to have escorted her to her hotel; but the *Pacific* came in three hours before its time, and the musicians were not ready. They did their best by fetching their instruments and serenading her after she had gone to bed; but the necessity of resuming the clothes which she had just taken off, in order to bow her acknowledgments from the balcony, can hardly have been agreeable to a weary woman.

About ten days later the campaign began; and the illusions on which Raphael had based his arithmetical calculations evaporated. Rachel, it became clear, was not destined to achieve Jenny Lind's success, or anything resembling it, for reasons which might perfectly well have been foreseen.

One reason was that Jenny Lind had been "run" by Barnum; and Barnum was a showman by whose side Raphael was but an ignorant child groping in the dark. The other reason was that American playgoers were, with rare exceptions, ignorant of the French language and indifferent to the master-pieces of French dramatic literature. They had no more needed to know the language of Jenny Lind than to know the language of the nightingale, and had been delighted to listen to her night after night. They only wanted to hear Rachel once, in order to be able to boast of having heard her. And this difference of attitude towards the two artists was inevitably reflected in the receipts. Rachel's first house was her best—at the Metropolitan Theatre, on September 3, she drew £1,053 7s. 2d. But Jenny Lind's first performance had drawn no less than £3,751 8s. 9d.

Artistically, it is true, the beginning seemed to be good. The few who understood were rapturous in their applause; and the many who did not under-stand took their hint from the leaders of taste, and applauded also. There is a pen picture of the scene in *Harper's Magazine* for November, 1855, from which an extract may be taken—

" The audience received her with solid applause. There was no hooting, no whistling, no tumult of any kind. One indiscreet brother tried to yelp, and was instantly suppressed. The reception was generous and intelligent. It was the right reception for a great artist. It acknowledged her previous fame by courtesy. It expressed the intelligence which could approve or revise that fame.

" Yes, astonished friend, approve or revise even a Parisian decision."

That when the curtain rose. Then, afterwards—

" For an hour and a half the curtain was up, and the eyes of the audience were riveted upon Rachel. For an hour and a half there was the constant increase of passionate intensity, until love and despair culminated in the famous denunciation; the house hung breathless upon that wild whirl of tragic force— and Camille lay dead, and the curtain was down, before that rapt and amazed silence was conscious of itself.

" Then came the judgment—the verdict which was worth having after such a trial—the crown, and the garland, and the pæan. The curtain rose, and there, wan and wavering, stood the ghost of Camille, the woman Rachel. She had risen in her flowing drapery just where she had fallen, and seemed to be the spirit of herself. But, pale and trembling, she flickered in the tempest of applause. The audience stood and waved hats and handkerchiefs, and flowers fell in pyramids; and that quick, earnest, meaning ' bravo ' was undisturbed by any discordant sound. It was a great triumph. It was too much for the excited and exhausted Rachel. She knew that the news would instantly fly across the sea —that Paris would hear of her victory over a new continent—that, perhaps, Ristori's foot would be

found too large for the slipper. She wavered for
a moment. Then some one rushed forward and
caught her as she fell—and the curtain came down.

"There was no attempt at a recall. There was
something too real in the whole scene. The audience
silently arose and slowly separated. Ladies sat
in groups upon the benches with white faces and red
eyes. They all thought her beautiful. They all
forgave everything, and they all denied everything. It was a rare triumph. We so love what
we greatly admire that we all longed to love
Rachel."

Decidedly a "notice" to be treasured in a press-
cutting album. If everybody had been of the same
mind as the writer, Rachel would decidedly have
scaled loftier heights of glory in the new world
than in the old. But the voice was the voice of
the elect, not of the multitude. The multitude
shouted with the elect because it seemed the correct
thing to do; but in selecting the entertainments for
which it would "keep its money," it consulted its
own tastes. And this in spite of the fact that the
name was good enough for tradesmen to use it for
purposes of *réclame*. Puddings "à la Rachel" appeared in the restaurants; ices "à la Rachel" were
sold by the confectioners; gaiters "à la Rachel"
figured in the boot-makers' windows; the green-
grocers offered melons "à la Raphael Félix." But
these devices were more effective in advertising the
shopkeepers' wares than in advertising Rachel's
entertainment. The receipts had touched high-water
mark, and were never to touch it again. On the

second night they fell to £792 9s. 8d; on the third
night to £724 1s. 8d.

In part, it may be, the decline was due to the
fact that Rachel was poorly supported and that
her pieces were cheaply staged. Beauvallet, her
leading man, who afterwards wrote a relation of
the adventure, was the only one of her company
who counted. The others, especially Dinah and
Leah and Sarah of the Supper-parties, were spoken
of disdainfully as "Hebrew sticks." The supers,
recruited on the spot, excited even greater derision.
Habited as Roman lictors, they showed their
Republican independence by declining to shave, but
strutted their little hour upon the stage, embellished
with goatees, saluted by a sputtering fire of chaff
from friends and acquaintances in the cheaper seats.

Rachel was advised to court popularity by sending
a large subscription for the relief of the sufferers
from an epidemic of yellow fever then raging at
Norfolk and Portsmouth. It was a counsel of
despair; and she was soon complaining that for all
the good the investment had done her she might
just as well have thrown her money into the sea.
There were playgoers who wanted to see the jewels
which she wore in *Adrienne Lecouvreur*, and playgoers
who were eager to hear her sing the *Marseillaise*;
but the number of playgoers who desired to follow
her in her classical repertory was limited and tended
continually to diminish.

Moreover, there were dissensions, feuds and
disagreeables of various kinds. There was an occasion on which Sarah of the Supper-parties slapped
little Dinah's face, and another occasion on which

Rachel

Raphael told Sarah that the sooner she returned to Europe the better he should be pleased. Raphael, too, got into trouble with the critics by curtailing their privileges, and with the public by speculating in the seats. The strangers were denounced as "European blood-suckers"; and a boycott was organized, with the result that, one night, the receipts fell to £168. Raphael only partially saved the situation by offering humble apologies and promising never to offend again.

At Boston, however, Rachel, on the whole, did fairly. It was on her return to New York that she became fully conscious that she was ceasing to attract. She appeared, this time, at the Academy of Music—a bare, ugly and unpopular house; and there the receipts melted rapidly; *Adrienne Lecouvreur* drawing only £345, and *Lady Tartufe* only £344 12s. Raphael made haste to transfer his company to another house—a music hall known as Niblo's Garden; but though they did better there they were very far from realizing their dreams of wealth. *Angelo* drew £560 6s. 6d.; *Virginie* £517 12s. 10d; *Mlle. de Belle-Isle* £630 4s. Not until the farewell performance did the figures rise to £824; and against this gain there was quickly to be placed a drop at Philadelphia to £395 8s. 10d.

The end was now near, however, for Rachel was already ill, and was rapidly getting worse. On September 25 she had written to her mother to say that she was eating and sleeping well and " getting fat," and that it suited her better to be braced up in New York than to be sent south in search of sunshine. She had not understood, however, the danger of the sudden changes of temperature to which New York is liable. Early in October a sharp east wind caught her and gave her a cold. She neglected it, in order to accept an invitation to a reception given in her honour, and made it worse. She continued to neglect it, and the climax came when, at Philadelphia, she played in a theatre which had not been warmed.

She coughed painfully all through the performance, took to her bed, and did not leave it until she left the town. Raphael made the company play without her; but the results were disastrous. For the four nights on which they appeared the takings only averaged £40 a night. It was decided to cut the tour short and go at once to Charleston, and thence to Havana, where the climate might be expected to be kinder. Rachel was so weak that she would willingly have gone home, but Raphael would not hear of it. She could only bear the fatigue of the journey by taking it in easy stages; and the first thing which she did on her arrival was to call in a doctor.

It is not certain whether the physician told her all that he diagnosed. If so, he was a bad blunderer; but it is more likely that he thought it discreet to spare her the full truth. His prescription, at any rate, was six months' absolute rest; and she would not take it—perhaps Raphael would not let her take it. The frame of mind in which she faced her illness at this stage is shown in a letter addressed to her mother from Boston—

" If laurels preserve one from lightning, they do

not protect one from colds in the head. . . . I caught
cold in the train; and since I have been here I have
been coughing like a consumptive, though I am
nothing of the kind, as I beg you to believe, in spite
of the fact that I am looking pale and thin."

Her company at Charleston had been billed to
appear without her; and the *fiasco* had been even
worse than at Philadelphia. A big fire had happened
to break out at the hour announced for the performance; and the inhabitants of Charleston had
thought that the fire would be a more attractive, as
well as a cheaper, entertainment than the play.
They ran to see the fire, and the box-office took no
money that night. That was on December 10. A
week later Rachel herself—her passage to Cuba
already booked—was billed to make her "last
appearance in America" in *Adrienne Lecouvreur*.

Her last appearance in America was, in fact,
to be her last appearance on any stage; and there
was a pathetic propriety in her selection of her piece
and part. Adrienne was an actress like herself,
cut off, like her, in her prime. In representing
her, she enacted, as it were, a scene from her personal
life. She had never been able to render the part
without feeling the sensation of her mortality and
the presage of her death. It has already been told
how she dissolved in tears when she rehearsed it.
She could only struggle through it now—her lines
punctuated with a hacking cough; but her pain and
her feebleness only made the rendering more realistic.

"Ah, quelles souffrances . . . ce n'est plus ma

Rachel

tête, c'est ma poitrine qui est brûlante . . . j'ai
là comme un brazier . . . comme un feu dévorant
qui me consume. . . .
  "Ah! Le mal redouble. . . . Vous qui m'aimez
tant, sauvez moi, secourez moi . . . je ne veux pas
mourir . . . à present je ne veux pas mourir. . . .
  "Mon Dieu, exaucez moi! Mon Dieu, laissez moi
vivre . . . quelques jours encore. . . . Je suis si jeune,
et la vie s'ouvrait pour moi si belle!
  "La vie! La vie! Vains efforts! Vaine prière!
Mes jours sont comptés! Je sens les forces et l'existence qui m'échappent!
  "O triomphes du théâtre! mon coeur ne battra
plus de vos ardentes émotions! Et vous, longues
études d'un art que j'aimais tant, rien ne restera de
vous après moi. Rien ne nous survît a nous autres
. . . rien que le souvenir."

It was her own case to an iota. The theatre
was all in all to her; and she clung to its
pleasures and triumphs, frantically and frenziedly,
as she saw them escaping from her, having no
inner life, whether of religion or of philosophy, to
fall back upon—no contentment in the thought of
continuing to live in the life of the Universal Spirit,
of which she had been the transient, ebullient
manifestation. And therefore she played to a thin
and almost indifferent house as she had never
played before.
  Among the few who saw, there were some who
understood. Her fellow player, Chéri, who took
the part of Michonnet, did so for one. "I had a
niece," he said, "who died of consumption, and

I know the signs. So mark my words. Rachel, I tell you, will never play again."

But she meant to. In spite of the Charleston physician's warning she would not give up the fight yet; and it was with the firm intention of continuing to play that she embarked for Havana on December 19, 1855.

CHAPTER XXV

Life at Havana—Rachel's ill-health there—Return to France and departure for Egypt.

IF Rachel had been able to play at Havana the profits would have been great. For the performances announced, tickets were sold to the value of £2,400. Her " benefit," too, would have been very lucrative if she had conformed to the custom of the place. It was expected that she would pay a round of visits to the notables of the city, and would afterwards sit, attended by one of them, in front of the house, with money-boxes or trays before her, to receive offerings and oblations. She found it physically impossible, however, to do anything of the kind; and her position was made more painful by the unsympathetic scepticism of those about her.

Every physician whom she consulted ordered her to rest; but she had so often pleaded indisposition as an excuse for evading engagements that neither the Havaneros nor her company believed that she was really as ill as she said; and there was a good deal of bad feeling when she announced that the tour was over, that the money taken must be returned, that salaries must cease, and that the troupe must go back to Europe, while she remained to bask in Cuban sunshine. She insisted, however, being not only ill but frightened; and as Beauvallet puts it, "the shores of two continents were strewn with the wreckage of the expedition."

Even her sisters did not remain with her. Dinah and Leah went to New York, and Sarah repaired to Charleston, where, no doubt, there were supper-parties at which she was made welcome. Some of the others, after arranging to give performances on their own account, were alarmed by reports of an epidemic of yellow fever, and booked their passages to Europe. Rachel herself wrote pathetic letters home, constrained at last to admit the truth about her health—

"I am ill, very ill indeed—equally broken down in body and mind. I shall never play at Havana; but, as I have come here, the manager of the theatre, standing on his rights, demanded 7,000 piastres damages. I paid him, and I have paid my company up to date. I have to bring my poor army back, routed, to the banks of the Seine; and perhaps I shall myself, like another Napoleon, come to the Invalides to die, and beg for a stone on which to rest my head. But no—not that. There are my two guardian angels, my two sons. I hear them calling me. I have been too long away from their kisses, their caresses, their dear little arms. And God, who protects my angels, compels me to return home. I no longer regret the money I have lost; I no longer regret my fatigue. I have carried my name as far as I could, and I bring back my heart to those who love me."

"My dear father, I am so glad that I stayed at

Rachel

Havana. Such motherly care is being taken of me in a new family which has adopted me that I really ought to be well towards May, when I hope to return to France. Next week we are setting out for a sugar plantation—an immense estate, two and a half days' journey from Havana. They have their own doctor on the estate, and he is said to be very good. I still cough rather often, but my spirits are better than they were. I am doing my best to forget this terrible journey to America and the two thousand leagues which separate me from my children and my parents. I get through the time without boring myself too much. God grant that I may continue to do so. I read, I write, I do needlework, I lunch at ten, and I dine at six. As I have to dress twice a day, that task occupies a good deal of my time. In the evening the young people give us a little music, and the ladies chatter to me and try to prevent me from talking. The interest that they take in me is incredible. Reports of the state of my health are published daily in the papers. It is at night that I feel tired. I sleep very little, and such sleep as I get is troubled. It is thought that I may cure my insomnia by means of baths."

A fortnight later there is a complaint of pain in the left side—an old pain returning, and not to be exorcised by blisters, or any other of the old remedies: also complaints of cold feet, and nightly perspirations which, though not painful, were exhausting. The modern reader knows the symptoms at a glance as those of pulmonary consumption; but Rachel

Rachel

was not so certain. She could still fluctuate between despair and hope, persuading herself that she felt well when, in truth, she was only feeling warm, mistaking every rally for recovery, still hugging the intention of returning to the theatre when she had rested a little longer.

She remitted her profits—about £6000—to France, and presently she followed the money which she was now too ill to care about. The term of the vacation accorded to her by the Comédie Française not having expired, she settled down to rest in a country house at Meulan, where several of her friends visited her. Her letters to some of them, though little more than notes, give glimpses of her life, and show us how her cheerfulness still flickered, from time to time, into a flame. For instance :—

" If you really want to see me at Meulan, take the Rouen train at Saint Lazare, two steps from your own door. You like the country sunshine, don't you ? Very well. Take the eleven-thirty, and you will be here at one; and since I am pitilessly forbidden to have more than two hours of your conversation, you shall leave me at three and get home in time for dinner. I never go out, so you may choose your own day.

" When the north-east wind stopped blowing on the banks of the Seine I felt better for a day or two. Unhappily the improvement did not continue. During the last three days I have felt quite knocked up. You can boast that you have a battered old hulk for a friend."

Rachel

"Nothing would please me better than to dine with you and the very amiable and gracious *Niche* (Mme. Doche); but, my poor friend, I am not yet fit to go to Paris. In order that I may convince you of that, you must come and dine with me at Meulan, in a charming farm, in which I am practically at home. The hospitable proprietor receives my friends as if they were his own. . . .

"If you bite at this proposal, name your day, and arrive in the country at sunrise. The weather is marvellously fine and warm, and I want you to give me a long day."

"I have been better since I have followed the treatment prescribed by Dr. Rayer. I cough less, and that is a great improvement. I shall take the waters somewhere in June. The Faculty of Medicine, more serious than in Molière, and assembled, if I may say so, for a sadder case than that of Argan, advises me to spend a season at Ems. At first they wanted to send me to Eaux Bonnes; but I could never recover my health in the place in which I saw my dear sister Rebecca die."

And then to Arsène Houssaye :—

"My dear Conversationalist (for all the others are mere babblers), come here and gossip with me under the trees of the days that are past. Sometimes I really think I have had no past. Life is a dream following a dream. We are never quite awake to the realities."

Rachel

Arsène Houssaye accepted the invitation. Rachel played billiards with him for five-franc pieces, and won. Then she talked of the old days when she had strummed the guitar for coppers. She took the instrument down, and struck a few notes, and then dropped it, and pretended to chase a butter-fly, pirouetting like a ballet-girl as if reaching out for it. And then—

"It has flown away," she said. "Alas! Life slips away, running after butterflies—love, happiness, glory; but who catches them ? "

Who, indeed ? Or rather, who, having caught them, holds them ? Not those assuredly who only seek them on the glittering surface of things; for to such accident is cruel, and illness and age are pitiless.

A report circulated, at about this date, that Rachel was going to be married. The author of it was Jules Lecomte—the tenor beloved by Marie-Louise, whom we last met at a supper-party where Rachel and the other guests chaffed him about the Empress's favours. Rachel charged him with having invented the rumour and with trying to amuse the Parisians at "poor Rachel's" expense. "Why," she asked, " do you credit me with any such absurd intention ? " And then she went on—

" I have two sons whom I adore. I am thirty-two, and I look fifty. Eighteen years of passionate tirades on the stage, mad expeditions to the ends of the earth, winters at Moscow, treasons of Waterloo, perfidious seas and ungrateful lands—all these things have aged the poor weak little woman that I am. . . .

" By Jupiter, I think it is very nice of me to write to you like this; for my letter certainly is not from the pen of a great tragédienne, but from that of the good-hearted girl whose name is RACHEL."

One can trace the slow progress of the relentless malady in these letters—the tide rising continually in spite of the constant illusion that it is turning. It was quite clear—nothing could be clearer—that Rachel could not go back to the theatre for the present. It was, no doubt, quite clear to every one but herself that she would never go back to it at all. But she still persisted in hoping, and still refused to do more than postpone the date of her return. To that end she wrote to Achille Fould, the Minister of Fine Arts—the same Achille Fould to whom she had sold for a thousand louis the guitar on which she had *not* strummed for coppers in her childhood—asking for an extension of her leave of absence—

" My health, which was already impaired when my leave of absence began, has obliged me to return to France. For ten months I have been taking care of myself, solely in the hope of resuming my place at the Comédie Française on the day fixed by you.

" It is with grief, as you may suppose, that I find myself compelled to postpone my reappearance, as the state of my health does not allow me to think

Rachel

of playing on November 1. Dr. Rayer, however, having assured me that I may hope for a complete recovery if I spend a few months in a warm climate, I have consented, without hesitation, to expatriate myself, in order that I may be able, at the earliest possible date, to demonstrate my eagerness once again to receive the applause of my public."

The permission which she sought was granted. She decided to sell her mansion in the Rue Trudon, together with its art treasures, and she set out for Egypt. Jules Janin, who had lately denounced her with indignation for singing the *Marseillaise* to an American audience, now sped her on her way with a friendly letter :—

" My DEAR CHILD,
  I cannot let you depart without sending you my best, my most sincere, my most paternal expressions of tenderness. I regard you as my child. I saw your artistic birth, and watched you grow up and set out for your goal and reach it. At present a little fatigue, a great distress, and your regrets for the theatre from which you are absent, are a cruel trial to you. But you must be strong and of a good courage. Fill your soul with hope, and entrust your body to the warm and favourable winds, to your journey, to the Orient, to the sun, to the clement stars which await you, and will give you back, happy and inspired, to us who love you, and to the great art of tragedy which you have revived, and which has no future save in you."

Rachel

It was well meant, albeit a little overdone; but that could not be helped, for Jules Janin always overdid things. No doubt he knew better, but thought that Rachel wished to be deceived. Her letter to her mother, written on board the steamer, shows that she deceived herself. She had sat next to the captain, she wrote, and had managed to eat a little; and she coughed less at sea than on land. The Mediterranean was beautifully blue; she felt her lungs expanding; she had no doubt that her journey would do her the good she hoped from it.

And so to Cairo.

CHAPTER XXVI

THE journey into Egypt was, naturally, devoid of incident. One can make no incident out of the fact that Rachel drank asses' milk, or out of the fact that a necklace was discovered for her in an Egyptian tomb, and that the discoverer attached to it a legend of his own invention to the effect that it had been worn by Cleopatra—a legend to which Jules Janin devoted a paragraph of his dramatic gossip. The story that she offered Sarah 15,000 francs to go home and leave her alone, and that Sarah refused to depart for less than 20,000 francs is probably a legend also. Certainly it has all the marks of one.

In truth there is nothing to be recorded except that Rachel, failing to get better at Cairo, hired a dahabeah and travelled up the Nile, attended by a private physician; and that she slowly got worse instead of better, and came back again. Beyond that one has only the chronicle of her alternating hopes and fears—the invariable accompaniments of her malady—set forth in her letters to her family and her friends. " In the shadow of the Pyramids," for instance, she wrote to Arsène Houssaye—

" I chose to live like a *gourmande*. In the course of a few years I devoured my days and my nights.

Rachel

But the thing is done, and I am not going to say,
like the penitents : ' It was my fault; it was all
my own fault.'

" When one has not kindled one's heart to warmth
in one's best days, one cannot make the flame blaze
up at thirty-five. No, no. It is over. Ah ! if I
had not two sons, who are all that I love in the world,
I should not be sorry to die. But I shall come back.
The God of Israel will permit me, in the entr'actes
above, to come to earth again and kiss my children
and revisit my friends at the Théâtre Français which
I have loved so well.

" You live in the Champs Elysées. Every day
you pass the Obelisk. Think then of the poor
exile.

" At the foot of the Pyramids I look upon twenty
centuries buried in the sands. Ah, my friend, I
clearly see here how a tragédienne must disappear
into nothingness. I thought myself like a pyramid,
and, behold, I am no more than a shadow which
passes—which has passed. I came here to find
a fresh hold on the life which is escaping from me,
and, all around me, I see nothing but death. When
one has known what it is to be loved at Paris it
is time to die. Dig me a little hole at Père Lachaise—
and in your memory. Have you forgotten ? I, at
any rate, remember.

" I write this without really knowing what I say;
but I use the dust of the queens of Egypt to dry
my ink. That dust is the most eloquent thing in
my letter.

" The departing
RACHEL."

Rachel

She was to meet Arsène Houssaye once again, and to boast to him that the letter " wasn't so bad." It was self-conscious perhaps; but the writer nevertheless had made a little literature without knowing it, her correspondent being a more inspiring man than the majority of the managers of theatres, and with something of the sincerity of a guardian angel hidden only a little way beneath the exterior of a man of pleasure. Other letters, less literary, exhibit her fluctuating expectations.

" The weather continues to be splendid, and I write to you from the midst of a fairy-like garden. Fancy that, on the 14th of November! I am no worse. I hope to see you again. I embrace you. If that does not please you, send my kiss back to me. My remembrances to your neighbour."

That is to a friend whose name is not given. On her way up the Nile we find her writing cheerfully to her boy Gabriel—

" I continue to improve, thanks to the continual warmth of this beautiful climate. . . . I am sitting in my little bed, in my little cabin, with the windows open.

" The Nile is like a lake. Not a breath of wind ruffles the surface. The sun itself, as if it were too hot, plunges its rays into the water. . . . I am filling my lungs with the life-giving air of Upper Egypt. I still cough; but instead of growing weaker I am gaining strength. My appetite is always good; my nights are more comfortable, though I am still feverish this evening. My doctor does not appear in the least anxious about me, but every day gives me the best possible report of my health. . . .

" Good-bye, dear. Take care of the kisses which I send to the family and to our friends. It will be a double pleasure to them if I make you my messenger.

" For yourself, dear, I send you all the love of my heart—there will always be love there for my sons. So great are the joys which God bestows on the mothers who love their little ones! "

From Thebes she writes to her mother, whom she tells that her doctor feels her pulse five or six times a day, but has nothing else to do except to pace the deck of the dahabeah with his hands in pockets. She adds, however, that her cure is a " martyrdom," and continues—

" God is taking pity on me. My health is not getting any worse. I have been a little feverish; and, for two nights, my cough kept me awake; but the doctor assures me that that is only a temporary inconvenience, and that I shall soon be convalescent. It was rather cold all through February at Thebes, and the wind made it impossible for me to leave my room. My appetite is not so good as it was, but I still have all the appetite I need; and though I have to admit that I am dreadfully bored, my spirits are tolerably good, and I can laugh."

One easily reads between the lines and sees that the note of cheerfulness is being forced. The proof,

Rachel

if proof be needed, is in a letter written a few days later to a friend to whom it was easier to tell the truth. Rachel writes that she can hardly stand on her feet, and is longing for the day when she will lie down for ever.

" I am not yet dead, but I am almost as good as dead. I no longer wish for anything or expect anything, and I am tired of the merely animal life which I have been leading ever since this long and painful illness attacked me. Better a hundred times to be nailed up within four boards, and treated as they treat the Egyptian mummies. If I do not die of consumption, I shall assuredly die of boredom. . . .

" . . . I received your letter of the 8th of September just as I was being put on board for Alexandria. You would have shed a real tear for me if you had seen me then. They had to carry me on to the boat. Really I do not know what my poor fragile body is made of. What a lot it takes to kill me! I did not think one could suffer so much without dying a thousand times over.

" And now I must leave off. My cough—it makes me first hot and then cold."

One would not have expected her to rally and recover her spirits after that; but she did so. The next letter shows her once more making plans— looking, in fact, quite a long way ahead.

" I am coming back to Cairo for April and May, and then I shall embark on the Mediterranean.

Rachel

I shall be at Marseilles in the first fortnight of June, and shall go on to Montpellier, a place equally renowned for its warm climate and its doctors. I shall spend a portion of my children's holidays at Paris, winding up some business which requires attention, and then, at the first sign of cold, I shall go south. Perhaps I shall return to Egypt; or perhaps I shall pass a month or six weeks at New York, and the rest of the time at Charleston, where, I remember, the climate was so agreeable."

So she proposed; and the end was not even yet so near but that it was possible for her to carry out a part of the programme. She pulled herself together and appeared bright and even coquettish on board the steamer which brought her home; but the truth about her condition is in a letter from Joseph Autran, who saw her land, to Pontmartin—

"Ah! My dear friend! What a power have suffering and misfortune to tame the haughtiest pride! I saw the poor woman in a state which left no room for any emotion but pity—shrivelled to a skeleton, livid, hollow-eyed, unable to speak four words without a fearful fit of coughing. Who would believe that that voice, which issues with effort from her breast like a last sigh, is the same voice which made the rafters of the theatre ring and kept the most brilliant assemblages in Europe hanging on its words!"

And so to Montpellier!

Rachel

A house had been taken for her there belonging to a M. Coffinières, an advocate practising at the Montpellier court. With her were her maid Rose, her physician, Dr. Farrat, and Dr. Farrat's brother-in-law, Lieutenant Aubaret of the French navy.

The last-named was the last of the men who fell under the spell of her charm—or perhaps it was of her fame ; a simple honest man, without any sort of guile or subtlety, who not only sentimentalized at her feet, but laid plans for the salvation of her soul. If only she would become a Catholic ! he urged. If only she, a Jewess, would be born again of water and the spirit !

The idea, as we know, was not quite new to her. She had toyed with it sufficiently to set the theatre and the boulevard talking. Her reception into the Church, it had been rumoured, was to be of the most ornate character, attended by a choral service and a gift of jewellery from a devout admirer. " May I ask, madame," some mocker had inquired, " for whose benefit the performance is to be given ? " But it was not to be given for any one's benefit, or at all. There had been nothing but *réclame* in the rumours then, and there was nothing whatever in them now. The only reference to the subject in Rachel's letters is an account of her presentation to a bishop on her way home from Egypt.

The bishop, we gather, said a mass for Rachel's recovery. She thanked him, but, at the same time, dropped a hint that she desired no religious discussions. He took the hint and changed the subject, talking thereafter only of food and the best way of cooking it.

Rachel

"He was a regular glutton of a prelate. One day he asked me point-blank—alluding no doubt to my first appearances on the stage—whether I had even eaten the Gymnase sweetmeats. 'I never fail to fill my pockets with them when I go there,' I replied. That, I admit, was somewhat of the nature of a confession; but it is the only time in my life that I have had anything to do with the Catholic ritual."

Possibly she became more disposed to have something to do with it a little later. It is said, at any rate, that Lieutenant Aubaret nearly persuaded her to become a Christian, but that his counsel was, in the end, overruled by that of her friend Plon-Plon; but that is doubtful. All that is certain is that a Rabbi boasted over her grave that she had been " too intelligent not to die in the religion of her fathers "—as if " intelligent " meant " impervious to argument," or as if it were possible to arrange the different sectarians in order of intelligence.

Nor can it be said that Rachel's life at Montpellier was the life of a woman who accepted without demur the teachings of her experience concerning the vanity of terrestrial things. She spent the long days basking in the sun on the terrace of her villa, occasionally playing backgammon with her brother, but more often emptying her jewels out of their cases, running them through her fingers, spreading them on the table, passing them in review.

They were her trophies, won in all the capitals of Europe—trophies of her art and of her charm—

Rachel

the gifts of emperors and empresses, and kings and queens, and princes and princesses, and admirers, rich and poor, titled and undistinguished. They bound her with gold chains to the glorious days when the joy of living and triumphing had at once delighted and surprised her. They mocked her, doubtless, with the memories which they evoked; for she had lived no inner life, independent of incidents and gauds. She could not even find comfort and repose in the thought of enduring achievement and a great work done which would survive her. Her glory had been the most evanescent kind of glory. Already it was becoming a memory; and these precious stones which she had not brought into the world and could not take out of it were all that remained to her.

Yet not quite all—for there were also certain friendships. Arsène Houssaye, to whom she had written that, after flattering herself that she was as firmly established as the pyramids, she had learnt that she was only a shadow " which was passing—which had passed," was her very good friend still. So was Ponsard, who had loved her, and to whom she had written that, seeing life about to escape from her, she clung to it with desperation. The two men took a journey to see her, and lunched with her, and spent an afternoon with her, pretending to believe that she was getting better, and talking in epigrams, just as in the old days of the suppers after the play.

It seemed as if their talk galvanized her back to life. She dragged herself out of her chair and made plans. She would go back to Paris; her mother

Rachel

must take a house for her—one of the houses in the Rue de la Pompe at Passy would suit her.

" I intend to start on June 18. It would be useless and tiring for you to come to me here. As soon as my business is wound up you shall follow me wherever my health compels me to go.

" I shall see you soon. My kisses to my father and yourself.

RACHEL."

And so once more to Paris !

CHAPTER XXVII

THE last sojourn in Paris was of brief duration. It was a period of farewells, more or less formal and final. Rachel spoke of the house in which she stayed as a station on the road to Père Lachaise. It was a spacious house in the Place Royale, to which all her personal effects which had not been brought to the hammer had been removed; and she smiled and said, with a flicker of playfulness, that there would be plenty of room there for the funeral feast. Then she made her preparations to depart—some of them on the assumption that she would return, but most of them in the belief that she would not. A letter to Empis, who had succeeded Arsène Houssaye as Director of the Comedié Française, finally severed her long connection with the theatre—

"It is with deep regret that I inform you that the state of my health forbids me to hope that I shall be able to return to the Théâtre Français in the immediate future. I will accept, therefore, any decision that the committee may arrive at with regard to my resignation."

The letter covered Dr. Rayer's medical certificate, couched, with kind intentions, in phrases which,

Rachel
From a photograph.

Rachel

while hardly encouraging hope, did not quite exclude it—

" Mlle. Rachel is ill. She is better than she has been, but it is imperative that she should leave Paris, and winter in the South. Her physician could not think of allowing her to reappear on the stage before June 1, 1858."

The next thing was to sort and docket her correspondence, so that every letter might be returned to its writer after her death—an injunction duly obeyed. Then, with a weakening hand which did not easily hold the pen, she wrote her own letters of farewell : letters which seem to be punctuated by tears—letters in which the writer cries out against the cruelty which snatches her away prematurely from the world which she has found so good—

" Dear friend, I am very ill; and I am taking my departure, not yet for the other world, but for a better climate, to which they are sending me for the sake of the warmth which is lacking here. My spirits are as much broken as my health; and the whole of my poor body needs rebuilding—supposing that it is not too late. Sometimes I fancy that night is suddenly falling, and I feel, as it were, a great void in my head and in my mind. Of a sudden, all the light goes out, and your poor Rachel quite ceases to exist. Alas ! poor me ! the poor *me* that I was so proud of—too proud, perhaps—it is so feeble now —hardly anything is left of it. So this letter, my friend, is to wish you good-bye. . . .

" What things have happened, my friend, since

Rachel

our last meeting! And what a cruel journey was
mine! Even now I cannot speak of it without
tears, and without reminding myself of its deceptions
and delusions, due to the terrible illness which is
so fast breaking me up. But how could I foresee
this melancholy end to an enterprise which began so
prosperously and only failed at the hour when success
seemed assured? And this pitiless disease—this
shirt of Nessus which I cannot tear off—how easily
I might have prevented it! But I trusted my
strength too much—I believed too confidently in my
star—and, without taking any precautions, I started
on that interminable journey from New York to
Havana, the last stage of my fatal odyssey. And
now, my friend, I do not know whether I shall ever
return from the country to which I am going. I do
not know whether God will take pity for me for the
sake of my poor dear children and my friends, or
whether He will call me to Himself.

"Farewell, my friend. Very likely this will be
the last letter which you will receive from me.
You who have known Rachel so brilliant—you
have seen her in luxury and splendour—who have
so often applauded her triumphs—it would be very
hard for you to recognize her to-day in the skeleton
which she has become and the spectre which attends
her wherever she goes."

Simultaneously she wrote to her colleague, Augustine Brohan, who had been too jealous of her ever
to be her friend, and had said many bitter things at
her expense, but was none the less moved to commiseration now—

Rachel

" Patience and resignation—that is my motto in these times. I am very grateful to you, dear Mlle. Brohan, for the kind interest which you take in me; but only God can help me now. I am just starting for the South. I hope the pure air and the warmth may do something to ease my sufferings."

And so to Cannet, on the Riviera—though there was one more farewell to be said first.

On the day fixed for her departure all the grey gloom and clammy damp of November were in the air; but Rachel rose early and came down, dressed to go out. They told her that it was too soon to start. She replied that she knew it, but that she had an expedition to make before starting, in fulfilment of a vow, and wished her carriage fetched. They offered to accompany her, but she put them off, insisting that she must go alone. They wondered, but let her have her way. She got into the carriage and drove off.

It was the pale hour of a November dawn, and the streets were empty. " Drive slowly," Rachel said. " First to the Gymnase, then to the Français." Before each of these theatres in turn she halted for a few silent minutes, abandoning herself to the thoughts which came and went; and truly there was much there for meditation as well as tears. In the former house she had emerged from the gutter, proving her great gifts, complimented and encouraged by those patrons of the arts in whose power it was to make reputations. In the latter she had found herself famous at an age when most girls are still at school—the acknowledged queen of the greatest theatre in the world. For eighteen years she had reigned there without a rival, rejoicing in her glory and her power to please; the multitude applauding, while princes laid their hearts and their diamonds at her feet. And now it was all over, so soon, so completely, so irrecoverably. Another had succeeded to the glory. The flames of the passions of her lovers had burnt themselves out, even faster than the fire of her own energies had failed. The jewels, indeed, remained; but though these had once meant much to her, they could mean very little now. There were mockery and irony in their cold glitter; and they could only give point and poignancy to the reflection : "What shadows we are! What shadows we pursue!"

The particular shadow that was Rachel, however, had ceased the pursuit of shadows, and was not to resume it. She lay back in her carriage, indulging the luxury of regret and grief, and not unconscious of the drama of it, until the cold of the early morning began to chill her through her furs. Then drying her eyes—

"It is enough," she said. "Drive on—to the Gare de Lyon."

She was so weak when she got there that she had to be helped, and even lifted, into the train.

And so southwards, with Rose, and Sarah of the Supper-parties, on the last of all her journeys; Plon-Plon, who had been her lover, and was still her friend, having promised to send his yacht to pick her up at Marseilles.

CHAPTER XXVIII

Life on the Riviera—Last illness and death.

THE villa prepared for Rachel was at Cannet, near Cannes, with a view of the blue sea on one side, and of the blue Esterel hills on the other. It belonged to Professor Sardou, the uncle of Victorien Sardou, then a young man whose first play had just failed ignominiously at the Odéon. The bedroom to which the invalid was shown was furnished in strangely chilling taste. The bed was of alabaster, —the sort of bed on which it seemed less natural for the living to sleep than for the dead to lie in state.

"Not yet," Rachel shuddered with a cough. She added that she had dreamt, when in Russia, that she would die in such a bed, and that the recollection of the dream had haunted her ever since. She fell asleep in it, but awoke at midnight, shrieking for help.

She knew that she was dying—all the world knew it. All the world seemed to have paused in its work to watch her die—to beg a souvenir, or to offer comfort or counsel. Strangers begged for her autograph, and she gave it them, writing—

"Dans huit jours d'ici je commencerai à être
Mangée par les vers et par les biographes."

All the amateur and quack physicians of Europe

Rachel

and America proposed remedies which they believed might succeed where those of the orthodox practitioners had failed. Milk, in which a calf's foot had been boiled, sweetened and flavoured with orange flowers, to be sipped from a teaspoon continually, was one suggestion. Roasted chestnuts, pounded to a powder, were recommended by another counsellor. A third thought that iron pills would be efficacious. A fourth declared that it would be a good idea to sleep with the cows in a stable, and offered to lend his own stable for the purpose. A fifth advised baths of gelatine. A sixth wrote, with pompous imbecility—

" Believe me, mademoiselle, the doctors of to-day care nothing about healing their patients. Their one idea is to enrich themselves at their expense. As nothing is impossible to God, you had better consult a somnambulist if there is a good one in your neighbourhood. If not, send a lock of your hair to Mme. Morelle, at Niort (Deux-Sèvres), who, last August, cured a young soldier of the Army of Africa, who had only one lung left. She gave him a prescription which she had written in her sleep."

And so on, and so forth, for even this list of medical recommendations is incomplete. Every post brought a handful of them, each more fatuous than the one which had preceded it; but Rachel wasted away without being deluded into false hope by any of them.

She only once got beyond the grounds of the villa on an occasion on which the peasants organized a country dance for her amusement. She sent for

Rachel

the photographer, and had her portrait taken in the garden—it is the likeness of a withered old woman, though in truth she was only thirty-seven. She returned some of her friends their letters, packed in baskets of fruit or flowers, as offerings for the New Year, post-dated because, as she wrote to Plon-Plon, " it seems as if that would give me strength to live until the date I have put on them."

A few friends called—among others Legouvé, with whom she had made her peace. She told him how she passed the time : " For six hours of the day I hope, and the rest of the time I despair." She also complimented him on the dramatic character of the women in his plays, adding that she hoped he would write a piece for her return to the stage; but that can only have been said in playfulness, and for the sake of saying something. Three days after she had said it she was dead.

The only regular visitor was Lieutenant Aubaret, who was then stationed at Toulon, whence he journeyed to Cannet as often as his duties suffered. He had not even yet abandoned the hope of persuading the Jewess to become a Christian. It is said that he nearly succeeded—that preparations were actually made for her private baptism, but were interrupted by the unexpected arrival of Prince Napoleon, and were not resumed. But that is uncertain, and hardly matters; for it is only because the Truth is hidden in mystery, that death-bed conversions are possible. The essence of all religions is, after all, the same : that death is not the end— that the shadows pass not into nothingness, but to new conditions; that the seen and the unseen are one in spite of the curtain between them, the causes

Rachel

on one side producing effects upon the other—and that our unfulfilled resolutions will still have their chances of fulfilment. And therefore, for this solemn moment of transition, every religion provides its ritual.

And so, as the hour approached, it was felt that Rachel must die in accordance with the ritual of her forefathers. Sarah, who had so often been the companion of her frivolities, now hurriedly set the telegraph wires in motion and summoned Hebrew functionaries from Nice to chant psalms in the dying woman's ear.

" Listen, Israel, the Eternal, our God, the Eternal is One.

" Go, then, whither the Lord calleth thee. Go, and may His mercy assist thee. May the Eternal, our God, be with thee. May His immortal angels guide thee to Heaven, and may the righteous rejoice when the Lord receiveth thee in His bosom !

" God of our fathers, revive in Thy mercy this soul that goeth to Thee; unite it to those of the holy patriarchs, amid the eternal joys of the heavenly Paradise ! Amen ! "

So they intoned. Perhaps Rachel understood— more probably she did not. It does not matter; for the great use of ritual lies in its power to soothe the ears even of those who do not understand it. But the course was run; the vigil between the two sleeps was over; the sojourn in Vanity Fair, where no man has an abiding habitation, had reached its end. Rachel had passed through Vanity Fair, and learnt its lesson, and passed on.

INDEX

275

Index

Noailles, Duchesse de, 65
Nye, Captain, 234, 237

Plessy, Madame, 157, 161
Poirson, Auguste, 19, 21-22
Ponsard, François, 193-198, 200, 264
Provost, Jean Baptiste François, 19

Rachel, Mademoiselle, introductory survey of her character, 1-9; birth, parentage, and childhood, 10-15; theatrical training, 16-26; her *début*, 26-27; reception by public and critics, 38-45; quarrel of Janin and Musset over her, 45-47; her impromptu supper-party, and subsequent quarrels with Musset, 48-57; quarrel with Dr. Véron, 58-60; her relations with the Faubourg, 61-62; her disposition to revert to type, 62-64, 105; performance at Windsor, 73-76; reception in London society, 76-80; symptoms of pulmonary disease, 80; quarrel with Crémieux, 86-89; relations with the Prince de Joinville, 90-92; with Walewski, 92-94, 97-100; with Dumas, *père*, 94-98; her palatial mansion, 101-105; quarrel with Walewski, 105-109; relations with Déjazet and with Bertrand, 110-119; failure of *Judith*, 122; appears with Mlle. Maxime in *Marie Stuart*, 125-129; Charlotte Brontë's criticism in *Villette*, 131-135; relations with Viennet, 136-137; her methods of plundering, 138-141; Larmartine's appreciation of, 141-143; her singing of the *Marseillaise*, 144-152; secures for Houssaye directorship of Comédie Française, 153-161; betrothal to and quarrel with Hector B——, 175-192; her German and Austrian tour, 184-190; relations with Ponsard, 193, 198; tour in Russia, 198-204; return to Paris, 205; death of her sister Rebecca, 208; relations with Legouvé, and subsequent quarrel, 209-222; refusal to appear in *Médée*, 217-222; resumes friendship with Crémieux, 220; litigation with Legouvé, 221-222; failure of *Rosemonde*, 223-224; rivalry of Ristori, 226-232; Dumas' onslaughts, 228-230; decides to go to America, 232; reception in London, 233; indifferent reception in New York, etc., 237, *et seq.*; illness, 242, *et seq.*; at Havana, 246-249; return to France, 250; departure for Egypt, 255; return to France, 262; last days in Paris, 266, *et seq.*; farewell to the theatre, 269; departure for the Riviera, 270-271; last illness and death, 271 to end

Récamier, Madame, 65 (*mentioned*)
Ristori, Adelaide, 222, 226-232, 235
Romanticism, 28-37, 167
Rosemonde, 223
Rothschild, Baron James de, 170

Sainte-Aulaire, 14-17, 19
Sainte-Beuve, Charles-Augustin de, 44, 59, 225
Samson, Joseph Isidore, 18, 22-25, 43, 80, 209
Samson, Madame, 23-24
Scribe, Eugène, 209-211, 225
Soulié, Frédéric, 38

Talma, François Joseph, 22 (*mentioned*)
Tattet, Alfred, 110

Vacquerie, Auguste, 233
Véron, Dr., 18, 58-60, 86 - 87, 140, 155, 212, 225
Victoria, Queen, 73
Viennet, Guillaume, 136-137
Vigny, Alfred de, 164, 167
Villette, 131-135

Walewski, Comte, 62-63, 92-94, 97-100, 105-109, 140